INVITATIONS AND INVESTIGATIONS

An Isle of Man Ghostly Cozy

DIANA XARISSA

ISBN: 1725745763
ISBN-13: 978-1725745766

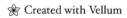 Created with Vellum

For my readers. I'm grateful for each and every one of you.

AUTHOR'S NOTE

As I begin this ninth book in the Isle of Man Ghostly Cozy Series, I'm thinking about gratitude. (It was just Thanksgiving here.) I'm hugely grateful that many of you enjoy spending time with Fenella and her friends. I'm having a wonderful time writing about them all. I recommend reading the books in order (alphabetically), but each should be enjoyable on its own.

The stories are primarily written in American English, although the characters who are British or Manx use British English. I try to keep this consistent, but I'm sure I make mistakes. Fenella grew up in the US, although she now lives on the Isle of Man, where these stories take place. It is a UK crown dependency and a very unique and special place.

This is a work of fiction. All of the characters are products of the author's imagination. Any resemblance to actual persons, living or dead, is entirely coincidental. The shops, restaurants, and businesses in this story are also fictional. The historical sites and other landmarks on the island are all real; however, the events that take place within them in this story are fictional.

I love hearing from readers and would be delighted if you'd take the time to get in touch. All of my contact details are available in the back of the book. I have a monthly newsletter that will keep you informed about upcoming releases. If you are interested, you can subscribe to the newsletter from my website.

❧ I ❧

"I t all sounds terribly exciting," Shelly said as she and her friend, Fenella, walked slowly down the Douglas promenade.

"I don't know about exciting," Fenella replied. "I'm just hoping for delicious."

Shelly laughed. "Is that truly all that this holiday is about? Food?"

"Not at all. It's about giving thanks, really. The food is secondary, although very important. Thanksgiving commemorates one of the earliest successful harvests by colonists in what would one day become the United States. They had a feast and invited the local Native Americans to join them."

"Whom have you invited, then, to your feast?" Shelly asked.

"Just about everyone I could think of," Fenella laughed. "It's going to be strange, being here on the island for Thanksgiving. I've nearly always spent my Thanksgivings with my brothers and their families."

"All of them?"

"Pretty much. As John is the oldest, he's always had everyone come to his house. The other three sometimes come late or leave early if they have to spend time with their in-laws, but usually we all just go to John's for the day."

"What about Jack?"

Fenella made a face. Jack Dawson was her ex-boyfriend. They'd been a couple for over ten years, but Fenella had always known that the relationship wasn't going to last forever. She'd met Jack after a painful breakup and they'd quickly fallen into a comfortable but dull life together. Her decision to move to the Isle of Man after inheriting her Aunt Mona's estate had finally given her the excuse she'd needed to end the relationship. "He used to spend the day with his mother," she told Shelly. "Actually, once she moved out of Buffalo, he used to go and spend the week with her."

"And she didn't mind that you didn't come with him?"

"She never liked me and the feeling was mutual."

Shelly laughed. "My in-laws were lovely and we always got along really well. I miss them almost as much as I miss my own parents."

"I've never had good luck with the parents of anyone that I've dated," Fenella told her. "None of them ever seemed to like me."

"That's odd, as I find you incredibly likeable," Shelly replied.

Fenella smiled. She'd only met Shelly in March, when she'd moved to the island, but the pair had already become close friends. They lived next door to one another in a luxury apartment building in Douglas and spent time together nearly every day. One of their favorite things to do was walk together, and they had an informal arrangement to do so most mornings. Today marked the third time in three days that they'd taken a morning stroll together.

"Why aren't you going back to the US to have Thanksgiving with your brothers, then?" Shelly asked as they reached the end of the promenade and turned around.

"I was thinking about going back, but then Joseph and his wife decided to travel to California to spend Thanksgiving with their daughter who is working there at the moment. Their other daughter is going to join them as well. Jacob and his wife are going on a cruise to celebrate his early retirement. That just left James, and he's so busy writing that he told John not to count on him coming, either. Once John found out that no one was coming to his house, he and his wife decided to spend Thanksgiving in Colorado with some of her family. They all invited me to join them, but since everyone is so spread out, I decided it was probably easier to just stay here."

"Easier, but different."

"Yes, it's going to be very different. I'm not sure how I'll feel on the day."

"It isn't too late to fly to California or Colorado," Shelly suggested. "Surely you can afford it."

Fenella nodded. Aunt Mona had left Fenella considerably more than Fenella had been expecting when she'd first arrived on the island. It seemed that Mona had managed to amass a large fortune over the years, much of it coming from Maxwell Martin, the man with whom she'd been involved for most of her life. Fenella had been shocked to learn that she'd not only inherited a luxury apartment and a sleek red sports car, but also several bank accounts, multiple properties around the island, stocks, bonds, and a pair of safe deposit boxes that Fenella had yet to visit.

"I thought about it for a long time," she told Shelly. "I decided it's time to start making some new traditions for myself here. I love the island and it's my home now. It just took some time for me to find somewhere to have the feast."

"And then you found a place right next door," Shelly laughed.

"It is, or at least very nearly." Fenella felt as if she'd called almost every restaurant on the island, trying to find somewhere that could make a huge turkey dinner for her and her guests on the fourth Thursday in November. Nearly everyone told her the same thing. They were getting ready for the Christmas dinner parties that would start in early December. Some offered to prepare their standard banquet menu meals for her, but she had her heart set on turkey and all the trimmings, including some American items for which she'd happily supply the recipes. She'd been thrilled when she'd finally found a restaurant in Douglas that was prepared to make what they considered "Christmas dinner" in November and even to attempt to duplicate a few of Fenella's American favorites.

"So who is on the guest list?" Shelly asked.

"As I said, I think I've invited just about everyone I know. I mailed the invitations on Friday, so they should get delivered today, I suppose. I invited you and Peter from our building."

Peter Cannell was Fenella's other next-door neighbor. In his early fifties, he was semi-retired, although he seemed to work a great deal, at least as far as Fenella could see. When she'd first arrived on the island he'd taken her out once or twice, but their relationship had settled into a warm friendship rather than anything romantic.

"Did you tell him he could bring a guest?" Shelly asked.

"I've told everyone that they're welcome to bring a guest. Do you think Peter will bring someone?"

"He's never around any more. I know he works a lot, but I can't help but think that he's found himself a girlfriend, as well."

"If he has, I hope he brings her to Thanksgiving. I'd like to meet her."

"Me, too. After his disastrous second marriage, he deserves some happiness, even if he did treat his first wife badly."

"At least he seems aware and apologetic for how he treated her. They have dinner together once in a while, too, so it sounds as if she's forgiven him."

"I hope so. But who else is invited?" Shelly repeated her earlier question.

"I invited Mel, my former driving instructor. I don't know if he'll come or not, though. Donald isn't coming, although I did mention it to him."

Donald Donaldson was a wealthy and sophisticated man in his late fifties. He and Fenella had gone out several times, but when his daughter had been badly injured in a car accident, he'd gone to New York to be with her. He called Fenella occasionally, but he was unlikely to be back on the island before the new year.

"Is he still miserable in New York?" Shelly asked.

"He hasn't called me in a week or more, which leads me to believe that he's finding ways to amuse himself," Fenella replied dryly.

Shelly nodded. "That doesn't really surprise me."

"Me, either," Fenella sighed. "Anyway, I invited Harvey, and I told him to bring the dogs, too."

Shelly smiled. "That will be fun."

Harvey Garus was an older gentleman who lived in the apartment building next door to Fenella's. He had two dogs, a large beast called Winston and a tiny girl called Fiona. Fenella had found herself looking after the two animals once under odd circumstances. She'd enjoyed the experience, but had been happy when the dogs had returned to their rightful home. In October she'd looked after them again for a week and she'd promised Harvey to repeat the favor whenever he had the need.

Fenella rattled off a list of the other people who had been sent an invitation for Thanksgiving. It felt like a short list to her. "I really should know more people," she said with a sigh. "I've been here for what, eight months? I must try harder before next year."

"If everyone comes and they all bring guests, it should be a pretty large party," Shelly countered. "As Gordon is away with work, I thought I might bring Tim with me, if that's okay with you?"

"Of course it is. You're welcome to bring anyone you'd like. I thought about sending Gordon an invitation, but I didn't want to make things awkward for you."

Shelly had been widowed not much more than a year earlier. In the first days and weeks after her husband's unexpected death, she'd sold the home that they'd shared, taken early retirement from her teaching job, and moved into Promenade View Apartments. Fenella's Aunt Mona had helped the woman through the worst of her grief, helping Shelly rediscover her love of life. When Shelly had reconnected with Gordon, a man who'd been friends with both her and her husband, she and Fenella had both expected a romance to develop. Before that could happen, Gordon had begun traveling a great deal for work, leaving Shelly to start noticing other men.

Tim Blake was a member of the local band, The Islanders. They occasionally played at the Tale and Tail, Shelly's and Fenella's favorite pub. When Fenella began dating Todd Hughes, a musician who sometimes filled in with the band, Shelly had gone out with Tim a few times.

"How are things with you and Tim?" Fenella asked.

"We're taking things slowly," Shelly replied. "Unlike with Gordon, where I wasn't sure if he just wanted to be friends or something more, Tim makes sure that I know how he feels. I'm just not sure I'm ready for anything more serious yet. He's being very patient with me, I must say."

"Because he's smart enough to know that you're worth working to win."

"I'm not sure about that," Shelly laughed. "We're having fun together and he's not shy about holding my hand or kissing me good-night, anyway."

"Good for you."

"How are things between you and Todd?"

"He's going to be spending Thanksgiving in Hawaii," Fenella told her. She named a very famous Hollywood actor. "He's having a big Thanksgiving feast and he's invited Todd to be part of the band as well as a guest for the week-long festivities," she explained.

"Too bad he didn't invite you to come along. That sounds amazing."

"Oh, he invited me, but I don't want to spend my Thanksgiving surrounded by strangers in a strange place."

"Normally I'd agree with you, but Hawaii? With famous people? I'm not sure."

"I'm not really fond of sun, sand, and beaches," Fenella told her. "I think if I ever met any famous people I'd probably forget how to talk or do something equally embarrassing, anyway."

"Todd's pretty famous."

"Yeah, I know, but I didn't know that when I met him. I still feel a little, I don't know, intimidated by him, now that I do know who he is, though."

"Is that the full guest list for your dinner, then?"

"It's most of it," Fenella replied. "I sent an invitation to Daniel, too." She blushed bright red as the words left her lips.

Shelly grinned. "I hope he comes and you two get a chance to talk."

Fenella shrugged. Police inspector Daniel Robinson had been one of the first people that Fenella had met after her arrival. The handsome man in his late forties had also only recently moved to the island. They'd met over a murdered man, and over time they'd begun dating. If Fenella was being totally honest with herself, she'd started falling for the man. Before things could get too serious, though, Daniel had been sent to take some classes in the UK. When he'd returned to the island, he'd brought a young and very pretty blonde friend back with him. While the woman, Tiffany Perkins, had since returned to the UK,

Fenella hadn't yet had a chance to actually speak with Daniel. They both seemed to be avoiding one another.

"I don't know that I want to talk to him," she told Shelly.

"Then why did you invite him to your feast?"

"I invited everyone I've met on the island, or nearly. I invited Constable Corlett and his wife and the baby, and I invited Inspector Hammersmith, even though I think he hates me. Not inviting Daniel would have looked odd."

Shelly gave Fenella a skeptical look. "Or maybe you invited Constable Corlett and Inspector Hammersmith so that you'd have an excuse to invite Daniel," she suggested.

Fenella thought about arguing with her friend, but she knew that Shelly was probably right. "I doubt any of them will come."

"You might be surprised. Your little party will probably be the talk of the island once word gets out about it. It may well be the social event of the month. Mona's parties always were."

"Mona had a lot more friends than I do, and her friends were rich and famous. Anyway, it's just dinner, not a proper party."

"Regardless, I'd be very surprised if anyone turned you down. This is the first party you've held since you've been here, after all. And you are Mona Kelly's niece. That gives you a good deal of social status on this island."

"Aside from the people who hated Mona," Fenella added.

"No one hated Mona," Shelly countered. "There were a lot of people who were jealous of her and some that didn't approve of her, but no one hated her."

Mona had never married or held down a job. From what Fenella could tell, she'd relied on gifts from generous men to support her over the years. Allegedly, at least some of those men had been married to other women. "I suspect there might be a few women out there who hated her," Fenella said. "Women whose husbands slept with Mona."

"Mona was never as wild as everyone seems to think," Shelly told her. "I think she was far more devoted to Max than anyone knew."

"You may be right about that."

They'd made their way back to their apartment building, and Shelly stopped. "I'm not walking any further today, or at least not now. I have errands to run and then I'm having lunch with Tim."

"Good for you. I suppose I should be home this morning in case anyone calls about the party."

"If the invitations are going to be delivered today, it's probably too soon for anyone to ring, but you never know."

The pair crossed the road and made their way into the building. Shelly stopped to check her mailbox in the small room off of the lobby.

"Oh, look," she exclaimed. "I appear to have received a party invitation."

Fenella laughed. "I didn't get one," she complained.

Shelly opened the envelope and pulled out the printed card. "This is lovely," she told her friend after she'd read through it. "It was smart of you to include a brief history of Thanksgiving on the back. I'll be there for sure, and I'll probably bring a guest."

"I actually invited everyone from the band," Fenella told her. "Tim won't count as your guest. You can bring someone else, if you'd like."

"I'll think about it, but right now I can't imagine who else I would ask."

They rode the elevator to the sixth floor and then made their way to their respective apartments. "Tomorrow morning at eight?" Shelly asked.

"I won't promise, but probably. Maybe tomorrow Katie will let me sleep in, though. You never know."

"I'll see you tomorrow," Shelly laughed.

Fenella let herself into her apartment. "You might let me sleep in tomorrow, right?" she asked her tiny black kitten.

"Mmmeerrrooowww," Katie replied.

"I think that's a no," Mona said from her seat near the window.

Fenella sighed. "Too bad you can't feed her. You never sleep."

Mona shrugged. "Ghosts don't need to sleep. That's just one of the things I like about being dead."

Fenella still wasn't completely convinced that the woman who frequently appeared in her apartment was the ghost of her dead aunt, but that was just about the only explanation that seemed possible. That the woman might merely be a figment of her imagination did cross her mind sometimes, but there were reasons why that didn't seem likely.

"What else do you like about being dead?" Fenella asked, wondering if Mona would choose to answer or not.

"All manner of things," Mona shrugged. "You'll find out yourself in good time."

The woman could be infuriating, which was one of the reasons why Fenella didn't think she was imagining Mona. Surely her own imagination would dream up someone a good deal nicer and less difficult. "I don't suppose you could work out a way to feed Katie," Fenella said, dragging the conversation back to where it had started.

"I could probably manage it, if I had to, but only in an emergency. Katie is your pet, not mine. She's your responsibility."

Katie had walked into Fenella's apartment uninvited not long after Fenella had arrived. The kitten had promptly made herself at home, and now Fenella couldn't imagine life without her. "I don't mind the responsibility," she objected. "I love that she's my pet. I would just like to sleep late once in a while. When I was working, I nearly always had a class at eight o'clock. Now that I'm retired, it would be nice to get up at eight, or even nine, once in a while."

Fenella had been a professor in the history department at the same university where she'd studied. A few years shy of her fiftieth birthday, she was far too young to actually be retired, but Mona's millions meant that she didn't ever have to work again.

"Except that would probably turn into ten or eleven, and you'd soon find that you weren't getting out of bed until noon most days," Mona suggested. "By which time you'd have wasted many useful hours."

"Were you an early riser?"

"I never needed a great deal of sleep. I was usually up by six or seven, regardless of the time I went to bed. I often had very early nights as well, actually. Despite my reputation, the wild parties were usually confined to weekends or special occasions."

"Shelly thinks that my Thanksgiving dinner might generate some excitement on the island."

"Of course it will. You are my niece and this is the first social event that you're having. Everyone who is anyone will want an invitation."

"Oh, dear. I didn't invite everyone, only people I actually know and like."

Mona shrugged. "I should have helped you with the guest list. There are probably a few important people you should have included."

"It's just a dinner for my new friends. It isn't anything important."

"If Todd were going to be there, it would be more important, of course. He's one of the island's most famous residents."

"But he's going to be in Hawaii."

"I'd have gone with him, if I were you."

"Of course you would have," Fenella sighed. "But sitting on the beach all day isn't my idea of how to spend Thanksgiving."

"I have some wonderful bathing suits in my wardrobe," Mona told her.

Along with the properties and money that Fenella had inherited, she'd also been left a huge wardrobe full of Mona's clothes. Nearly everything in the wardrobe had been designed and made for Mona by a local designer called Timothy. Every item of clothing that Fenella had tried from the wardrobe had been beautifully made of the finest fabrics and, perhaps due to exquisite tailoring, everything seemed to fit Fenella perfectly, even though she was built rather differently than Mona had been.

"It should be cold on Thanksgiving, preferably with snow," Fenella replied. "It's the official start to the Christmas season, after all. Everyone knows that snow makes for the best Christmases."

"You are going to be disappointed if you stay here for Christmas," Mona warned her. "It very rarely snows on the island."

"At least it will be cold. Todd is talking about going to the Bahamas for Christmas."

"And I was so sure that you two were perfect for one another," Mona sighed. "He seems like such a lovely man."

"He is lovely, but he doesn't seem to be able to stay in one place for very long," Fenella sighed. She liked Todd a lot and when they were together, he seemed nearly perfect, but they were very rarely together for more than a few days before one of his friends would call to ask him to play at a party or attend a special event halfway around the world. As far as Fenella could tell, Todd never said no to anyone.

"You could go with him sometimes," Mona suggested. "You've plenty of money if you wanted to pay your own way, even."

"I'm happy here, at least for now, especially now that I have research to do."

Fenella had moved to the island intent on writing a fictionalized autobiography of Anne Boleyn. It was an idea that had been in her head for many years, but once she'd actually begun doing the necessary research, she'd discovered that it was going to be hard work. She hadn't completely given up on the idea, but she had recently made contact with Marjorie Stevens, the Manx Museum's librarian and archivist. Marjorie had a long list of topics that she was hoping someone might research and several of the items on the list were of interest to Fenella.

After a lengthy discussion with the woman, Fenella was now digging through some of the original island records from the time of the English Civil War. The chance to work with original seventeenth century documents was exciting for Fenella and she found herself spending more and more time at the museum each week.

"I can't imagine spending hours with dusty old documents," Mona said. "People are so much more interesting."

"The documents teach me about the people, though," Fenella countered. "I'm trying to learn what I can about what life was really like on the island during the English Civil War. Not life for the Earl of Derby and his family, but life for the ordinary men and women who were simply trying to keep their children fed and a roof over their heads. Did you know there was a famine on the island during the period?"

"I did, because you've mentioned it at least a dozen times. I'm sure it's all very interesting, but if that's what you want to talk about, I'm going to go and find Max. He's usually getting up around now. Maybe he'll want to do something enjoyable."

"Why is it okay for Max to sleep late in the morning, but not me?" Fenella demanded.

"The poor man is dead. You must make allowances."

"I thought you said the dead didn't need to sleep."

"We don't, not when we know we're dead, anyway. I'm not sure that Max fully understands that he's passed away, though. When I'm ready to move on to the next stage of my afterlife, I'll probably try to explain it all to him. For now, I'm just grateful for his company."

Before Fenella could comment, Mona faded away. "I wish she wouldn't do that," Fenella told Katie.

The cat blinked at her and then seemed to shrug. A moment later she jumped up onto the couch and curled up exactly where Mona had been sitting.

"And you get to sleep whenever you want," Fenella complained. "You'd be less tired if you hadn't woken me at seven." Katie didn't bother to reply.

Fenella sat down with a few photocopies from her most recent trip to the museum. Reading seventeenth century handwriting was a difficult skill and it wasn't one that Fenella had yet mastered. She spent an hour with a magnifying glass trying to read one document after another, but never feeling as if she were actually making any progress. Marjorie was going to be teaching a class in reading old handwriting in the new year and Fenella had already signed up.

She put the magnifying glass down and sighed. While she was eager to dig into more documents, it was probably best to wait until she'd taken the class, or at least the first week of the class, before she tried reading anything. All she was doing at this point was frustrating herself and getting a headache.

A few pills helped with the headache. Fenella made herself a light lunch and then decided that she needed a trip to the grocery store before dinner. "There's plenty of cat food," she assured Katie as she poured out the kitten's lunch. "But there isn't much people food."

Katie didn't look at all concerned. As Fenella ate, she wrote out a short list for the store. Since she was hungry, she found herself adding all sorts of ingredients for complicated meals that she doubted she would actually ever bother to prepare. Still, if she had the ingredients to hand, she might cook at least some of them. She was just putting on her shoes when the phone rang. Letting the machine answer was tempting, but as she was standing right next to it, she picked up.

"Hello?"

"Fenella? It's Daniel, er, Daniel Robinson."

"Oh, hello."

"Yes, hello. I, um, that is, I had the morning off, so I was here when the post arrived. Thank you for the invitation to your Thanksgiving banquet."

"You're welcome. I've invited just about everyone I know on the island," Fenella said, not wanting the man to think that he was anything special, not after Tiffany.

"Have you? That's great. I'd like to attend. Thank you again for inviting me."

"Will you be bringing a guest?" Fenella asked. She held her breath while she waited for his reply.

"A guest? No, I don't believe so. I don't really know many people on the island."

"I thought maybe Tiffany would be back by then," Fenella said. As soon as the words were out of her mouth, she regretted saying them. No doubt they'd make Daniel think that she cared. And she didn't care, she reminded herself.

"Tiffany? No, I don't think she'll be coming back to the island. It didn't really suit her."

"No? That's a shame. I can't imagine living anywhere else."

"Yes, well, the island does seem to have that effect on some people, but it didn't work on Tiffany. She's gone back to London. I'm sure she'll be happier there."

"Good for her."

The silence that followed was just starting to get awkward when Daniel spoke again.

"I never did thank you for your help with Phillip Pierce's murder," he said suddenly. "We were focusing our inquiries on the person you identified, but were missing that inconsistency that you spotted. It was the key to getting the confession that we needed."

"I was happy to help," Fenella replied.

"Yeah, and you have great instincts with these things. I'm looking into another cold case. I think it might be really helpful to run it all past you, if you have some spare time."

"I could probably make some time," Fenella said hesitantly.

"Maybe we could meet at the pub tonight," Daniel suggested. "I'm working a short shift today, so I finish at seven. Maybe we could meet around eight? Mondays are usually quiet at the Tale and Tail, aren't they?"

"They have been the last few times I've been there on a Monday. They sometimes have a band on Tuesdays or Sundays, but not Mondays."

"Are you free tonight, then?"

Fenella thought about her answer for a minute. Part of her desperately wanted to see Daniel again, but she was scared. She'd come to care for him a great deal in the months they'd known each other. Seeing him with Tiffany had been difficult and she wasn't certain that she was ready to give him another chance.

"If not tonight, then what works for you?" Daniel asked after a moment.

"I can do tonight," Fenella let her heart decide. "I'll see you around eight at the Tale and Tail."

"Great. I'll try to get there a little early and get a table upstairs. Hopefully it will be quiet."

"Okay. I'll see you then."

Fenella put the phone down with her head spinning and her heart racing. "I'm going to see Daniel tonight," she told Katie. The kitten didn't even bother to open her eyes.

2

"What am I going to wear?" Fenella wailed as she walked back and forth across the bedroom floor. "I want to look fabulous, but I don't want to look as if I tried to look good."

"Maybe you should wear something fabulous and tell him you have a date for later," Mona suggested from where she was sitting on Fenella's bed.

"I don't want to play those sorts of games," Fenella replied. "Things are already a mess between us. I'd rather not make them any more complicated."

"Men love games. I remember once when Max was angry with me about something insignificant. I flew off to Paris with another man. We were having dinner in the Eiffel Tower when Max stormed in, pulled me into his arms, and carried me away. It was incredibly romantic."

"It sounds horrible. I wouldn't want a man carrying me out of a public place like that."

"No offense, my dear, but I don't know that a man would be able to lift you. I was very petite, really, and that was simply Max being Max. It was all about dramatic effect, nothing more."

"What did the other man do?"

"What could he do? He finished his dinner and then went back to his hotel. Knowing him, he probably took the waitress back with him. Max paid for the meal that he'd interrupted, at least, which was kind of him."

"Some day you're going to have tell me your whole life story in detail," Fenella said. "Maybe I should write your biography. I'll bet everyone on the island would buy a copy."

"I'm not sure you're old enough to hear every detail of my life," Mona laughed, "but we need to focus on what you're going to wear tonight."

"It's just the Tale and Tail. I don't usually dress up when I go there on a Monday night."

"But tonight you are meeting the man you were falling in love with a few months ago. That needs a very special outfit indeed."

"I wasn't falling in love."

Mona sighed and gave Fenella a sympathetic smile. "You should be able to admit it to me, if anyone. You know I won't repeat anything you say. I do tell Max quite a bit, actually, but he doesn't speak to anyone other than me, so all of your secrets are safe with me, or with us, rather."

Fenella shook her head. "I did care about Daniel, but I wouldn't say I was falling in love with him. Anyway, it really doesn't matter what happened in the past. I'm more worried about what's going to happen tonight."

"Tonight you're going to go and talk to him, and he's going to apologize for behaving like an idiot and beg you to forgive him," Mona predicted. "Then you're going to tell him that you've been too busy with Todd and Donald to have noticed his absence. Really, it's a shame you agreed to meet him on such short notice. You should have told him you were busy until one day next week, or even next month."

"I told you I'm not playing games. Anyway, he wants my help with a cold case. This isn't a date, it's work."

"You don't work for the police. This is a date, whatever else you might want to pretend."

"Whatever it is, what am I going to wear?"

Mona sighed. "Second dress on the left side of the wardrobe. It's blue, which makes it less formal than black can be, and it's casual but still elegant."

Fenella had already learned not to argue with Mona when it came to clothes. She pulled the dress out of the wardrobe and held it against her torso. "It's pretty," she said, "and surprisingly modest for one of your dresses."

Mona chuckled. "I did go to events where short skirts and plunging necklines weren't appropriate."

"Did you? From everything I've heard about you, I can't imagine you cared what was appropriate."

"I wish I could say that I didn't, but actually, Max was very concerned with what people thought. He took me just about everywhere with him and he always insisted that I be appropriately dressed. That was one of the reasons why he paid for such an extensive wardrobe for me, of course."

Fenella took the dress off its hanger and slid it on. "It's gorgeous," she said as she twirled in front of the mirror. "And just right for tonight."

"I told you it would be. The shoes and handbag are in the drawer."

It seemed that Mona had matching shoes and a matching handbag for every single item in her wardrobe. They'd all been made by a man called Samuel, who'd worked with leather to make shoes and bags. He'd been a genius with dye as well, managing to perfectly match every fabric that Timothy had used.

Fenella slipped on the matching shoes and sighed. "They're so comfortable. How did Samuel manage to make high heels that are so comfortable?"

"I've no idea. He never shared his secrets with me and I never asked."

Moving the things she might need from one handbag to another didn't take long. It was still far too early to head to the pub.

"Do stop pacing," Mona suggested a short while later. "Samuel made good shoes, but you'll wear them out if you keep up at that rate."

"I'm nervous," Fenella admitted.

"Yes, I can see that, but you said yourself that this is just work, not a date. You've no reason to be nervous. Daniel just wants to share a cold case with you, not the rest of his life."

"Why does he want to share a cold case with me, anyway?" Fenella demanded.

"What did he say?"

"That I have good instincts."

"There you are, then. You have good instincts. Besides, I've solved a few of his murder cases for him. You have me on your side, even if he doesn't know about me. I suppose that's why he thinks you have good instincts."

"We've helped him solve a few cases, but he hasn't spoken to me in weeks, not since he interrogated me when I was last caught up in a murder investigation. Why does he suddenly want to discuss anything with me?"

"My dear child, the man was just looking for an excuse to ring you. The Thanksgiving invitation gave him the perfect excuse, but simply replying to the invitation didn't let him see you and that's what he really wants to do. He was probably afraid to simply ask you to dinner, so he invented a cold case he wants your help with as a reason to see you."

"You don't think he really has a cold case?"

"I'm sure he's found one now, since he's spoken to you, but I doubt he had one this morning when he rang."

"I don't know," Fenella sighed. "I mean, maybe I shouldn't have even invited him for Thanksgiving."

"Of course you should have. So far he's the only one coming, isn't he?"

"Shelly is coming."

Mona laughed. "Of course Shelly is coming, but she's known about it for weeks. Daniel is the only one who has replied to the posted invitations, though, isn't he?"

"So far, yes, but it's early days yet."

"It is. While I'm not entirely convinced that a Thanksgiving feast is appropriate on the island, I do hope that most, if not all, of your friends attend. I know it means a great deal to you."

A knock on the door kept Fenella from replying. "Shelly? Hello."

"I just got back from lunch with Tim," she said, "and I was thinking that a trip to the pub might be in order."

"You just got back from lunch?" Fenella repeated. "It's nearly eight o'clock."

"We started talking and, well, found a lot to talk about," Shelly replied, blushing. "After lunch we went for a long walk and then we sat on the promenade for a while and talked some more. Then we got dinner and had a few drinks. We probably would have just gone to the pub together, but Tim wanted an early night. He has to work in the morning and tomorrow will be a late night because the band is at the pub."

"Daniel called to accept my Thanksgiving invitation," Fenella told her. "He asked me to meet him at the pub tonight, too. He has a cold case he wants to discuss with me."

"A cold case? But what else did he say? Did he apologize? Did he explain Tiffany?"

"He didn't say much else, really. He told me that he'll be coming for Thanksgiving and that he wasn't planning to bring anyone. Then he suggested that we meet to go over a cold case he's been working on and I agreed."

"I wouldn't have agreed," Shelly said. "I'd have told him he can solve his own darn cold cases or maybe he could share them with Tiffany. I'm sure she'd be more than happy to talk crime with Daniel all night long."

"Well, I agreed to meet him. Maybe I shouldn't have, but I was so surprised by the invitation that I said yes."

"And now you're all dressed up and looking fabulous for him. I hope you tell him all about Todd and how he's been taking you all over the island for wonderful meals and all sorts of other things."

"I'm just going to talk cold cases, that's all. You know I enjoyed helping Daniel with the ones that he discussed with me in the past."

"I hope his cold case isn't another murder investigation. You've dealt with quite enough of those."

"I agree. I've no idea what Daniel is working on, though. Anyway, it's nearly time for me to meet him. You're welcome to join me."

"I don't want to be in the way."

"You won't be in the way. This isn't a date, it's a criminal investigation."

"In a pub. With drinks and a bit of romantic tension."

"There won't be any romantic tension." Especially if you're there, Fenella added to herself.

It took her another minute to persuade her friend to join her. Having Shelly along made Fenella feel slightly less nervous about seeing Daniel again. If Daniel didn't want to discuss the case in front of Shelly, that would be his problem.

The Tale and Tail was only a short walk down the promenade from their apartment building. It had once been a private library in a huge seaside mansion. New owners had converted the mansion into a luxury hotel. After adding a large bar in the middle of the library's ground floor, they'd opened the library as a pub. What they hadn't done was remove the bookshelves lined with books that covered every wall. The pub was one of Fenella's favorite places on the island. Just inside the door, she always stopped to look around and sigh happily.

A pair of young cats raced up and began to shout loudly at them as Shelly and Fenella crossed the room.

"Don't mind them," the regular bartender called. "They're new and they seem to think that everyone who visits needs to admire them immediately."

Fenella laughed and then gave both cats a thorough petting. Shelly followed suit. Satisfied, the cats raced away, snuggling up together in one of the cat beds that were scattered throughout the room. Fenella had never tried to count how many cats called the pub home, but she knew that they were all well looked after and loved by the pub's staff.

The bartender poured them each a glass of their favorite wine before they headed for the narrow winding staircase to the upper level. It was there that groups of couches and chairs surrounded small tables. Nearly all of the seats were within reach of at least one bookshelf, which made the arrangement all the more wonderful.

When they reached the top of the stairs, Fenella took a quick look around. There were six other people in the space. There was no sign of Daniel.

"Let's sit in the quietest corner," Shelly suggested.

She and Fenella settled together on a couch. While they sipped their wine, Shelly told her friend a few of the stories that Tim had shared with her during their day together. It was about twenty past eight when Daniel finally appeared at the top of the stairs. Fenella was sure she didn't imagine the look of relief on his face when he spotted Shelly with Fenella.

"I'm sorry to have kept you waiting," he said, stiffly, as he joined them.

"We would have been here anyway," Shelly laughed. "I hope you don't mind that I came along. I can leave while you discuss your case, if you'd prefer."

"Not at all," Daniel assured her. "I'm not going to share anything with Fenella that isn't public record. You'll probably remember the case from the local paper once I mention it."

"What's the case, then?" Shelly asked.

"The disappearance of Ronald Sherman," Daniel replied.

"That sounds like a book title," Shelly said, "but maybe only because I'm rather obsessed with books at the moment."

"Have you been reading a lot lately?" Daniel wondered.

Shelly blushed. "Not exactly," she replied vaguely.

Fenella knew that Shelly had been working on writing, not reading, over the past few months. Shelly was trying her hand at writing a romance novel where the heroine was somewhat older than was typical in the genre. The last Fenella had heard, Shelly was stuck somewhere in the middle of the story, but trying to add at least a few hundred words each day.

"But I do remember something about Ronald Sherman," Shelly added. "Didn't he disappear about six or seven years ago?"

"He did, yes," Daniel said. "Well remembered. It got a lot of coverage in the local paper at the time, but it's been years since he disappeared."

"I think I simply assumed that he'd come back at some point," Shelly said. "If you're reopening the case, then I guess he hasn't."

"No, he hasn't come back," Daniel sighed. "Let me start at the beginning, or rather the middle, and we'll go from there."

"Maybe we need another round before we start," Shelly suggested.

"I'll go." She got up and headed for the elevator, leaving Fenella alone with Daniel.

"That's a pretty dress," Daniel said eventually.

"Thanks," Fenella replied. The monosyllable seemed inadequate. "It was Mona's," she added.

Daniel nodded. "She left you everything, didn't she? Houses, cars, money, clothes, an absolute fortune as I understand it."

"She left me very well provided for, yes," Fenella agreed, not really wanting to discuss it with Daniel, but knowing that Mona's will was a matter of public record. He could do a little bit of digging through the island's property records and discover a great deal. "I didn't realize how well provided for until recently, though. Doncan was quite vague when we first met."

Doncan Quayle had been Mona's advocate, and now he was Fenella's, though she always thought of him as her lawyer rather than using the Manx term. When she'd first arrived on the island, he'd simply told her not to worry about money and to come to see him when she wanted to know more. Now Fenella was grateful that she'd had some time to adjust to life on the island before she'd found out just how wealthy she truly was. That suddenly discovered wealth was proving more difficult for her to adjust to than life on the island had been.

"I had no idea," Daniel said. "Mark was happy to fill me in when we first talked about you."

Fenella frowned. Inspector Mark Hammersmith had investigated a few cases that Fenella had found herself caught up in while Daniel had been in Milton Keynes taking his classes. If she'd known that he was the one who'd told Daniel about her money, she never would have invited him for Thanksgiving. The money was one of the issues causing the distance that had grown up between her and Daniel over the past few months. Tiffany was another issue, though. Maybe it was time to ask Daniel about the girl.

"Here we are," Shelly said brightly. She set drinks on the table and then sat back down next to Fenella. "I hope I didn't miss anything."

"Not at all. We waited for you to get back," Daniel told her.

"Excellent. Thank you," Shelly smiled. "So, tell us all about Ronald Sherman."

"As I said, I'll start in the middle. Ronald was reported missing by his cousin, Gary Mack. According to Gary, they were meant to be having lunch together one day and Ronald never turned up."

"Did they have lunch together often?" Shelly asked.

"Gary gave an interview to the *Isle of Man Times*. According to the article, Ronald was the only child of two only children. Gary was also an only child. His mother had a brother, but he'd died young and Gary's father was an only child. Gary and Ronald were only distantly related, through a mutual great-grandfather, but they were the closest thing to family that either of them had. As such, they tried to meet for a meal at least once a month or so, usually on a Saturday."

"I hope that doesn't mean that Ronald was missing for a month before anyone noticed," Shelly exclaimed.

"No, not at all. At first the constable Gary spoke with didn't even want to file a report because Ronald had only been missing for a few hours, but when the man didn't show up for work on the following Monday, the police opened a full investigation."

"Where did he work?" Fenella asked.

"He worked for a local computer company," Daniel replied. "It's a small company that does a little bit of everything from selling hardware to installing software and supporting it, mostly for small businesses, but sometimes for residential customers or larger companies with fairly simple computer needs."

"Was there anything going on there that might have made the man want to disappear?" Shelly wanted to know.

"The local paper gave that idea a lot of column inches. The reporter who covered the story seemed to be convinced that Ronald had stumbled across something on a customer's computer that had led to his disappearance."

"Like what?" Shelly asked.

"The reporter, Dan Ross, seemed to have two basic theories. One was that Ronald had uncovered something illegal and had been silenced by whoever was behind whatever was happening. The other theory he advanced was that Ronald found access to a fortune somehow and disappeared with someone else's money."

"Surely that someone would have reported the missing money," Shelly suggested.

"Unless he or she had come by the money illegally," Daniel replied. "If you have a pile of stolen money and someone else takes it, you probably don't ring the police to complain."

"Was there ever any evidence for either of those scenarios?" Fenella asked.

Daniel shrugged. "Not hard evidence, just lots of hints and shadows. There may have been something shady going on at the company, but no evidence was ever found to link that with Ronald's disappearance."

"Why else might he have disappeared?" Shelly wondered.

"The first question is whether he went voluntarily or not," Daniel told her. "There was no sign of foul play, but that doesn't mean that he left voluntarily, either. Nevertheless, the investigating officer started by looking at that possibility."

"If he simply decided to leave, surely he'd have told his only family member," Fenella said. "Unless they'd had a disagreement or something."

"According to Gary, everything was fine between them. He insisted throughout the entire investigation that Ronald never would have simply left the island without telling him."

"If he was right, then something must have happened to Ronald," Shelly sighed.

"If he was right," Daniel said. "Ronald's girlfriend told a rather different story. Her name is Cassie Patton and she told the police and the local paper that Ronald had been talking for months about leaving. According to her, he was fed up with life on the island and wanted a change. He'd been taking computer classes and was hoping to find a job across that would offer good pay and a chance for advancement, neither of which were available in his current position, apparently."

"If he'd talked with her about wanting to leave, though, surely he'd have told her when he was actually going?" Shelly asked.

"Except Ronald and Cassie had a big fight about a week before the man disappeared. Unfortunately for Cassie, who insisted from the beginning that she and Ronald were very much in love, they had their fight in the middle of a crowded pub. There were plenty of people who were happy to share the entire story with the police and the local paper. I've read all of the different reports of the fight, and some of what Ronald reportedly said was just vague enough to be confusing."

"What do you mean?" Shelly wanted to know.

"He may have been saying that he was leaving the island, but he also may have simply been threatening to leave Cassie," Daniel said. "Cassie insisted that he was seriously planning to go across, but she still insisted that he would have told her, fight or not."

"If he'd simply gone across, surely you could have found him, though, right?" Fenella asked.

"We should have been able to find him," Daniel agreed. "It's a fairly common name, but if he'd tried to change his Manx driving license for a UK one, we would have been notified. Once it became apparent that he was truly missing, we were able to get access to his bank accounts. If he'd withdrawn any money from any of them, we would have been notified."

"So he's never used his bank accounts again?"

"He hasn't. He left behind a car, and a flat in a nice building. Cassie was still living in the flat, but she moved out a few months later because she couldn't afford the rent on her own. Ronald's car was repossessed because he stopped making payments on it, or rather his bank stopped making payments once the man's bank account reached a zero balance."

"No overdraft?" Shelly asked.

"Not in this case," Daniel replied. "Once the bank was notified that the man was missing, they canceled any overdraft limit that the man may have had before he'd disappeared."

"That all suggests that something awful happened to him," Fenella said.

"It does, rather, although Dan Ross put together a strong argument in favor of the man leaving voluntarily and simply cutting all of his ties. Dan seemed to think that Ronald had stumbled across a fortune, stolen it, and then gone underground with his newly found fortune," Daniel said.

"Do you think that's a possibility?" Shelly asked.

Daniel shrugged. "One of Ronald's work colleagues, a man called Eugene Matthews, seemed convinced that that was exactly what had happened. He said he and Ronald found all sorts of things on computers when they repaired them. Mostly it seemed to be pornography that he was talking about, but he told Dan that Ronald had said something to him a few days before he'd disappeared about finding a fortune in a most unexpected place."

"You are going to lend me copies of all of the newspaper reports, right?" Fenella asked. "I want to read all of this for myself."

Daniel grinned. "I have copies of every article for you here," he replied, handing Fenella a large envelope. "I should probably tell you to read through it all before we even discuss the case. I'd rather hear your thoughts than share mine, anyway. It's your insights I'm looking for, after all."

Fenella glanced inside the envelope. It was fat with photocopied sheets of paper. "There was nothing to suggest that he'd been taken anywhere against his will?" she asked.

"Nothing. As far as we could tell, nothing in his flat had been disturbed. Cassie insisted that everything was normal there. Ronald had been sleeping on the couch since their argument, but from what she told the papers, that wasn't unusual."

"If you wanted to make someone disappear, how would you do it?" Shelly asked.

"If I wanted to make someone disappear, I'd probably get them on the ferry with me and then simply push them overboard," Fenella said. "That seems reasonably easy."

Daniel frowned at her. "It sounds very much like you've been giving the matter some thought," he said.

Fenella laughed. "It was just the first idea that popped into my head," she told him. "Remember that Robert Grosso's killers were planning to dump his body off the ferry. I suppose that's where the idea came from when you asked."

Daniel nodded. "It isn't a bad idea, really. If the person was still alive when he or she hit the water, you might even manage to persuade the police that it was an accident or even suicide, assuming there was a police investigation. Depending on how long it took for the body to reach land somewhere, it's possible it might never be identified."

"So maybe that's what happened to poor Ronald," Shelly suggested.

"It's possible, although no ferry tickets were issued in his name in the six months prior to his disappearance," Daniel said. "That fact didn't make the papers, but as it's negative evidence as such, I don't think it matters."

"What about any of the others? The cousin, or the man from work, or the girlfriend? Did any of them take a ferry anywhere around that time?" Shelly asked.

"Not according to the ferry's records," Daniel said, "but there are a lot of private boats around the island. None of the principals in the case owned a boat at the time, but anyone could have borrowed or even stolen one, I suppose."

"Do you think that's what happened to him, then?" Fenella asked Daniel. "Do you think he was thrown off the ferry or another boat?"

"I don't know. That's certainly one possibility, although no unidentified body has ever turned up, if that is what happened. It's possible he went across voluntarily and something happened to him that prevented him from returning to the island. Again, though, there aren't any unidentified bodies in the UK that match his description."

"Maybe he moved to France or Germany or even Canada," Shelly suggested.

"He didn't take his passport when he left and he's never applied for another one," Daniel told her. "If he did leave the UK, we have to assume he did so using someone else's passport."

"His cousin isn't missing a passport, is he?" Shelly asked.

"I don't believe so, but that's an interesting idea. I'll have to check on that, actually," Daniel said.

"Did they look like one another?" Fenella wondered.

"There are pictures of both of them in the paperwork I gave you," Daniel replied. "They both had dark hair and eyes, and I suppose if you'd seen them together you might suspect that they were related. I think they probably look enough alike that Ronald could have used Gary's passport and not been caught, considering how terrible most passport photos are, anyway."

Fenella flipped through the papers until she found the photos. "They both look like ordinary middle-aged men," she said, passing the photos to Shelly.

"I know Gary Mack," Shelly said, sounding surprised. "I shouldn't say it quite like that, actually, as I didn't even know that was his name, but he did some work on my house, the house I used to have. He was just one of the crew that came and remodeled our kitchen. I'm almost certain I recognize him, anyway."

"He did work for a company that does that sort of thing," Daniel said. "What do you remember about him?"

"Nothing," Shelly sighed. "I mean, I recognized him, but I don't really remember him specifically. There were four men that came to do the work, and as far as I was concerned, they were pretty interchangeable. They did a decent job, cleaned up after themselves for the most part, and they came in on budget. I really only ever spoke to the man who was in charge of the crew. His name was Lloyd something or other."

Daniel made a note in his notebook and then looked at Fenella. "Read through all of the newspaper articles and other information in the envelope. The paper was kind enough to give me complete transcripts of the interviews that they conducted, which gives more information than what they actually printed. As those transcripts are considered public records, I've included them for you. Read it all and then let me know what you think."

"May I read all of it, too?" Shelly asked.

"Of course. We should all get together again in a day to two to discuss everything," Daniel said.

"The Islanders are playing here tomorrow night," Fenella said. "It will probably be too busy to talk. How about Wednesday evening?"

"That would work for me," Daniel said after checking his phone.

"I can do Wednesday," Shelly agreed. "Is Todd playing tomorrow night?" she asked Fenella.

"He's agreed to play a few numbers with them, as Henry still isn't back to performing. They've replaced him with someone else, but the new guy is still learning some of the songs, so Todd has agreed to help out where he's needed," Fenella replied.

"If people know that Todd is playing, it will be really busy tomorrow night," Shelly sighed. "I was hoping for a quiet evening, really."

"Todd hasn't told anyone he's going to be here," Fenella told her. "It shouldn't be too bad."

"I hope not," Shelly said.

"I've been hearing about Todd Hughes and The Islanders ever since I got back. Maybe I should make the effort to come and see them tomorrow night," Daniel said.

"They're very good," Shelly told him.

Fenella finished her drink to avoid speaking. She really didn't want Todd and Daniel in the same place together, but there was no way she could tell Daniel that. He had to know that she and Todd had been dating. The whole island was probably talking about it.

"I may see you both tomorrow night, then," Daniel said as he got to his feet. "Otherwise, we'll meet here around eight on Wednesday."

"Great," Fenella muttered as Daniel walked away.

❧ 3 ❧

"**S**hould we have another round?" Shelly asked.

"While I'd love to have several more, I think I should go home," Fenella told her. "That was depressing."

"What did he say to you when you were alone together?"

"That he liked my dress and that Mark Hammersmith was the one who'd told him all about Mona's money."

"Oh, dear. That's a shame. It seems as if the money might be a problem for him."

"It shouldn't be. I didn't even know I had money when we first met. I'm more concerned about Tiffany than anything else, but we didn't have time to talk about her."

"I shouldn't have come," Shelly fretted.

"Nonsense. Things were difficult enough with you here. You're coming again on Wednesday, no arguing."

Shelly shrugged. "I can, if you're sure you want me here."

"I definitely want you here. If Daniel really wants to talk to me, he knows where I live. If he just wants to talk about missing people and cold cases, then he can't complain if I bring a friend along."

"I can't wait to read everything in that envelope," Shelly told her. "I hope we can work out what happened to poor Ronald Sherman. I'm quite worried that he's dead."

"Yes, I am as well. It seems to be the only solution that makes sense, although I've no idea why the body hasn't turned up."

"Maybe the murderer buried it somewhere on the island and it simply hasn't been found yet."

"Maybe. Let's go home." Fenella got to her feet and grabbed the envelope that Daniel had given her. She and Shelly took the elevator back down to the ground floor. They waved to the bartender and then made their way outside.

"It feels a lot colder than it did when we went in," Shelly remarked as a strong breeze blew past them.

"It is November. If I were in Buffalo, we'd probably have snow now," Fenella replied. She felt quite warm and snug inside her heavy winter coat. She'd brought it with her from the US and she was fairly confident that it would be able to get her through the worst weather the island could throw at her. After many years of Buffalo winters, including one where a single storm had dropped more than seven feet of snow overnight, she wasn't worried about rain and wind.

"When are you going to read through the papers?" Shelly asked as they walked off the elevator on their floor.

"Probably tomorrow morning," Fenella replied. "I'm having dinner with Todd before he needs to head to the pub for the show, but that gives me most of the day to read through everything Daniel has given us."

"If I come over just after lunch, do you think you'll be done?"

"If I'm not, you can start with the articles I've read while I finish the rest. Then we can discuss it all either tomorrow or Wednesday."

Shelly grinned. "I'm awfully excited about being included in this," she admitted. "I feel like I'm being given inside access to a police investigation."

"Remember, everything Daniel has given us is public record. He isn't giving us inside access."

"I know, but it's still exciting," Shelly laughed. "Maybe I'll learn something about police investigations that I can use in my books.

Maybe once I've finished the romance I'll try my hand at writing a murder mystery."

"That sounds difficult. I think I'll stick to doing historical research."

Fenella let herself into her apartment and put the envelope on the table near the door. Katie was already fast asleep in the middle of Fenella's king-sized bed. Fenella got ready for bed as quietly as she could, not wanting to disturb the sleeping animal. Of course, Katie woke up as Fenella climbed under the covers.

"Meerrrooww," she said sleepily.

"Sorry to bother you," Fenella replied, "but it is my bed, after all."

Katie stared at her through narrowed eyes for a minute and then put her head back down and went back to sleep. Fenella turned off the light.

"Hey, stop that," she said what felt like a minute later. Katie was gently tapping on Fenella's nose. "It can't be seven o'clock already," Fenella protested.

She opened one eye and squinted at the clock. It was seven, and Katie was hungry. As Fenella wondered why she'd ever let the kitten into her apartment, Katie dashed into the kitchen and began to shout loudly.

"Okay, I'm coming," Fenella shouted at her. "I just need a minute to wake up, that's all."

She stumbled her way into the kitchen and got Katie her breakfast. "Coffee would be good," she said loudly. "Lots and lots and lots of coffee."

"You really are quite addicted to coffee, aren't you?" Mona said from behind her.

Fenella jumped. The water that she'd been pouring into the coffee maker went everywhere, including all over Katie.

"Yoooowwwlll," Katie shouted, dashing out of the kitchen, leaving a trail of water behind her.

"Must you always sneak up on me like that?" Fenella asked her aunt as she reached for the roll of paper towels on the counter.

"You walked right past me on your way to the kitchen. I shouldn't have assumed that you saw me, I suppose," Mona sighed.

"I didn't have my eyes open," Fenella snapped.

"Go and shower," Mona told her. "By the time you're done, the coffee will be ready. Once you've had a cup of coffee, you'll be human again and we can talk about Ronald Sherman."

"What about Ronald Sherman?"

"I've been reading the papers that Daniel gave you. It's a fascinating case. I've several different theories as to what might have happened to the man."

"How could you read the papers?" Fenella demanded. She walked into the living room and found an empty envelope on the table by the door. The papers that had been inside it were neatly spread out across the table in the corner.

"I'm going to go and visit Max for a short while. I'll be back before midday so that we can talk before Shelly arrives." Mona faded away before Fenella could ask her any additional questions.

"Midday is noon, that much I know, but how did you know that Shelly was coming over this afternoon?" Fenella asked the empty room. "And how did you move all the papers?"

Mona didn't answer, and Katie simply shook her head at Fenella. After a shower and three cups of coffee, Fenella began to feel better. She still wanted answers to her questions, but she knew Mona well enough to know that she'd never get them. After a slice of toast and a clementine for breakfast, she sat down with the papers from Daniel.

Mona had arranged them by the date the various articles had appeared in the paper. Fenella read the first article, which simply reported that Ronald Sherman was missing. It gave a brief description of the man and then requested that anyone with any information about him should contact the police.

Two days later, the tone of the article in the paper seemed a bit more concerned. A photograph of the missing man was included and the article gave the police hotline number and more details about Ronald. His cousin, Gary, was quoted insisting that Ronald would never have simply disappeared. Gary was adamant that something awful must have happened to Ronald.

The articles that followed approached the story in different ways. There were interviews with various people who'd known Ronald, but

there were also several articles that seemed filled with pointless speculation as to what might have happened to the man.

"Dan Ross has missed his calling," Fenella muttered after a while.
"He's come up with several dozen different possibilities for what might
have happened to Ronald, only two or three of which seem at all
possible."

"Meeroow," Katie told her.

"What are his ideas? Well, he seems quite happy to speculate about
the various ways someone could kill a man and get rid of the body,"
Fenella told the animal. "Some of them seem a little far-fetched to me,
but I've never tried to get rid of a body, either. His other theory was
that Ronald found or maybe stole a whole lot of money. He then talks
about all the places in the world where someone could successfully
disappear. I didn't realize there were places like that anymore, at least
not places like that where anyone would actually want to live."

Katie had obviously grown bored with the subject. She got up and
left the room, heading for the spare bedroom where she liked to nap
on lazy mornings.

Fenella read for a while longer and then stopped to get paper and a
pen. She took a few notes as she continued to make her way through
the papers.

"Ahem," Mona said loudly. "I have arrived. Do not be frightened. It
is just your Aunt Mona."

"Very funny," Fenella told her. "You don't have to announce yourself
when you appear right in front of me. It's when you appear behind my
back that you startle me."

"I shall endeavor to always appear in front of you in the future,"
Mona told her. "If I can't manage that, I'll be extra noisy."

"Great," Fenella muttered.

"Have you finished all of the articles yet?"

"Nearly. I have one or two more to look at, but they're all much the
same, really. After a few days of fevered speculation, Mr. Ross seems to
have settled for simply reminding people that Ronald was still missing
and castigating the police for not solving the case."

"Yes, the last few articles were nearly identical and not at all helpful," Mona agreed.

"Then I just have to read the transcripts of the actual interviews with the various people involved."

"Those were boring, too," Mona complained. "Mr. Ross put everything interesting that anyone said into his articles. Reading the entire transcripts is a waste of time."

"I have another hour before Shelly will be here. I can probably get through them by that time. I'd hate to miss something, and you never know what's important."

"I'll be back at one when Shelly is due, then," Mona told her. "You're wasting your time reading them, though."

When Shelly knocked an hour later, Fenella was forced to admit to herself that Mona had been right. Everything that was at all interesting in any of the interviews had been included in the newspaper articles she'd already read. Fenella couldn't imagine the entire case hinging on any of the more mundane comments that were buried in the transcripts.

"I'm here, ready to learn everything I can about Ronald Sherman," Shelly said brightly when Fenella opened the door.

"Good luck," Fenella replied. "I've read everything and I don't think I know anything about the man."

Shelly frowned. "What do you mean?"

"From everything that everyone said about him, he was incredibly ordinary. No one could suggest any serious reason why he would have chosen to disappear, but no one could imagine why anyone would want to kill him, either."

"I'd better start reading. I'm sure you missed something," Shelly said, winking at Fenella.

"Good luck to you," Fenella replied. "I'm going to have lunch. Can I make you something?"

"I ate before I came over. You go and get yourself something," Shelly said, barely glancing up from the first article.

Fenella made herself a sandwich and ate it while standing over the sink. No doubt Mona wouldn't have approved, but it was quick and efficient. When she was done, she rejoined Shelly in the living room.

"May I borrow a sheet of paper and a pen?" she asked Fenella. "I want to keep track of the main suspects."

"I believe they're called witnesses, not suspects," Fenella told her as she handed her a pen and a small notebook.

"I can call them whatever I like," Shelly laughed. "In my mind, they're suspects, whatever the police say about the matter."

"I made a list, too. We can compare them when you're done."

"Are the transcripts interesting? I was thinking that I might skip them for now."

"If I weren't such a nice person, I'd lie and tell you to read them all, but they're incredibly dull. As we talk about each person, I'll tell you if there was anything interesting in their transcripts."

"That sounds good," Shelly said. "Give me five more minutes and I'll be ready."

Fenella got them each a cold drink and then sat down with her page of notes and waited for Shelly.

"Okay, I'm ready," Mona said, dropping into the chair next to Fenella. "Maybe I need a notebook, though. You and Shelly are both taking notes. I'll be right back. Don't start without me."

Biting her tongue to stop herself from replying to Mona, Fenella wondered if the woman really could get a notebook and pen from somewhere. Shelly couldn't see or hear Mona, but what if she could see the notebook and pen? It seemed impossible, but then Fenella still wasn't sure that she believed in ghosts anyway.

"I think I'm ready," Shelly said a moment later.

Mona reappeared in her chair, a small notebook in one hand and an expensive-looking fountain pen in the other. Fenella relaxed when it became clear that Shelly couldn't see Mona or anything she was holding.

"I have to say, I didn't get any flashes of inspiration while I was reading the articles," Shelly sighed. "There didn't seem to be any clues at all, really. From what the paper said, Ronald was here one day and gone the next. He never told anyone he was leaving and he's never contacted anyone since."

"Maybe it was aliens," Mona suggested.

"It wasn't aliens," Fenella snapped.

Shelly raised an eyebrow. "Who said anything about aliens?" she asked.

Fenella shook her head. "Sorry. I had a colleague back in the US who always blamed everything that happened on aliens. Mostly it was when things disappeared from the office, like food and drinks from the staff refrigerator or miscellaneous office supplies. Every time someone asked her about anything that was missing, she'd always suggest that it was aliens."

"And it was never aliens?"

"She ended up moving to a different university and then getting fired for taking home office supplies. We only found out about it because when the police searched her apartment they found hundreds of pens and notebooks with our university's name on them."

"Did you just make that whole story up?" Mona demanded.

Fenella gave her aunt an enigmatic smile. "But if it wasn't aliens, what do you think happened to Ronald?" she asked Shelly.

"I really hope he left voluntarily, even if he stole someone else's money in order to fund his travels. The other obvious answer is that something horrible happened to him."

"But it could be some combination of the two, as well," Mona said. "Maybe he left of his own accord and then got run over by a car somewhere in the UK."

"If he met with an accident, either here or in the UK, surely the body would have been identified, if not immediately, then eventually. The man's been missing for nearly seven years," Fenella said thoughtfully.

"I did some research into missing people this morning," Shelly said, flushing when Fenella looked at her. "I was curious, that's all. According to the UK Home Office, about 250,000 people go missing in the UK every year."

"That's a lot of people," Fenella said. "That's over twice the island's population."

"Yes, but again according to the Home Office, ninety-nine percent of the cases are solved within a year."

"So Ronald is unusual in that he's not been found."

"Exactly. Which suggests that something has kept him from coming back," Shelly said. "I started looking at ways to get rid of a body, but then I started to worry about someone seeing my search history and locking me up."

Fenella laughed. "Let's talk about the various witnesses. Maybe that will give us an idea or two."

"As I said yesterday, Gary Mack helped install my kitchen. He seemed like a perfectly ordinary man."

"And he was the one who reported Ronald missing, so it seems unlikely that he had anything to do with the man's disappearance."

"Did he say anything in the press transcripts that was at all interesting?" Shelly asked.

Fenella shook her head. "He said something about having met with Ronald every month for many years, and that the man had never even been late for a single meeting. That was why he went straight to the police on the Saturday afternoon. From what he said, he thought maybe Ronald had been in an accident. He tried Ronald's mobile and didn't get any reply, which was also apparently unusual."

Shelly nodded. "Ronald was in his forties, so maybe less attached to his mobile than a teenager would have been, but he'd still have kept it with him, and I would have thought he'd have answered it when his cousin rang. Did I read in the paper somewhere that his mobile never turned up?"

"Yes, that was in there somewhere," Fenella said. "Or at least it hadn't turned up by the time Dan Ross stopped covering the story. That's something we could ask Daniel, though. I suppose once the bill stopped being paid, the phone would have been disconnected or whatever the phone company does under those circumstances."

"The number has probably been reassigned to someone else by now," Shelly speculated. "That's what usually happens, I believe."

"Right, so Gary Mack is our first and best witness. He was supposed to be having lunch with Ronald on the day he disappeared."

"His supervisor at the computer company was interviewed and he told the papers that Ronald had been at work on Friday as normal."

"That was Eugene Matthews," Fenella said. "He claimed that Ronald left at six, same as always, and that they'd made plans to start a new project together on the Monday, which suggests that Ronald wasn't planning to go anywhere that weekend."

"He's the same one who said that Ronald had told him about finding a fortune, though, isn't he? Maybe he killed Ronald to get his hands on that money," Shelly said.

"Surely, if that were the case, he wouldn't have told the police about it," Fenella countered. "No one else heard anything about any fortune."

"Including the other man who worked with them. Lucas Hardy had only just started at the company a few months before Ronald disappeared, though. Maybe he and Ronald hadn't had time to become friends yet."

"Maybe. The papers interviewed Lucas but he didn't say much. As you say, he'd only been with the company for a short while, and he claimed that he'd barely spoken to Ronald in those few months."

"Manx Computing Innovations," Shelly said thoughtfully. "The name is vaguely familiar. I wonder if I've ever used them for anything."

"It would be interesting to find out if Eugene and Lucas are still working for them," Mona said. "You could spill water on your laptop and take it in to get it fixed."

Fenella frowned at her aunt. Her laptop was getting old. No doubt spilling water on it would kill it, no matter how many experts she tried to consult. "I may need a new laptop," she told Shelly. "Maybe we should pay them a visit."

"Daniel won't like it," Shelly warned.

"Surely Eugene and Lucas aren't even still working there," Fenella argued. "I'm sure shops like that go through staff at an enormous rate. There probably isn't anyone there who even remembers Ronald Sherman."

"You could be right, but then we'd be wasting our time visiting," Shelly replied.

"Except maybe I could get a new laptop."

"Do you really need one? I thought you were just making an excuse to visit the shop."

"I truly could use one," Fenella said. "Or rather, I'd really like one and I seem to have enough money to afford it. My old one is about six years old, which is about seventy-five in computer years."

Shelly laughed. "I have an old desktop that my husband bought about ten years ago. It seems to be doing the job for my writing, so far, anyway, touch wood."

"Touch wood? Is that like knock on wood?"

"I suppose so, but why would you knock on wood?"

"I've no idea. I suppose to scare away the spirits that might take away your good fortune."

"Now that you've said that, maybe I should start knocking instead of just touching," Shelly mused.

"Spirits don't interfere in the lives of the living," Mona said. "I believe the saying originated because people believed that supernatural beings lived in trees and would help people if asked."

"Really?" Fenella said.

"Well, yes, really, I mean, if that's the reason why you knock," Shelly replied, looking slightly confused.

Fenella frowned at Mona, who was laughing at her. "Anyway, maybe you could do with a new computer, too, then," she said to Shelly. "Maybe something new would help you write faster."

"Ha. I don't think anything can help with that, but a new computer is tempting. As is a visit to Manx Computing Innovations, just in case any of the suspects, er, witnesses still work there."

"Daniel can't possibly object to our doing some shopping," Fenella said. "Trying to track down the other witnesses would be a different story, of course."

"I would love to have my kitchen redone," Shelly said. "I wonder if Gary still works for the company I used all those years ago."

"I think Daniel might get suspicious if we go looking for too many witnesses," Fenella said. "I have two others on my list as well, and I've no idea where to find either of them."

"That would be the girlfriend and the ex-girlfriend, right?" Shelly asked. "I have them on my list, too."

"Yes, Cassie Patton was Ronald's girlfriend when he disappeared, although by the sound of it they weren't getting along very well at the time. Helen Campbell was his former girlfriend. She gave the papers a long interview, but they only printed a little bit of it."

"I assume you read the whole thing. Is there anything interesting in it?" Shelly asked.

Fenella shook her head. "She complained a lot about Ronald. Apparently he never wanted to do anything fun and he didn't have any ambition. You're welcome to read the transcript yourself, but it seemed to me as if she was just venting her frustration after a failed relationship."

"I wonder where she is now," Shelly said.

"She was working for one of the banks when Ronald disappeared. I believe I have an account there, or rather Mona did," Fenella told her.

"I had accounts at every bank on the island," Mona said. "You should go and visit some of my money."

"So maybe we do have an excuse to visit her," Shelly replied. "What about Cassie? She was the current girlfriend. I'd rather talk to her, anyway."

Fenella checked her notes. "She was working for the ShopFast in Ramsey when Ronald disappeared."

"I doubt she's still there," Shelly sighed. "Shop assistants don't tend to stay in one place for very long. Anyway, we have a ShopFast right down the street. I'm not sure what excuse we could use for going to the one in Ramsey."

"Daniel just wanted us to read through the articles and see if we could come up with any insights into what might have happened to Ronald Sherman. I'm sure he doesn't want us trying to talk to any of the witnesses."

"Well, he's going to be disappointed, then, because I don't have any idea what happened to the man based on what I read in those articles," Shelly replied. "Do you think there will be something in the paper about him reopening the case? Maybe some of the witnesses will make new statements if there is."

"I suspect if someone at the paper hears that Daniel is reopening the investigation, then the paper will try to track down everyone involved," Fenella said. "They'll be able to find out where people are working now and they'll probably put that information in the paper."

"So we can find an excuse to go and talk to whomever they find," Shelly said happily. "We have a good reason to visit Manx Computer Innovations, anyway. Let's do that now."

Fenella glanced at the clock. "I'm supposed to be having dinner with Todd in an hour," she said. "He has to eat early because the band is hoping to get a bit of practice in before the show tonight. I don't think we have time to go computer shopping today."

Shelly frowned. "How about first thing tomorrow, then?"

"Sure, as long as first thing is ten or eleven. The band will probably play until midnight or later, so I'm hoping to sleep late tomorrow."

"Manx Computer Innovations probably doesn't open much before nine, anyway, so ten or eleven is fine."

"I don't think we're going to be able to help Daniel much based on what was in the papers seven years ago," Mona said. "Let's hope word does get out that Daniel is reopening the investigation. That's probably the easiest way for us to track down the other suspects, and you're going to have to talk to everyone if you're going to solve the case."

"I don't think I'm going to be able to solve the case," Fenella said.

"I don't think Daniel is expecting you to solve it," Shelly told her.

Fenella sighed. She needed to learn not to respond to Mona, no matter what the other woman said. "No, I know, but I'm sure he'd be happy if I did."

"And you're interested in making him happy."

Blushing, Fenella shook her head. "I'm interested in finding out what happened to poor Ronald Sherman. I mean, it would be nice to solve the case for a whole lot of reasons."

"Including impressing Daniel," Shelly suggested, "but you have Todd to worry about in the meantime."

"Todd isn't a worry. He's fun, but he isn't really looking for a serious relationship. I don't think he's ever quite recovered from his wife's death."

"That's a shame. If you'd have asked me eighteen months ago, I would have insisted that I'd never recover if anything happened to John, but now that he's been gone for over a year, I do feel as if another man might find a place in my heart eventually. John and I were very happy together. Maybe I just miss being part of a couple."

"You are coming to hear the band tonight, right?"

"Yes, of course. I, um, promised Tim that I'd come early, actually," Shelly said, blushing.

"So tell me about Tim. Todd said something about him having been married before, but I don't know much else about him."

"He was married twice. His first wife cheated on him. Todd mentioned that, didn't he? She cheated with Mark, who's also in the band. Apparently that caused some trouble for a short while, but they all get along now."

"Weird," Fenella said.

"I should say that Mark and Tim get along now. It probably helps that the woman in question also cheated on Mark and is no longer on the island."

"Yeah, that would make a difference," Fenella agreed.

"Anyway, Tim reckons he was better off without her. He lost his second wife to cancer about three years ago."

"How sad."

"Yes, from what he's said about her, they were devoted to one another. I get the feeling that he hasn't really been involved with anyone since her passing."

"What about children? And what does he do for a living? Surely being in the band doesn't make him enough money to live on?"

"He never had any children in either marriage," Shelly replied, "and he's actually an architect, believe it or not."

"An architect? Really?"

"Yes. He works for ShopFast, designing their shops and other things. I didn't realize large companies sometimes employ their own architects on a full-time basis, but apparently they do."

"How interesting. And he plays with The Islanders in his spare time."

"He's been playing with them for most of his life," Shelly told her. "He simply loves music and loves to perform. He's quite content on the island, playing with a local band once in a while. He's not chasing fame and fortune like Paul."

"And you like him a lot," Fenella suggested.

Shelly blushed. "I do like him a lot. He's right around my age, attractive, and we always have fun together. I sort of feel as if I'm cheating on Gordon when I'm with him, though."

"Have you mentioned him to Gordon?"

"Not exactly. I haven't spoken to Gordon in weeks. We've simply exchanged texts a few times. Basically, he texts something exciting like 'hi' and I respond in kind. There really isn't an easy way to casually drop Tim into that sort of exchange."

Fenella nodded. "You shouldn't feel as if you're cheating, then. If the man isn't bothering to ask you how you are and what you've been doing, then he can't be upset if you don't tell him things."

"I suppose so."

"And now I must find something to wear," Fenella said. "We're just going to that little Italian place on the promenade for dinner, so nothing fancy."

"You should still dress as if he were taking you somewhere wonderful. Men like to feel that they are appreciated," Mona said.

Fenella rolled her eyes at her aunt and then headed for the bedroom with Shelly on her heels. No doubt the perfect dress for the evening ahead would be hanging in Mona's wardrobe.

❦ 4 ❧

"You look gorgeous," Todd said when Fenella opened the door to him an hour later. "Far too nice for a casual meal." He named the very expensive and exclusive restaurant that was a few doors away from the Italian place they'd been planning to visit. "I haven't been there yet, but I understand the food is wonderful."

"I've been there a few times," Fenella said. Donald had taken her when it had first opened, and then she and Shelly had visited more recently. On that visit their waiter had insisted on putting their meals on Donald's account, something that Fenella still needed to discuss with Donald. The last thing she wanted to do was have her dinner with Todd billed to Donald. "It's usually really busy. We probably can't get a table on such short notice."

Todd laughed. "There are some advantages to the small amount of fame that has come my way over the years," he told her. "I'm pretty sure we can get a table."

Fenella nodded and then picked up her handbag. "Be a good kitty," she told Katie as they left the apartment.

Todd held her hand as they rode the elevator down to the lobby. "Are you sure you have time for something fancy?" Fenella asked as they began to walk toward the restaurant.

"I can make time," Todd assured her. "No one will mind if I turn up late, anyway."

Fenella knew that was true. The Islanders were always grateful to Todd when he stepped in to help out when someone else was missing. Todd usually brought in a much larger audience for them to perform in front of, and there was always a chance that one of his music industry friends might attend and offer someone in the band his big break.

The doorman at the restaurant seemed to be arguing with a well-dressed man in his forties when Fenella and Todd reached the building.

"I can't believe you don't know who I am," the man was saying angrily. "I could buy this building and every other building in this town, and then I could shut your fancy restaurant. You wouldn't be nearly so smug if you lost your job, would you?"

"I'm sorry, sir, but the restaurant operates on a very strict bookings-only system. We wouldn't even let the Queen herself get a table without a booking. I believe we have an opening next week on Wednesday if you'd like to come back."

The pretty blonde woman who was hanging on the angry man's arm sighed deeply. "Let's just go. I heard the food isn't that good here anyway."

"I'm not going to just go," the man shouted. "I demand to see the owner."

"I'm sorry, but the primary owner is in America at the moment," the doorman said. "I can get the manager for you, if you'd like."

"Yes, I'll see the manager," the man agreed.

The doorman said a few words into his attached headpiece, and then smiled at Fenella.

"Ms. Woods, it's lovely to see you again. And Mr. Hughes, I didn't realize you were joining us tonight. Chef is a huge fan of your music. Your table is ready for you." He opened the door behind him and let Fenella and Todd enter the restaurant. They nearly ran into a harassed-looking man in an expensive suit who was heading outside.

"Ms. Woods, Mr. Hughes, thank you for joining us tonight," he said quickly. "I have to go and deal with a difficult customer, but I'll be back in a moment. If you need or want anything, just ask."

Todd looked at Fenella. "It seems as if they know you here."

"I came with Donald once," Fenella replied. "I believe he has a financial interest in the place."

Todd nodded. "Maybe he'll pick up the bill for us, then," he said lightly.

"Ah, Ms. Woods, Mr. Hughes, let me show you to your table," one of the waiters interrupted.

They were shown to a small table for two in the back corner of the building. "Will this do?" the waiter asked.

"It's fine," Todd replied. He held Fenella's chair for her and then sat down beside her.

"Chef is very excited that you've decided to dine here tonight," the waiter told Todd. "He understands that you were served a special ten-course meal at the new restaurant in the north of the island."

"We were. The chef and owner is a friend of mine," Todd replied.

"Chef would like to do something similar for you tonight, if you have the time," the waiter said. "Including wine pairings, of course."

Todd looked at Fenella, who shrugged. "That would be fine," he told the waiter. "As neither of us is driving, wine pairings sound good, too."

"Is your life always like this?" Fenella asked as the man walked away.

Todd shrugged. "It wasn't, not for many years. I worked hard to get to where I am professionally. Now that I've achieved some level of success, yes, life is often like this, and I fully enjoy the advantages that come with my fame. There are downsides, of course, but that's one of the reasons why I like living on the island. People here don't generally seem all that impressed with me."

Fenella laughed. "Except the chef here."

"I never complain when people want to make me delicious food."

The first course arrived a moment later, along with the first glasses of wine. "Delicious," Fenella sighed after her first bite. "I'm sorry I had lunch today. If I'd known what we were in for, I wouldn't have eaten since Sunday."

Todd chuckled. "Maybe you won't like one or two of the courses."

"I feel terrible saying it, but I rather hope so."

Every course was delicious, however, and Fenella found herself feeling stuffed by the time they arrived at the dessert course. All the wine was starting to make her feel a little bit tipsy, as well.

"While Chef can do fancier puddings, he thought a hot chocolate sponge with a molten center would be best," the waiter said as he set down their dessert plates.

Fenella sighed with pleasure. "It almost looks too good to eat," she told the man.

"It tastes better than it looks," he assured her.

"The waiter was right," she said to Todd after her first bite. "This is amazing."

"It's good," Todd shrugged, "but I don't usually eat much pudding."

Fenella made a mental black mark next to the man's name. How could anyone not like dessert?

"We're going to be terribly late," she said as the waiter cleared their last plates.

"Chef was hoping he might have a quick word," the waiter said.

"After that gorgeous meal, of course he can," Todd replied.

Fenella was only half listening as the chef told Todd what a huge fan he was and Todd complimented the meal. "I'm so glad you enjoyed it," the chef said when Todd was done. "Everything is with my compliments tonight."

"Are you quite sure?" Todd asked. "We ate a lot, and drank a lot as well."

"I'm quite sure. If you feel you must do something, I'll take an autograph, but only if you feel you must."

Todd laughed. "I'm more than happy to give you an autograph," he said. The waiter brought over a menu and Todd signed it with a flourish. "Thank you again," he told the man as the chef took the menu and headed back toward the kitchen.

Todd put a generous tip on the table. "And now we must dash," he said, glancing at the clock on the wall near the bar.

Fenella took his arm and they rushed out of the building. There was a short line of people waiting to get inside, and Fenella noticed that the angry man from earlier was in the line.

"I wonder if they'll find him a table," she murmured to Todd.

"I doubt it, not after he shouted at the doorman like that," Todd replied. "As he's still waiting, maybe they've agreed to do something, though."

There was also a line of people waiting to get into the pub. Todd sighed as they approached. "Someone must have told someone that I was playing tonight," he said. "We'll have to sneak in the back way."

Fenella followed the man into the hotel portion of the building and then up and down the corridors and stairs that led to the hidden door at the back of the pub.

"It's busy," Fenella said, "but not as bad as it's been before."

Todd nodded and then led her over to the small stage on the back wall. The band was already on stage, but they were talking together, not playing. Shelly was sitting in a small roped-off area by herself.

Todd led Fenella into the area and then pulled her close. "I may not get a chance to talk to you between sets," he whispered. "We'll sneak out together at the end, okay?"

"Sure," Fenella agreed.

Todd gave her a casual kiss and then released her. As Fenella dropped into the chair next to Shelly, she glanced around the room. When her eyes met Daniel's she muttered "fudge" under her breath.

"Fudge?" Shelly asked.

"When I first started teaching, I forced myself to substitute nicer words for the swear words that I'd used when I'd been a student," Fenella explained. "It was never as satisfactory as letting loose with a proper curse, but I was worried about keeping my job in those early days. Anyway, it became habit."

"Should I ask why you felt the need to curse just then?"

Fenella looked at her. "I just spotted Daniel in the crowd."

"Fudge," Shelly exclaimed. "Do you think he saw Todd kissing you?"

"I'm pretty sure he did," Fenella sighed.

"He was living with Tiffany," Shelly reminded her. "Lucky for you, it was a pretty innocent kiss."

Fenella nodded. "Both of those things are true, but I still feel pretty awful," she admitted. "Let's talk about something else."

"How was dinner?" Shelly asked.

Fenella told her friend about their change in plans and the lavish feast that had been prepared for them.

"I want to start going to dinner with you and Todd," Shelly complained. "I've never been fed a fabulous ten-course meal prepared especially for me by a world-class chef."

"After the first few courses it all sort of runs together," Fenella told her. "I do remember the dessert really well, though."

Shelly laughed. "Why am I not surprised?"

"I drank too much, though. I didn't mean to, but the waiter brought out a different glass of wine with each course. I should have just taken a sip or two of each rather than finishing them all, but they were all really good. Now I'm a bit giddy and I feel very much like confronting Daniel about Tiffany. Make sure that I behave, okay?"

"The good news is that Daniel is stuck in the crowd somewhere," Shelly told her. "No more drinking for you. Hopefully you'll sober up before the night is out."

"Todd is going to walk me home. I hope Daniel is long gone by that time. I'd rather he not see me and Todd together again."

"You've every right to be with Todd," Shelly said firmly.

"And what if Gordon walked in right now? How would you feel about him seeing you with Tim?"

Shelly blushed. "That's different," she muttered.

Before they could talk any further, the band began the first song. Forty-five minutes later Fenella was feeling a bit less giddy and a lot more tired.

"Todd isn't going to be happy if I leave early, is he?" she asked Shelly as the band took a break.

"Probably not, but you look really tired," Shelly replied.

"I am really tired. Maybe I'm coming down with something. I may just go home."

"I'll walk home with you," Shelly offered. "Tim won't mind."

"Tim won't mind what?" a voice said from behind Shelly.

"If I leave now and walk Fenella home. She's tired," Shelly told Tim, who sat down next to Shelly and took her hand while she was speaking.

"You do what you need to do," Tim replied. "Fenella does look really tired."

"I can walk myself home," Fenella told the pair. "You stay and enjoy the show. We only live a few doors away and it's still early. I'll be fine on my own."

Shelly frowned. "Are you sure?"

"I'm very sure," Fenella said firmly. "Can you give Todd my apologies?" she asked Tim. "I'm not sure what's wrong with me, but I really think I should go home."

"I'll tell him," Tim replied.

"Tell him that I'm going straight to bed, so I'd rather he didn't ring me until tomorrow morning," Fenella added as she stood up. She yawned and then looked at the stage. Todd was surrounded by people and he looked energized as he laughed at something someone had said.

"I'll ring you in the morning," Shelly told her. "I'm a little bit worried about you."

"Don't be. I ate too much rich food and drank too much wine. I just need to sleep it all off," Fenella said.

"Do you think I should go with her?" Shelly asked Tim as Fenella began to make her way around the ropes. Determined to leave Shelly behind, Fenella tried to walk quickly, but the crowd made that impossible. When she was halfway across the room she glanced back. Shelly was still sitting with Tim.

Fenella sighed with relief and then tried to find a way through yet another group of people who seemed determined to block her way.

"Leaving so soon?" a voice said at her elbow.

Fenella felt her heart race as Daniel took her arm. He steered her through the crowds and out into the fresh sea air. "Thank you," she said.

"You're very pale," he said. "Are you okay?"

"I'm fine. I had too much food and way too much wine at dinner and then came here where it was too crowded and loud, that's all. I think I probably have a migraine coming on."

The fact that she was feeling slightly disconnected from everything that was happening made that seem more likely. What she needed to do was get home, take a few pills, and then go to bed.

❦ "I'll walk you home," Daniel said.

Fenella thought about objecting, but that seemed far too much effort. Instead, she fell into step next to the man.

"I'd heard that you and Todd Hughes were a couple, but I wasn't sure if it was true or not," he said a moment later.

"We go out sometimes," Fenella replied. "It isn't anything serious, though. He travels as much as he's here, really."

"Like Donald, then."

"Sort of. Donald is in New York until the new year. His daughter was in a bad car accident there."

"I'd heard that. I hope she improves."

"We all do."

"Todd's very talented and he's been very successful, I understand," Daniel said.

"Yes, I believe he has."

"He'll have lots of money, then, to fund all of his travels."

"I suppose so. I think his trips are often paid for by his famous friends, though. He's spending Thanksgiving in Hawaii." She told Daniel whom Todd was visiting there.

Daniel whistled softly. "I can't even imagine what it would be like to have famous friends," he said as they walked into Fenella's building.

"Me, either," she replied.

"Too bad Todd didn't invite you to join him in Hawaii," Daniel said as they boarded the elevator.

"He did," Fenella sighed. "Someone has been smoking on the elevator."

"How can you tell?"

"It smells of smoke," she replied. When Daniel shrugged, she sighed. "That's another sign that I'm getting a migraine," she told him. "I get a lot more sensitive to smells. As the pain is starting to set in, though, I really don't need any more signs."

Daniel took her arm as the elevator seemed to lurch to a stop. She took a few deep breaths before she started walking.

"Are you okay?" Daniel asked as she walked slowly down the corridor.

"It's too bright in here," she complained. "I'm sorry. I haven't had a migraine in months, and this one seems to be coming on very quickly and very badly. I just need to get to bed."

The first wave of nausea hit as Fenella tried to find her keycard. Don't throw up on Daniel, she chanted to herself as she fumbled through her bag. Tears of frustration sprang into her eyes. "Where is the stupid key?" she asked through gritted teeth.

Daniel took the bag out of her hand and looked inside. "I can see it," he told her. "May I?"

"Yes, please," she said, leaning against the doorframe as another wave of pain washed over her.

Daniel opened her door and then stepped back as she rushed inside, fighting the urge to vomit. "Are you going to be okay?" he asked.

She looked at him and then nodded before rushing past him to the nearest bathroom. A few minutes later her stomach was empty and she was feeling slightly better. Her head was still pounding, but the sick feeling was gone, anyway. Daniel was standing at the window when she walked back into the living room.

"I'm sorry about that," she said. "It's a bad one. I need to take some pills and go to bed."

"I was going to just leave, but I wanted to be sure you were okay first," Daniel replied. "I hope you feel better in the morning."

"I'm sure I will," Fenella replied. "Sleep is the best cure."

Daniel looked as if he wanted to say something more, but after a moment he simply nodded at her and then walked to the door. "Good night," he said softly before he let himself out.

Fenella locked the door behind him and then found her headache medicine. She took two tablets with a few sips of water and then crawled into bed with a cool washcloth over her eyes. She felt Katie jump onto the bed a moment later. The kitten curled up against Fenella's back and they both fell asleep.

Fenella felt fuzzy-headed when she woke up the next morning. Katie was staring at her with a concerned expression on her little face.

"What time is it?" she asked.

Katie looked at the clock on the bedside table and then shrugged. Fenella squinted at it. "It's nearly nine," Fenella exclaimed. "You lovely little creature. Thank you for letting me sleep off my headache."

"Merrow," Katie told her. She jumped down off the bed and headed to the kitchen. Fenella wasn't far behind her. No doubt the tiny animal was starving; she was used to having breakfast at seven. Fenella filled her food bowl and refilled her water bowl. She added a few treats as well, still feeling grateful to Katie for the extra hours of sleep.

"Good morning," Mona said quietly. "Are you feeling better this morning?"

Fenella took a moment to consider the question before she replied. "I think so. I still feel slightly removed from everything, as if I'm viewing the world through a filter of some sort or something, but that often happens after a bad migraine."

"The pain is gone, though?"

"Yes, the pain is mercifully gone."

"I was here when you came in last night, but you didn't seem to notice," Mona told her.

"My head was throbbing, and I was busy throwing up, as well," Fenella sighed. "I'm sure Daniel was very impressed."

"He mostly just looked worried. He wasn't the only one. Katie was beside herself."

"It was just a migraine. I've been getting them since I was a child, but I usually have more warning before they get that bad."

"What triggers them?"

Fenella shrugged. "It's usually related to my monthly cycle more than anything else, but I suspect last night's might have been triggered by the fact that I mixed red and white wine. I drank quite a lot of both, too."

"I thought you were going to the Italian restaurant?"

"Todd decided that I looked too nice to go there," Fenella told her. She explained about the change of plans and the ten-course meal with wine pairings that she and Todd had enjoyed.

"Ten different glasses of wine? That would probably give anyone a headache," Mona commented.

"They were more like half-glasses," Fenella told her. "I don't think I drank much more than half a bottle of wine, and we were there for over two hours. I felt a bit lightheaded, but not drunk. I'm pretty sure it was mixing the types, rather than the amount that I drank that caused the problem."

"What time are you meant to be meeting Shelly?"

Fenella sighed. "I told her ten. I'd better get through the shower."

She started a pot of coffee brewing and then grabbed a handful of cereal to keep her going while she took a quick shower. After she was ready for the day, she made herself a more substantial breakfast to go with her coffee. Once that was gone, she felt much better, almost back to normal.

Her mobile buzzed as she loaded her breakfast dishes into the dishwasher.

Just wanted to check that you are okay today, the text from Daniel read.

I'm fine. It was just a migraine. Thanks for checking on me, Fenella wrote back.

Do you get them often?

Occasionally. I can usually stop them before they get bad, but last night's caught me by surprise.

Are we still on for seven tonight, then? he asked.

Yes, of course. I don't think I have any helpful insights to offer, though. I didn't get much from the papers you gave me.

Never mind. Sometimes it's just helpful to talk things through with another person. I'll see you at seven.

Fenella put her phone down and sighed. "Daniel was just checking on me," she told Mona.

"As I said, he looked very worried last night."

"I can't believe I had a chance to talk to him and I didn't ask him about Tiffany."

"Did he ask you about Todd? Or Donald? Or Peter?"

Fenella shook her head. "He said something about Todd, but the whole conversation is something of a blur. Maybe I'll get a chance to talk to him about everything tonight."

"Just be sure that you're ready to hear his answers," Mona warned her.

"What does that mean?"

"How will you feel if you find out that he and Tiffany were intimately involved?"

"I'm sort of assuming that they were," Fenella replied dryly. "She stayed at his house for something like a month. Even if Daniel wasn't planning on that sort of relationship, I got the feeling that Tiffany was."

"Oh, yes. She was most definitely a woman with a plan," Mona agreed. "Since she's no longer here, I would suggest that her plan failed, but that doesn't mean that Daniel didn't care about her, at least to some extent. Be ready to hear about that if you start asking questions."

Fenella nodded. "I think I'd rather know than not," she said slowly. "Maybe not tonight, though, not after last night. I'm still feeling a little fragile."

A knock on the door kept Mona from replying.

"Are you okay?" Shelly demanded as Fenella opened the door. "You didn't look at all well when you left the pub last night."

"It was just a migraine," Fenella told her. "I get them occasionally, but I usually realize that they're coming and take something to stop them before they get too bad."

"I tried to follow you, but I couldn't get through the crowds," Shelly told her. "Then I saw Daniel take your arm and I knew you'd be okay."

"Daniel saw me safely home, and he stayed to make sure I was okay after I started throwing up."

Shelly gave Fenella a hug. "How awful for you. Are you sure you're okay now?"

"I'm fine. I slept like a log and didn't wake up until nearly nine. Katie didn't try to wake me for once, and I'm hugely grateful for that."

"She's a good kitty," Shelly cooed as Katie walked over to get some affection.

"Yes, she is," Fenella agreed.

"Do you still want to go and look at computers this morning?" Shelly asked after she'd fussed over Katie for several minutes.

"We may as well. I've nothing else to do."

The phone rang, startling Fenella. She jumped and then shrugged. "I'm a little on edge, I think," she told Shelly as she picked up the receiver.

"Hello?"

"Are you okay?" Todd demanded. "Shelly said that you weren't well."

"I had a migraine, that's all. I came home, took some pills, and went straight to bed. I'm fine today."

"Thank goodness for that. I got worried when I looked out at the crowd and you'd gone. I hope it wasn't our music that gave you the headache."

Fenella chuckled. "I think it was mixing all those different wines together that did it," she told him. "I don't usually drink red wine, so that might have been the trigger."

Todd sighed. "I really wanted a chance to spend some time with you last night after the show. Tonight I'm having dinner with the governor and some visitors from the UK. Are you free for dinner tomorrow night?"

"I can do that," Fenella agreed, "but maybe not ten courses with wine."

Todd laughed. "How about if I cook something for you?" he suggested. "I can't cook much, but I did learn how to make this great chicken dish with rice. It's my standby meal when I want to impress someone."

"Do you make it often, then?" Fenella had to ask.

"No, not at all. In fact, I haven't made it in years, but I'm sure I remember how. Anyway, it will give you a chance to see my house and for us to have some private time together. What do you think?"

"I don't want you to get the wrong idea," Fenella said hesitantly.

Todd laughed. "I don't expect you to swoon over my cooking and fall into my bed if that's what you mean. I'd just like to enjoy a meal with you and not feel as if the entire island's gossip network is watching."

"Okay, then. Where do you live and what time should I be there?"

"I don't live far from you, actually," Todd told her. "I'll meet you at your flat around seven. We can walk to my house from your place. That's easier than trying to explain how to get around my security."

"I'm intrigued."

"I hope that's a good thing," Todd laughed. "I'll see you around seven tomorrow. I'm really glad you're feeling better."

"So am I."

She put the phone down. "Todd is going to cook for me tomorrow night."

"Is he? That sounds romantic."

"I just hope he doesn't expect things to get too romantic."

Fenella's phone buzzed again as she was putting on her shoes.

I forgot to mention it, but there's an article in today's paper about Ronald Sherman. If you get a chance, read it before tonight.

Fenella read the text from Daniel to herself, and then read it out to Shelly.

"Maybe we should get a local paper before we go computer shopping," Shelly suggested. "It might tell us whether there's any point in going to Manx Computer Innovations or not."

"I really do want a new laptop," Fenella reminded her friend. "But yes, let's get a paper before we do anything else."

There was a small convenience store only a few doors away. Shelly bought a paper and then she and Fenella settled onto a bench to read the article.

"There's not much new in it," Shelly said once she'd finished.

"I don't know that there's anything new in it, aside from the fact that Daniel has reopened the investigation. We already knew that, of course."

"Dan Ross mentions that he's going to be reopening his investigation, too," Shelly pointed out. "Maybe he'll learn something interesting this time."

"He doesn't seem to have done anything yet," Fenella sighed. "There isn't any current information on any of the suspects."

"I thought you wanted to call them witnesses," Shelly laughed. "You're right, though. I was hoping that he'd tell us where to find everyone, but he hasn't."

"I suppose that means we'll have to start with Manx Computer Innovations and work from there," Fenella said. "Where is their shop?"

"In a little strip of shops in Onchan," Shelly told her. "Do you want to drive or should I?"

"Oh, I'll drive," Fenella said quickly. "I know it isn't far, but we may as well take Mona's car."

Shelly laughed. "You'll take any excuse to drive Mona's car."

"That's very true," Fenella agreed. "I love that car."

They took the elevator down to the garage and then climbed into Mona's racy red convertible. Fenella glanced at the far more sensible car that was parked in the space next to it.

"I do like my other car, too," she told Shelly. "It's perfect for things like grocery shopping, but it isn't nearly as much fun to drive."

"Let's put the top down," Shelly suggested as Fenella started the engine.

"It's pretty cold," Fenella said doubtfully.

"But it's much more fun," Shelly laughed.

Fenella felt invigorated and more than a little windblown when she parked in the lot at the row of shops a few minutes later.

"That was wonderful. We should take a longer drive after we've done our shopping," Shelly suggested.

"You know I'm not going to say no," Fenella laughed as she locked the car.

Manx Computer Innovations had a small storefront in the strip, which was about half-empty. "I can't imagine they do a lot of business out here," Fenella remarked as they approached the store.

"There used to be some interesting shops in the row, but most of them have gone now. There used to be a wonderful bakery, too, but they moved to a better location as soon as they started doing well."

Fenella nodded. She glanced at a large store that seemed to sell nothing but curtains and blinds, and a smaller shop with a window display full of suitcases and briefcases. The wind blew down the strip, stirring up a few empty potato chip bags and half of a torn sale flyer from the curtain shop.

"It's almost creepy," she said under her breath.

"As I said, it used to be nice," Shelly told her. "I've heard rumors that someone new is planning to buy it and bring in a few big UK retailers. I hope the rumors are right."

Fenella nodded. "Let's look in the window first," she suggested.

There wasn't much to see in the windows of the computer shop, though. There were a few signs about upcoming courses that were being offered and a large display of cardboard-cutouts of televisions.

"Do you need a television?" Shelly asked Fenella.

"We don't just sell televisions," a voice said. Fenella spun around and then forced herself to smile at the man who'd joined them. His dark hair was long and pulled into a low ponytail. He was wearing brown pants and a green polo shirt with the shop's name embroidered onto it. Fenella guessed that he was getting close to forty, with maybe a year or two to go. He looked as if he exercised regularly, and he seemed slightly arrogant as he grinned back at her.

"No?" she said.

"We sell complete home entertainment systems," he said. "Flat-screen tellys, projection models, surround-sound systems, gaming equipment. Everything you could possibly want for home entertainment."

"I don't even watch the television I have," Fenella told him. "I certainly don't need any of those other things."

The man shrugged. "Were you actually looking for something or just walking past?" he asked, sounding fairly certain that their answer would be the latter option.

"I need a new computer," Fenella told him.

His eyes lit up. "Really? Please come in," he said eagerly. He pulled open the shop's door and then held it for Shelly and Fenella. "Computers are to the left," he said loudly. "We have all of the latest models from all of the leading manufacturers."

Fenella walked into the store and looked around. There were about a dozen computers on display, about evenly divided between desktop and laptop models. As she walked toward them, the man spoke again.

"I'm Lucas, by the way. Welcome to Manx Computer Innovations. Were you looking for anything in particular from your new computer?"

Fenella shrugged. "I have a laptop now that's about six years old. I was thinking that I'd just get a new laptop, but maybe a desktop model would make more sense, as I have office space in my apartment."

The man nodded. "Tell me what sort of technical specifications you need," he suggested.

Fenella looked at Shelly, who shrugged. Since she'd known they were coming computer shopping, Fenella had done a bit of research the previous day. She pulled out her phone and read off the list of specifications she'd decided that she needed.

The man looked startled when she'd finished. "That's a pretty high-spec machine you're looking for," he said. "I don't know that we have anything in stock that meets those requirements. Where are you willing to compromise?"

"I'm not sure that I am," Fenella told him. "I found a machine with those specifications online last night." She told him the price she'd seen. "They included free shipping and handling with that price."

The man flushed. "But you don't get any support if you order from an online retailer," he said. "If you buy from us, you can also purchase a full support package that includes everything from setting up the machine to repairs or even replacement."

"Did you say that I can purchase a support package?" Fenella checked.

The man nodded. "We used to include it with every computer we sold, but many customers didn't feel as if they needed it, so now we sell the package separately."

Fenella nodded. "Show me what you have, then," she suggested.

As Lucas talked about one of the models on display, Shelly started playing around with the neighboring machine.

"Oh, look," she said a moment later. "The local news is all about that missing man."

Fenella looked over at the computer screen. Shelly had pulled up an article about Ronald Sherman. "The one we were reading about this morning?" she asked.

"Yes, him," Shelly replied. She looked at Fenella, and Fenella could see laughter in her friend's eyes. "He disappeared seven years ago. I can't believe that no one knows where he is, though."

"If you did want a laptop, some of them have higher specifications," Lucas interrupted.

"Hey," Shelly said. "According to this article, the missing man used to work here."

Fenella tried to look surprised. "Here? In this shop?"

"That's what it says. 'Ronald Sherman was employed at Manx Computer Innovations in Onchan.' That's this shop, isn't it?" Shelly asked.

"Yes, it is, and yes, the man used to work here," Lucas said. "I barely knew him, though. I'd only just started here when he disappeared."

"But you knew him? How fascinating," Shelly said. "What was he like?"

"He was just an ordinary man," Lucas replied. "As I said, I didn't really know him, and I have no idea what happened to him."

"He found the access codes to someone's Swiss bank account, stole the money and disappeared," another voice said.

Fenella looked up and smiled at the man who was crossing the room toward them. He was short, maybe five feet tall, with a rounded belly and grey hair. "Hi, there," he said brightly when he reached them. "I'm Eugene Matthews, the manager. I hope Lucas has been taking good care of you?"

"He's been great," Fenella said, "but do you really think Ronald stole money and ran away?"

Eugene shrugged. "We used to talk about it all the time," he told her. "We were always finding things on the computers that people brought in for repair. Apparently, if you spend a lot of time on pornography websites, you're likely to pick up a few viruses along the way." He winked at Lucas and then laughed. "Not that I think you ladies are using your computers for pornography," he added.

"Did you ever actually find access codes for Swiss bank accounts?" Shelly asked.

"I didn't, but I wouldn't be surprised if Ronald had. He was really clever with computers. He could hack his way into anyone's system."

"Oh, dear. I'm not sure I want hackers repairing my computer," Shelly said.

"It's a good thing Ronald isn't here anymore, then, isn't it?" Eugene laughed. "Seriously though, we have rules. We don't hack our customers, but Ronald didn't always play by the rules. He told me one day that he'd found an unexpected fortune. A few days later he disappeared."

"Maybe the person who actually owned the fortune realized that he or she had been hacked and got rid of Ronald," Shelly suggested.

"I suppose that's possible," Eugene conceded. "I'd rather believe that old Ron is alive and well and living the good life somewhere warm and sunny with his ill-gotten gains, though."

"According to the newspaper, he didn't tell his live-in girlfriend that he was going anywhere," Shelly said, gesturing toward the screen where the article was still visible. "Surely he would have told her if he were going to leave."

Eugene chuckled. "If you'd ever met Cassie, you wouldn't say that," he told Shelly. "If I were Ronald, I would have gone, stolen fortune or not, just to get away from Cassie."

"Disappearing seems a lot more complicated than simply breaking up with the woman," Fenella suggested.

"Again, you'd understand if you'd ever met Cassie. Ronald tried to break up with her a dozen times a month, but they always ended up back together again. I never really understood it, but Ronald once told me that he was going to have to run away and hide if he ever wanted to truly end things with the woman."

"Now I want to meet her," Shelly laughed.

"She's a fruit and veg buyer for ShopFast," Eugene told her. "I'm pretty sure she spends time at all of the different shops all around the island."

"Really? I'm going to have start hanging out in the broccoli, hoping for a chance to meet the woman," Shelly said. "She sounds fascinating."

"I'm not sure that's the word I would use, but she's definitely unique," Eugene said with a shrug. "Ronald always said he was sorry that he'd ever met her. He'd been seeing a lovely woman before he and Cassie first crossed paths. I'm pretty sure he was sorry he ever ended things with Helen."

"Oh, she's mentioned in the article, too," Shelly said excitedly. "She didn't have very nice things to say about Ronald, actually."

"She was pretty bitter when he dumped her for Cassie," Eugene said. "I don't know if she's mellowed any since, but I would hope so. As I said, she was a nice girl when she and Ronald first met, before he broke her heart."

"Now I want to meet her, too," Shelly giggled. "I'm a nosy thing, aren't I?"

"She works for one of the banks," Eugene told her. "She's a vice president now, but from what she's told me, it's just a fancy title. She deals with credit card and loan applications, I believe."

"Which bank?" Shelly asked.

When Eugene told her, she and Fenella exchanged glances.

"Have you kept in touch with both of them since Ronald disappeared, then?" Shelly asked the man.

Eugene shrugged. "I've kept track of them, if not exactly in touch," he said. "I liked Helen a lot. I wouldn't have minded a chance to help her through her heartbreak."

Lucas laughed and then tried to pretend that he was coughing instead. Eugene frowned at him. "Yes, well, I've kept track of Cassie so that I can avoid her, really. She seems to think that I know where Ronald went, you see."

"Why would she think that?" Shelly asked.

"Because we worked together," Eugene explained. "We were co-assistant managers of the shop in those days. We ran the place, although there was technically a manager over both of us. He was based in the UK, though, and never really came over here."

"I thought Manx Computer Innovations was a local company," Shelly said.

Eugene frowned. "It is and it isn't," he said. "We're managed locally, but sort of loosely part of a large UK chain. That lets us get better prices for our customers because we have a lot more purchasing power this way."

Fenella nodded. If they were part of a large UK chain, she wouldn't feel nearly as guilty about not buying anything from them, at least.

"Anyway, you don't want to hear about our corporate structure," Eugene said. "You want to hear about computers."

"I think I've probably heard enough for today," Fenella told him. "If you could write down the specifications and prices for your top two desktop and laptop models, including the pricing for the service plans, I'll go home and have a think about what I really need."

"What can we do to help you get a new machine today?" Eugene asked. "You can see the prices on the various models. Which one are you most interested in? Maybe I can help you out with the price."

"This one is closest to what I wanted," Fenella told him. "I found something similar for five hundred pounds less online, though."

"Similar, but not the same," Eugene grinned. "I'm sure ours is better."

"Actually, that one was from a major manufacturer with which I'm familiar," Fenella countered. "I've never heard of the manufacturer of these models."

"It's one of the UK's largest computer makers," Lucas told her. "Rebranded under a different name for us."

"Which maker?" Fenella asked.

"We aren't allowed to tell you," Eugene said. "You'll just have to trust us when we say that if we could tell you, you'd know exactly who they are."

Fenella looked at Shelly. She'd never heard of such a thing. "I'm assuming your list price on the machine doesn't include the service plan, either," she said after an awkward pause.

"Not usually," Eugene winked at her. "In this case, I might be able to make an exception. In fact, not only will I throw in the service plan, I'll even come out myself and install the system for you."

"I don't think I need a laptop installed," Fenella said dryly.

"Getting a new machine connected to your network can be more difficult than you might anticipate," Lucas said. "We charge a hundred pounds an hour if you don't have the service plan and you need us to come and help you with your connection."

Fenella turned her head so that the two men wouldn't see her roll her eyes. "What could you do with the price?" she asked.

"On that model? I could knock a hundred pounds off and throw in the service plan," Eugene said, "and I'll buy you dinner after I've helped with your network connection."

Shelly chuckled as Fenella struggled to work out how to respond. "I'm sorry, but I'm not interested in having dinner with you," she said after a long pause.

"Not even if I know where Ronald is?" he asked. "Oh, I know you aren't interested in finding Ronald, but maybe you'd like to help me track down his fortune."

"If you know where Ronald is, you should tell the police," Shelly suggested.

"I'm not totally sure exactly where he is," the man replied. "I have a good idea of where to start looking, though. His cousin, Gary, and I are mates."

"And you think Gary knows where Ronald is?" Shelly asked.

"He must. Ronald wanted to get away from Cassie, but he and Gary were close. He'll have stayed in touch with Gary, no matter what."

"But Gary was the one who reported Ronald missing," Shelly pointed out.

Eugene shrugged. "That was just for show, to put Cassie off."

"Filing a police report is pretty serious," Shelly told him.

"Anyway, if I can find Ronald, I can get my hands on some of his fortune. A hundred thousand pounds will make me a lot more attractive, won't it?" he asked Fenella.

She bit her tongue before she could reply with the truth. "I'm very sorry, but I'm involved with someone," she said eventually. "I'm not ready to buy that computer today, either. It seems overpriced for the specifications, especially since it's an odd brand."

"I can you assure you that it's excellent quality. The real advantage of buying from us is the service, though. If you have problems, and let's face it, everyone has computer problems, we're here to help you. For our very best customers, we'll even make home visits," Eugene said, winking at Fenella again.

The door to the shop suddenly swung open. A tall man who looked to be in his late forties strode in, carrying a large box.

"Right, here we are again," he said loudly. "This is the third time

I've brought this computer back to you. I want it repaired properly this time."

Eugene smiled nervously. "You can help the gentleman," he told Lucas.

"No way. I helped him last time," Lucas replied. "The motherboard keeps crashing. I've no idea what to do with it."

"Stop talking amongst yourselves," the man snapped. "I want this sorted and I want it sorted today. I'm paying a lot of hard-earned money for this machine and it hasn't ever worked properly."

"I think that tells me everything I need to know," Fenella said. "Thank you for your time," she added, nodding at Eugene and Lucas in turn.

"Wait. We can make you a deal," Eugene said.

"Don't do it," the tall man told her. "They told me they were giving me a good deal, but I found the same computer online for three hundred pounds less once I got home. It's only because of the payment plan that I bought it here, really. I wouldn't even mind the extra money so much, but I paid extra for the service package as well and they don't seem capable of getting the machine actually working."

"It was working when you left on Monday," Lucas said.

"Yeah, and it worked for about ten minutes once I got it home," the man replied. "Then it made a whirring noise, clicked a few times, and shut itself off. I can't even get it to turn back on now."

"I'm sure we'll be able to find the problem," Eugene said. "Leave the machine with us for a few days. I'll ring you when it's ready to be collected."

"Sure," the man agreed. "What can you give me to use in the meantime?"

"Give you to use? I'm not sure what you mean," Eugene replied.

"I need a computer to do my job and I'm making monthly payments for that one. If the one you sold me at overinflated prices isn't working, then I need another one. You'll have to lend me one so I can keep working until I get my machine back."

"We don't lend computers," Eugene said.

"Then I'll just wait here until mine is repaired," the man said.

Fenella looked at Shelly. The exchange was getting interesting, but maybe it would be best to take advantage of the distraction to get away.

Shelly nodded at the exit.

"Thanks again," Fenella called over her shoulder as she and Shelly walked quickly toward the door.

"At least leave me your name and number," Eugene called after her. "I can ring you if the machine you want goes on sale."

Fenella pretended that she hadn't heard the man. That seemed better than replying. She and Shelly walked as quickly as they could back to Fenella's car. Once they were both back inside it, Fenella looked at Shelly and then began to laugh.

"That was awful," she said.

"Yes, it was, wasn't it?" Shelly replied. "Maybe we should leave the investigating to the police. I'm sure Daniel doesn't have to deal with pushy salesmen or suspects who want to go out with him."

"And he can just ask straightforward questions, too," Fenella added. "Although, I don't know that Eugene would have given Daniel the same answers that he gave us."

"He thinks Gary knows where Ronald is, it seems."

"I'm not sure that I believe him. We should have asked him where we could find Gary. At least we know where to look for Helen and Cassie."

"We can start with them, at least."

"I don't know about that. We found Eugene and Lucas. Maybe that's enough interfering with Daniel's investigation."

"Maybe I need a new credit card," Shelly said. "I have my current account at the bank where Helen works."

"What's a current account?"

"Oh, dear, you'll call it something different, then," Shelly sighed. "It's the account that I use to pay my bills and from which I write checks, that sort of thing."

"So, a checking account," Fenella said. "I have at least one account there as well, and I truly do need a credit card. I'm still using my American cards and I'm sure it's costing me a fortune in foreign transaction fees every time I buy anything. There are probably rules against me even having the accounts now that I don't live in the US anymore, too. I've been meaning to get something sorted for months, but I keep putting it off."

"Maybe this afternoon you should go and talk to someone at the bank. As you're Mona's niece, I suspect your account would probably need to be handled by a vice president, don't you?"

Fenella sighed. "I really don't want Daniel to think that I'm interfering in his investigation. Maybe I should tell him what we're doing."

"You could do that," Shelly replied. "Or you could wait until after we've spoken to Helen to mention it. Don't they say that it's easier to get forgiveness than permission?"

Fenella laughed. "I need some lunch. Let's worry about what we do next after we've eaten."

"Do you want to go somewhere or just home?"

"I'm just hungry," Fenella replied. "Is there somewhere nice nearby?"

Shelly glanced out the car window. "The pub across the road used to have really good food, actually, but I haven't been in there for years."

"How bad can it be?" Fenella asked. "No, don't answer that."

They got back out of the car and walked across the road. Fenella's first impression of the pub was that it was very dark.

"This is what British pubs on television always look like," she whispered to Shelly.

"It's fairly typical. The Tale and Tail isn't, of course. I don't think there's any other place in the world like the Tale and Tail."

"Sit anywhere. Menus are on the table. Order from me when you're ready," the man behind the bar called out.

The women nodded and then crossed to a table in the corner. Fenella picked up a menu and read through it.

"What was good the last time you were here?" she asked Shelly.

"I don't remember, but it was probably steak and kidney pie or maybe chicken and leek. I usually order those in pubs because they're too much fuss to do at home."

"Chicken and leek pie sounds good," Fenella said after a moment.

"I'll go and order," Shelly told her. "You can try to work out how we're going to meet the buyer for fruit and veg from ShopFast."

Fenella frowned. What would Daniel say if he found out that she and Shelly were actively tracking down the various witnesses in Ronald Sherman's disappearance? He'd complained in the past about how she always seemed to have chance encounters with the men and women involved in his investigations, but going out of her way to actually find them was a step further.

"I did promise we could forget about the case over lunch," Shelly said as she returned. She handed Fenella her coffee before she sat down. "Tell me more about Thanksgiving while we wait for our food."

"When I was growing up, it felt like it was the most important family holiday of the year. It seemed as if people traveled all over the country so that families could spend Thanksgiving together. Christmas was often more about nuclear families, but Thanksgiving was for extended families, friends, anyone and everyone, really. I remember dinners with twenty-five or thirty people at them. And the food, my goodness, the food was amazing."

"How many are coming to your party, then?"

"So far only you and Daniel have replied," Fenella sighed. "I hope to hear from some of the others, though. It won't be much of a party with just three of us."

"After the show last night, the guys in the band were talking. I think they're all planning to come, well, all except for Todd, of course."

"Yes, I can't compete with Hawaii," Fenella laughed.

"Paul asked me about bringing a friend. I got the impression that he's started seeing someone, but he didn't seem to want to talk about it."

"He's more than welcome to bring a friend. I thought the invitations made that clear, but maybe they didn't."

"I told Tim that he wasn't allowed to bring anyone," Shelly said, blushing. "I'm sort of glad that Gordon is out of town."

"That might have been awkward, but you're going to have to tell him about Tim eventually."

"Maybe Tim will get tired of me before Gordon stops traveling all of the time. That could happen."

"I can't imagine anyone getting tired of you."

Shelly was still laughing when their food was delivered a moment later.

"It's delicious," Fenella said after a few bites. "And warm and comforting. Just what I needed."

"I'm so pleased it's good. I was worried that it might be awful after I suggested the place."

"I wouldn't have blamed you if it wasn't good."

"No, but I'd still have felt guilty."

Fenella was still talking about Thanksgiving traditions as they walked out of the pub a short while later.

"When I was a little girl my mother used to let me tear up the stale bread for the stuffing the night before Thanksgiving. That always seemed to mark the official beginning of the Christmas season to me," she told Shelly.

"It must be nice to have a clear beginning point for the Christmas season. Over here things just start whenever anyone wants to start them. I suppose the first of December is the unofficial start, but everyone seems to have their own ideas about it."

"When I was a child, no one put up any Christmas decorations until the day after Thanksgiving. Not at home and not in the stores, either. Now, though, I think they go up earlier every year, in the stores, anyway. I won't decorate at home until after Thanksgiving, though."

"Mona had gorgeous decorations," Shelly told her. "Wait until you see them."

"I wish I knew where they were," Fenella replied. Someone else had mentioned Mona's decorations to her, but she still hadn't remembered to ask Mona where she could find them. There certainly weren't any boxes of decorations anywhere in the apartment. She would have noticed.

"They're probably in her storage room," Shelly said. "That's where I keep mine."

"Storage room?"

"Every flat has its own storage room on the ground floor. It's a bit grand calling them rooms, really, as they aren't very large, but they're big enough for a few boxes of Christmas decorations, at least."

"I didn't know that."

"They should have told you about it when you moved into the flat."

"I didn't really talk to anyone when I moved in," Fenella said, feeling sheepish. "Doncan gave me the keycards and I made myself at home. I probably should have taken the time to speak to the building's manager or something, shouldn't I?"

"If you're going to talk to anyone, talk to Josh. He's the assistant manager, and he's much nicer than the manager. I don't think you need to speak with anyone, though. You know where to get your post and I can show you where Mona's storage room is. Your keycard should open that door, too."

"Now I'm curious to see what's in there," Fenella said. She and Shelly had walked back to Mona's car and climbed inside. "Do you think we could go there right now?"

Shelly shrugged. "I don't have any plans for this afternoon, aside from tracking down Cassie and Helen."

"Let's go and see what Mona had tucked away in storage. I think I'd rather wait and see how Daniel reacts when he hears about our visit to Manx Computer Innovations before we start hunting down anyone else, though."

"What if he tells us not to get involved?" Shelly asked.

"I don't know. I think I'd rather not get involved than have Daniel angry with me."

Shelly sighed. "I suppose you're right. I almost forgot how much Daniel means to you."

"We're just friends and likely to remain so, especially after last night's awkward encounter," Fenella said sadly.

"I'm sure it will all come right in the end," Shelly said soothingly. "If it's meant to be, you'll work it out."

Fenella started the car and drove slowly out of the parking lot. It was only a short drive to their building.

"Do you want to go up to our floor first, or should we go straight to the storage rooms?" Shelly asked as they boarded the elevator in the garage.

"Let's just go straight to the storage rooms," Fenella suggested. "For now I just want a peek at what's in there."

Shelly pushed the button for the ground floor and the elevator silently rose. She led Fenella past the mailboxes to a door that Fenella had never really noticed. It said "Residents Only" on it. Shelly pushed it open and then headed down a long corridor.

"This is mine," she said when she stopped in front of the door with her apartment number on it. "Mona's is next."

Fenella stopped in front of the door and took a deep breath. For some reason she felt as if she were intruding on Mona's privacy. She slid her keycard into the lock and then pushed the door open.

"Wow," Shelly said from behind her as Fenella switched on the light. "Mona's room is a lot bigger than mine."

Fenella looked around the massive space. A huge chandelier, one that would have once illuminated the grand ballroom when the building had been a hotel, lit up everything. There were stacks and stacks of boxes, all neatly labeled. Large shapes covered in cloths could only be furniture.

Shelly took a few steps into the room and then sighed. "I feel as if I've just walked into a cave full of treasures."

"I know what you mean," Fenella told her. "One day I'm going to have to go through everything. For now, though, there seem to be about ten boxes labeled 'Christmas.' The apartment isn't big enough for that many decorations."

"Do you want to open some of them to see what's inside?"

Fenella thought for a minute and then shook her head. "I'm going to wait until after Thanksgiving," she said. "Otherwise, I might be too tempted to start decorating early." And I want to talk to Mona about all of it as well, she added to herself. Perhaps her aunt could help her work out which decorations she should use.

6

Shelly headed for home to get some chores done before dinner.

"I'll cook something," Fenella offered. "Something quick and easy, so don't get excited."

"I always get excited when I don't have to cook," Shelly laughed. "When John and I were married, I cooked every night and never really gave it any thought, but now that I've only myself to look after, it seems an awful lot of bother."

"I used to cook for Jack, but I always secretly resented it," Fenella sighed. "I wouldn't have minded if he'd cooked for me once in a while, but he never even offered. I don't think the idea ever crossed his mind. For a very intelligent person, he's very dumb about some things."

"And you never asked him to cook for you?"

"I used to drop hints sometimes, but he wasn't very good on picking up on them. When he did finally get my point, he would insist on taking me out for a meal, but that wasn't easy either, as he's very fussy about what he will and won't eat. There were only about three restaurants in the whole Buffalo area that he was willing to visit, and he usually complained for much of the meal anyway."

"And you stayed with him for ten years?"

Fenella shrugged. "Sometimes when you're in the middle of something, you don't realize just how bad it is. He does have some good qualities, he truly does."

"I'll take your word for that," Shelly said with a grin.

Back in her apartment, Fenella curled up with a book and let herself relax. It had been an odd morning, and she was a little bit worried about telling Daniel about the visit to Manx Computer Innovations, but that didn't stop her from getting completely lost in the well-written murder mystery.

"What are you planning to make for Shelly?" Mona asked as she appeared next to Fenella on the couch.

Fenella's book flew out of her hands as she jumped to her feet. Her small scream startled Katie, who yelled loudly and then dashed out of the room. "You startled me," Fenella said as she tried to slow her racing heart.

"I didn't mean to," Mona replied with a shrug. "It must be a good book. You didn't even notice my arrival."

Fenella frowned. She was pretty sure that Mona had begun speaking before she'd appeared, but there was no way she could prove it. Rather than argue with her aunt, she walked over and picked up the book, quickly finding her place and sliding a bookmark into it. "It is a good book," she told Mona. "One of the best I've read in a while."

"Did you find it on my shelves?"

"Yes."

Mona looked at the cover as Fenella put the book on the table. "Ah, yes, I remember that one. I loved it right up until the end. The author was wrong about the murderer, though. That was disappointing."

"The author was wrong?"

"Yes. I knew who'd killed the victim throughout the entire story, but the author identified the wrong person in the last chapter."

"Perhaps, as the author wrote the book, she knows best?"

"Not in this case. I'm sure you think you know who the killer is, don't you?"

Fenella hesitated and then nodded. "I think I do, but I'm not certain."

"Well, see how you feel after you've read the ending. I think the author got it wrong, but you may not agree."

Fenella frowned. She was torn between wanting to finish the book to see if her theory about the killer was right and not wanting to read the rest in case Mona was correct. "What did you say as you came in?" she asked, shaking her head to try to clear it.

"What are you planning to make for Shelly?"

"My goodness. I nearly forgot that I promised to make dinner," Fenella exclaimed. "I don't know what to make. What do you think?"

"It might be nice to make her something American that she's not had before," Mona suggested.

"Like what?"

Mona shrugged. "What did you used to make at home that isn't typical over here?"

"Meatloaf?" was the first thing that popped into Fenella's head.

Mona made a face. "I've never had meatloaf. What is it?"

"It's ground beef with bread crumbs and spices and maybe an egg," Fenella said. "I like to add some tomato sauce and cheese to mine as well."

"Sort of like a giant meatball?"

"Yes, exactly like a giant meatball. Jack loved my meatloaf. Now that I've mentioned it, it sounds awfully good."

"I think it sounds terrible, but I'm sure Shelly will be polite about it."

Fenella made a face at Mona and then headed for the kitchen. "I can't believe I haven't made meatloaf in all the time I've been here. Not that I cook very often, but still, it was one of my favorites." She looked in the cupboards and the refrigerator and was happy to find that she had everything she needed.

"I'll serve it with mashed potatoes and roasted vegetables," she told Mona. "It will be delicious."

"I'm not sure if I want to watch or leave before you start," Mona said. "At least I don't have to smell it."

Fenella mixed up the meatloaf and put it into a pan. She slid it into a hot oven and then arranged carrots and parsnips on a baking tray. They went into the oven with the meatloaf before Fenella peeled the potatoes and set them on the stove. She set a timer to remind herself to turn the heat on under the potatoes and then cleaned up behind herself.

"Tell me what happened when you and Shelly went to the computer store, then," Mona suggested as Fenella worked.

"We met both of the men who used to work with Ronald. Lucas said he barely knew the man, and Eugene told us that he's sure that Ronald ran off with a ton of money and that he was pretty sure he would be able to find him if he tried."

"If Ronald is rich and Eugene knew where to find him, Eugene would have tracked him down years ago," Mona scoffed. "There's no way Eugene would still be working for Manx Computer Innovations if he had access to a fortune."

"I agree. He wasn't at all nice and I hope I never see him again."

"If you truly do need a new laptop, there's a very good computer shop in Ramsey that I would recommend." Mona told her. "Max used them for his business needs."

"I may just order something online. Anyway, I don't think we learned anything interesting, but we'll tell Daniel everything and see what he thinks."

"He'll probably think that you shouldn't be visiting suspects."

"He'll probably be right."

Fenella had everything ready when Shelly arrived a short while later.

"I hope you don't mind that I brought Smokey," she said as Fenella let her into the apartment. "She wanted to come and play with Katie."

"Of course I don't mind. Katie loves having her here."

The cats played together while Fenella served up generous portions of the dinner she'd made. "I hope you like it," she said as she put Shelly's plate in front of her. "It's meatloaf, which is very American, I gather."

Shelly smiled uncertainly. "It smells good," she said as she picked up her fork. A few minutes later she gave Fenella a much more genuine smile. "It's really good. It's like a giant meatball, isn't it?"

"More or less," Fenella agreed.

They had ice cream for dessert and then Fenella loaded the dishwasher and set it going while Shelly put Katie's dinner out for her.

"Yours is at home," she told Smokey, who seemed to be stalking Katie's food bowl. "Come on, it's time for you to go home anyway. Fenella and I have to get to the pub."

While Shelly was busy with Smokey, Fenella combed her hair and touched up her lipstick. She didn't want to look as if she'd fussed over her appearance, but she wanted to look good for Daniel.

"Put your hair up in a clip," Mona suggested. "It will look elegant, but casual."

Fenella did as she was told, smiling at the results in her mirror. "It's perfect," she told Mona.

"Maybe Daniel will share more information about the case with you. I want to hear everything when you get home."

"He just wants our impressions from what we read in the articles he gave us. He isn't going to be sharing any more information."

"I'll wait here, just in case," Mona replied.

Fenella sighed and then slid on shoes and grabbed her handbag. Shelly was at the door a moment later.

"You don't really think that Daniel will be angry with us for having gone to Manx Computer Innovations today, do you?" Shelly asked nervously as they rode the elevator to the ground floor.

"I've given up trying to work out what Daniel is going to do or say about anything," Fenella replied.

Shelly sighed. "I wish you two would just sit down and talk. I'm sure you can work everything out if you try."

"Probably, but for the moment we both seem to be avoiding talking."

"You're acting like small children or maybe teenagers who fancy one another and don't know what to do about it."

"It's awkward. We might have talked last night if it weren't for my headache. Maybe we'll get another chance soon."

"I don't have to come with you now," Shelly offered as they crossed their building's lobby.

"Oh, no. If Daniel's going to get upset about our visit to the computer shop, I want you there to help."

Shelly nodded. "I'll leave early, then," she offered.

"Let's see how it goes," Fenella suggested.

The walk to the pub only took a few minutes. The women got drinks from the bar and then headed up to the same quiet corner they'd used two nights earlier. Daniel was already there, sipping a soft drink, with a notebook on the table in front of him.

"Good evening," he said with a smile as they approached.

"Good evening," Shelly replied.

Fenella smiled and then sat down across from Daniel.

"I've been going back over all of the case notes from Ronald's disappearance," Daniel began. "I think the papers managed to report just about everything the police were told and maybe more. I hope one or both of you have some ideas for me."

"I don't know that I got any ideas from reading the papers you gave us," Fenella began. "It seems likely to me that something bad happened to the man, but if it did, I'm not sure where you should start looking to work out exactly what."

Daniel nodded. "No one seems to have a clear motive for wanting him dead, at least not as far as I know from what I've read so far. Tomorrow I'm going to start talking to the various witnesses. Maybe someone will change their story, even just a little bit."

Fenella glanced at Shelly. "We went to Manx Computer Innovations today," she said in a low voice.

Daniel raised an eyebrow. "Why?"

"I need a new laptop," Fenella told him.

"Do you really?"

"I do, actually. Mine is old and getting slow. Anyway, I'm pretty sure I can afford one."

Daniel made a face and then sighed. "I can't stop you from shopping, I suppose. I know from the work I did today that both Lucas Hardy and Eugene Matthews are still working there. Knowing you, you managed to speak to both of them about Ronald, didn't you?"

Fenella hesitated and then nodded. "While I was talking about computers with them, Shelly pulled up the news article about the case and dropped it into the conversation."

Daniel looked over at Shelly. "That was very clever of you."

Shelly flushed. "Thanks."

"Which is not to say that I'm condoning your decision to visit witnesses in a missing person case," he added in a serious voice. "But as it's too late to stop you, at least tell me what you learned."

"Lucas told us that he barely knew the man," Fenella replied "Eugene seemed confident that Ronald stole a lot of money and is now living comfortably somewhere exotic."

Daniel raised an eyebrow. He flipped back through several pages of notes in his notebook and then shrugged. "He said much the same thing when Ronald disappeared."

"He also told us that he's sure that Gary knows where Ronald is," Fenella added.

"Really? That's new," Daniel muttered. He went back through is notebook a second time. "Interesting."

"Is it?" Shelly asked.

Daniel shrugged. "Maybe. It's a point to discuss with the man, anyway. Obviously, I won't mention either of you when I speak to him, but if he doesn't mention Gary, I might press him a bit on the subject."

"Gary was Ronald's only family. I can't imagine Ronald disappearing and not keeping in touch with him," Shelly said.

"Eugene said one of the reasons why Ronald might have disappeared was because he wanted to get away from his girlfriend, Cassie," Fenella told Daniel. "We've not met her, obviously, but Eugene said Ronald was eager to get away from her but couldn't seem to manage it."

"That didn't make sense to me," Shelly said. "Why didn't he just break things off with her?"

Daniel looked through his notes again. "I'm looking forward to meeting Ms. Patton, actually. Everything I've read about her suggests that she's going to be interesting."

"I want to meet her, too," Shelly said. "Eugene told us that she's a buyer for ShopFast and spends some time in the different shops. I may have to start hanging around the carrots until I meet her."

"I can't stop you from visiting ShopFast," Daniel replied. "I do suggest that you avoid spending too much time simply standing around, though. That sort of behavior makes shop managers nervous."

Shelly glanced at Fenella. To Fenella it sounded very much as if

Daniel had just given them permission to speak with Cassie Patton. She raised her eyebrows at Shelly, who looked excited.

"We didn't ask Eugene where we could find Gary," Shelly said.

"I thought you told me that you'd met Gary before," Daniel replied.

"He helped install my kitchen years ago, but I don't know if he's still working for the same company."

"I've not actually started looking for Gary yet," Daniel told her. "I suspect Dan Ross will be hunting everyone down, though. If I were you, I'd watch the local paper. I suspect Mr. Ross will track everyone down as quickly as I will."

Shelly nodded. "Eugene said that Ronald was sorry he'd ended things with Helen Campbell."

"Did he? Helen didn't have very nice things to say about Ronald when she was interviewed by the papers," Daniel replied. "She didn't give the police any more information than she gave Dan Ross, either."

"Fenella needs a new credit card," Shelly said. "We were thinking she might try applying at the bank where Helen works."

Daniel looked at Fenella. "You need a credit card?"

"I'm still using my US ones, which means paying foreign transactions fees every time I buy anything. The currency conversion rates aren't great, either. I usually use the debit card that Doncan gave me for my main bank account here, but that has a fairly low daily limit," she explained.

"So you need a new, island-based credit card," he said.

"Yes, and some of my accounts are with that bank, so it makes sense to apply for the card through them," she replied.

"And of course, being how important you are, you'll have to speak to a vice president, won't you?" Daniel sighed.

"I don't intend to ask to speak with anyone in particular, but if I did happen to get a chance to speak with Helen, well, it would be interesting to hear what she's thinking after all these years," Fenella said.

Daniel took a long drink from his glass before he spoke. When he set the glass down, he frowned at each woman in turn. "I didn't share this cold case with you because I expected you to start trying to track down and speak to witnesses," he said in a stern voice. "I appreciate that you're interested in the case, but it's possible that something bad did happen to Ronald Sherman. Sticking your noses into everything could be dangerous."

"We aren't going to do anything foolish," Shelly replied. "We'll do all of our talking in public places and make sure we have other things to discuss so that the people we're speaking with don't realize that we're really just interested in Ronald."

"Did you buy a new laptop from Manx Computer Innovations?" Daniel asked Fenella.

"No, because they were overpriced, odd brands, and Eugene was creepy," she replied. "I wouldn't want them repairing anything of mine, either. There's no doubt in my mind that Eugene hacks into every computer that comes into the store."

"That's a worrying thought," Daniel said. "I may have to have our technology guys take a look at the company."

"He said he mostly finds porn," Shelly interjected.

Daniel nodded. "I'll have to see if we've had any complaints about them in the past. Not that that will help us find Ronald, of course."

"Is it possible that he found something criminal on someone's computer and that someone killed him to keep him quiet?" Fenella asked.

"It's possible, sure. There are any number of things that someone might have on a computer that they might not want anyone to know about, from Swiss bank accounts to child pornography to details of their scheme to embezzle a fortune from their employers or the government," Daniel told her.

Fenella sighed. "That's a depressing thought."

"Of course, if Ronald did uncover anything like that, he should have rung the police immediately," Daniel added.

"If he did find something, maybe he was bribed to disappear or he was made to disappear," Shelly said. "I'm not sure I like either idea."

"No, I'd much rather it was something more straightforward, but the amount of time that has elapsed suggests otherwise," Daniel said. "If he'd gone voluntarily, it's hard to believe that he hasn't bothered to get in touch with anyone on the island. It would be easy enough for him to send a card from somewhere, just to let his cousin know he was okay, for instance."

"You think he's dead," Fenella said flatly.

"I'm afraid I do," Daniel replied.

"Maybe he left voluntarily and then got run over by a lorry or something before he could let Gary know he was okay," Shelly suggested.

"We've never had a match on the missing person report, which was sent to every police station in the UK and on the continent. He didn't take his passport, so that should rule out his going any further afield," Daniel said.

"I think Shelly and I need to speak to all of the other witnesses," Fenella said after she'd emptied her glass. "I don't feel as if I have any idea what Ronald was like as a person, not yet."

"That may be part of my problem, too," Daniel admitted. "The papers talked about him a lot, but only in the most general terms. He came across as an incredibly ordinary, almost boring man. Eugene was the only one who suggested that Ronald enjoyed hacking computers. Cassie and Helen both seemed surprised by the idea, but then, I don't think either of them had ever given the matter any thought."

"I keep coming back to Gary," Fenella said. "He was Ronald's only relation. If Ronald were going to leave, he'd have told Gary, surely, especially when they were planning to have lunch together that week."

"I'm going to start speaking to witnesses tomorrow," Daniel told them. "I'm planning..." He was interrupted by a loud ringing noise. Sighing deeply, he pulled his phone out of his pocket. "I have to take this," he said.

Fenella sat back and watched as Daniel got up and walked a short distance away. As all the man said for the next few minutes was a series of monosyllables, she didn't think he'd actually needed to move. When he dropped his phone back in his pocket, he was frowning.

"I have to go," he said tightly. "I'll ring you in a few days, or maybe early next week."

"What's wrong?" Shelly asked.

"A group of young men decided to go out and drink heavily, and then two or three of them started fighting over a young lady that they all admired. One of the men had a knife. Now one man is dead and two others are seriously injured, and no one is willing to talk to the police, at least not yet. Of course, Dan Ross is already on the scene. He'll have his headline for tomorrow." Daniel sighed and then turned and walked away.

Fenella wanted to run after him and give him a hug and say just the right thing to encourage him, but she didn't have any idea what she might say. "Stay safe," she said to his back.

He turned and gave her a quick thumbs up before heading down the winding stairs.

"What a horrible job that man has," Shelly sighed. "I can't even imagine what he's going to go through tonight."

"He's far too nice to be a policeman," Fenella said.

"Did you want another drink? Maybe something stronger than soda this time?" Shelly asked.

"After last night, I'm staying away from alcohol for a while," Fenella replied. "We can have another round if you want. I'll just have another soda."

Shelly thought about it for a minute and then shook her head. "I think I want to go home and snuggle up with Smokey in front of the telly. I'll have to find an old movie or something to watch. I don't want to hear anything else about the real world tonight."

Fenella nodded. "I know what you mean," she said.

The pair made their way down to the ground floor and out of the pub, waving to the bartender as they left.

"My goodness, that's a lot of flashing lights," Shelly said as they emerged onto the promenade.

"There was a big fight down the road," a passing man told them. "Half a dozen teenaged boys started a knife fight, from what I heard. Three dead and six injured was the last body count. At least, that's what they're saying."

The man disappeared down the street before Fenella could ask him who "they" were or find out more about his sources for information.

"Poor Daniel," Shelly said.

"I feel sorry for the parents of all those young men," Fenella told her. "Whatever happened, it's terribly sad that someone died."

"Yes, sometimes I'm grateful that I didn't have children. I'm not sure how parents sleep at night."

There were dozens of people standing along the promenade watching the scene from a distance. Fenella and Shelly struggled to get through them so that they could get home. As they went, they heard increasingly awful reports about what had happened.

"The last comment that I heard suggested that there were at least a dozen dead," Shelly said as they boarded the elevator in their building.

"I heard that same number, along with two dozen injured," Fenella sighed. "I hope they're all wrong. The numbers Daniel told us were bad enough."

Shelly and Fenella parted ways in the corridor. When Fenella got inside, she grabbed Katie and gave her an extended cuddle. "Promise me you'll never go out drinking with your mates and get into a fight," she said to the animal.

Katie gave her a look that suggested that she thought Fenella had lost her mind, and then began to wriggle in her arms.

"Yes, okay, sorry," Fenella laughed at herself.

"What's going on down there?" Mona asked, gesturing toward the flashing lights.

"Apparently some young men who were out drinking got into a fight," Fenella told her. "One or more of them had a knife and someone got killed."

"How awful," Mona said. "I'm going to go and see what I can find out."

She faded away in front of Fenella's eyes. "How does she do that?" Fenella asked Katie.

Katie yawned and then headed for the kitchen. When she began to complain, Fenella joined her. She refilled her water bowl and gave her a few treats before making herself a bag of microwave popcorn and returning to the living room.

"What should we watch?" she asked Katie.

"Meerwoow," Katie replied.

"Yes, you're right. A nice animated classic with a happily-ever-after ending is just what I need," Fenella agreed, flipping through the channels. She didn't manage to find that, but she found an old comedy with a few of her favorite actors in it, so she settled in to watch that instead.

"No one is dead," Mona announced a short while later. "One young man is in very poor condition, but he's holding his own, at the moment, anyway. Two other young men are less seriously injured, although they will both need some weeks in hospital to recover. The man who was wielding the knife has surrendered to the police and is in hospital having his own injuries treated."

"Are you sure? Daniel told us that there was one fatality."

"Perhaps Daniel was wrong. It could happen."

"Perhaps. I hope you're right. It's still very sad, but far less so if everyone survives."

Mona nodded. Before she could speak, the phone rang.

"Ah, Fenella, darling, it's Donald. How are you?"

"I'm fine," Fenella replied automatically. "How are you?"

"Oh, I have good days and bad days," he told her. "I should say that Phoebe has good days and bad days, as how I'm doing is currently entirely dependent on how she is doing."

"I'm sorry."

"Thank you. This is far and away the hardest thing I've ever experienced. Losing my first wife was terrible, but I had my work and my children to look after. I didn't have time to sit around doing too much thinking. Now it seems that all I do is sit around and think."

"Any idea when you'll be able to come back to the island?"

"It may be longer than I was hoping for," Donald sighed. "Phoebe's next stop may be London, and she may need to be there for some time. At least she'll be closer to her brother, which will be nice for me, but I'd much rather be back on the island."

"You need to do what's best for Phoebe, but London is a good deal closer to the island than New York is, anyway. Maybe you'll be able to get away for a few days now and again."

"Maybe. But I didn't ring to complain about my life. Phoebe is actually doing better than the doctors expected, which is one reason why she's having so many bad days at the moment. She wants her recovery to go a good deal faster than it is, and she's struggling to see the small bits of progress she's actually making. At one point the doctors weren't certain that she'd ever be aware enough to realize that she'd been injured."

"I'm glad she's doing well."

"But how are you, really?"

"I'm okay. I've just sent out invitations for the American Thanksgiving banquet. You know you'll be more than welcome if you can manage to come."

"I hope I can make it next year. I'm afraid this year I'll be having whatever they're serving in the hospital cafeteria."

"Otherwise, I've been trying to help Daniel with a cold case," Fenella added. "A missing person called Ronald Sherman."

"Really? He hasn't turned up yet? I must say, when he first disappeared I assumed he'd turn up within days."

"You know him?"

"He once worked for me. I didn't know him well, but I'd spoken to him a few times, and I signed the paperwork when we let him go."

"You fired him?"

"We let him go when we restructured our IT department. That's the official line, anyway."

"But there's more, isn't there?"

"There were some concerns about the man's work. I'm sure the police spoke to my IT manager when Ronald disappeared. Daniel must know about the issues."

"What sort of issues?"

"Ronald's manager was concerned that Ronald was accessing parts of the system that were outside of his responsibilities. There was an email about a company buyout we were considering that was leaked to the press, for example. In the end we opted not to purchase, so it didn't do us any harm, but it could have caused problems under different circumstances."

"Ronald was hacking your systems."

"We didn't have any proof of anything, just suspicions," Donald said quickly. "His manager had a chat with him and they agreed that he would take a fairly generous redundancy package. In exchange, his manager agreed that he would do nothing more than confirm the man's employment with us if anyone rang for a reference."

"Daniel is considering whether it's possible that Ronald hacked a computer that was brought in for repair and found something he shouldn't have," Fenella told Donald.

"He certainly had the skills to do that. Does Daniel think his hacking got him killed?"

"Maybe, or maybe he managed to steal a lot of money from someone and ran away."

Donald chuckled. "I hate to say it, but I hope that's what happened. Even though I got rid of the man, I have to say that there was something I liked about him."

"I hope you don't mind if I tell Daniel everything you've told me."

"Not at all. As I said, my manager spoke to someone during the initial investigation."

The pair exchanged a bit more small talk before Donald sighed. "I really have to go," he said. "I like to have dinner each night with Phoebe. It's difficult for her, and it seems to go more easily when I'm there."

"I hope she continues to improve," Fenella told him.

"Thank you. Me, too."

He put the phone down and Fenella followed suit. Before she could move her hand away, it rang.

"Hello?" she said, expecting the silence that a glitch in the line would give.

"Hello," Daniel's voice replied.

"Oh, I wasn't, that is, I just hung up the phone and it rang immediately. I didn't really think anyone was there."

"Should I hang up and try again in a few minutes?" Daniel asked.

"No, not at all."

"That's good, because I really don't have time," he said in a tired voice. "I just wanted to take a minute to remind you to be careful, that's all. I know you and Shelly are determined to speak to everyone involved in Ronald Sherman's disappearance, and I want you to be very careful when you do so. It's just possible that one of them killed the man and hid the body. Remember that."

"We'll be careful," Fenella promised. "But I just had an interesting conversation with Donald," she added. She quickly told him everything that Donald had said about Ronald.

"How do you always manage to find out things that I don't know?"

"Donald said his IT manager spoke to the police seven years ago."

"I'll have to go through the notes again, because I must have missed that interview," Daniel sighed. "Anyway, I have a million more things I need to say to you, but right now I've half a dozen witnesses from the fight on the promenade to interview and about a hundred different reports to write. Then I need to go and sit beside a young man's hospital bed and hope that he'll recover enough to tell me what happened."

"I'm sorry."

"At least my initial report was wrong," Daniel replied. "Three badly injured, but no fatalities, at least not yet. I have to go. Sorry."

The line went dead in Fenella's ear. She sighed and put the phone down.

7

"How is Donald?" Mona asked. "From what I could hear, it sounds as if he's feeling very sorry for himself."

"Maybe a little bit, but he seems to be coping. I can't imagine how difficult this must be for him. He's used to being able to throw money at every problem that comes along, and this time he simply can't do that."

"He'll be able to use his resources to get his daughter the best treatment available. That's more than many people can do."

"True. He's probably going to move her to London next. He isn't sure when he'll be back on the island."

"He'll find someone else, either in New York or London," Mona predicted. "He's alone and I'm sure he's lonely."

"Next you'll be suggesting I should go to New York," Fenella muttered.

"No, not at all. Donald was never the right man for you. I should imagine you'll be relieved when he finally tells you that he's found another woman."

Fenella thought for a minute before she replied. "I suspect you're right. I do like Donald, but I never felt as if I fit into his world, even after I found out that I'm quite wealthy on my own."

Mona nodded. "You and Daniel are better suited, although he's rather too nice sometimes."

"Are you suggesting that's why he ended up with Tiffany?"

"You'll have to ask him about Tiffany. I'm not even going to speculate as to what happened there. Anyway, he was the second caller, wasn't he? What did he want?"

"To tell me to be careful if I go looking for Ronald Sherman's associates," Fenella replied.

"He worries about you."

"I suppose."

"I worry, too, but not as much," Mona told her. "Now, unless you've anything interesting to tell me from tonight's meeting with Daniel, I must go. Max is having a party in the ballroom and I must be there to welcome the guests."

"Will there be many?"

"Probably not, but hopefully Max won't notice. As long as I'm there and I look beautiful, he won't care, anyway."

"Have fun," Fenella said, wondering if Mona was telling her the truth or making things up again. It didn't really matter, she told herself as she washed her face and changed into her pajamas. Katie was curled up in the exact center of the king-sized bed when Fenella walked into her bedroom a few minutes later. She carefully climbed under the covers and switched off the light.

"You should buy this computer," Eugene Matthews said with a wink. "It used to belong to an African dictator. I'm sure I can hack it and find the access codes for all of his bank accounts."

"Let me guess, he was a Nigerian prince and if we give him my bank details he'll transfer ten million pounds into my account," Fenella said dryly.

"Maybe," Eugene shrugged. "There really are Nigerian princes in the world, you know. Anyway, you buy the computer and I'll hack it. We can split the proceeds fifty-fifty."

"If you can hack it, why don't you just do it and keep all of the money?"

Eugene frowned. "Because this is your dream, of course. If I really had access to an African dictator's computer, I'd hack it without consulting you."

"It's a dream?" Fenella frowned and looked around the room. She appeared to be in the Manx Computer Innovations showroom, but there was a large kitchen in the corner and Katie was sleeping in a cat bed on top of one of the counters, tucked between two large desktop models.

"Of course it's a dream," the man laughed. "I knew you'd be dreaming about me. Come and give me a kiss." He lunged at her, causing Fenella to jump and then sit up in bed.

"It was a dream," she told a startled Katie, "but then it turned into a nightmare."

"Meeoow," Katie sighed, and then curled up again and went straight back to sleep.

Fenella thought about getting up, but the nightmare hadn't been bad enough to warrant giving up on the sleep she needed. "No more Eugene," she told her subconscious firmly and then fell back to sleep.

"Meeeemmmeeeooowww," Katie said as she patted Fenella's nose gently.

"Is it really seven already?" Fenella asked, opening one eye. It was exactly seven. Fenella sighed and then slid out of bed. "Okay, I'll get your breakfast, but then I'm going back to bed," she told her pet.

Katie raced off to the kitchen to wait for Fenella. Once she'd filled the food and water bowls, Fenella found that she wasn't as tired as she'd thought she was. She felt restless, instead.

"I think I need a walk," she told Katie.

Katie just looked at her for a minute and then went back to eating her breakfast. Fenella set a pot of coffee brewing and then took a shower. By the time she was dressed and ready for the day, the coffee was ready to drink. She used it to wash down a few slices of toast before she headed for the door. A nice brisk walk up and down the promenade was exactly what she needed.

Police crime tape blocked off the entrance to one of the bars at one end of the promenade. Fenella shivered as she walked past it on the opposite side of the road. When she reached the end of the promenade, she turned around and nearly got knocked over.

"Woof, woof," the friendly dog said as he pressed himself against Fenella.

"Winston, how wonderful to see you," Fenella exclaimed. She fussed over the huge hairy beast for several minutes as Harvey caught up to the end of Winston's leash.

"It's a new lead," he told Fenella when he reached them. "I can let it out for much longer distances, which lets Winston have a good run ahead. He knows he's not to go on the beach and so far he's done very well with it."

Fenella grinned. There was nothing Winston liked better than splashing in the sea. He managed to get away from Harvey on a regular basis and while Harvey always complained about it, Fenella didn't think he actually minded. The local dog grooming business was always happy to give Winston a quick bath after his unplanned excursions onto the beach, and Fenella knew that Harvey didn't have to worry about the cost of an occasional extra visit to get Winston a bath.

"And what does Fiona think?" Fenella asked as she gave the much smaller animal her share of attention.

"She tries to chase after him for a few steps and then falls back into step with me and just watches Winston run," Harvey said. "As long as he's still on a lead, she doesn't worry, at least as far as I can tell."

Fenella nodded. The tiny animal seemed to idolize her larger friend. "She seems very happy," she commented.

Harvey shrugged. "I don't think she and Mortimer were ever very close."

Fiona had formerly belonged to one of Harvey's neighbors, a man called Mortimer Morrison. Everything that Fenella had heard about the man suggested that he'd never really wanted a dog, but had done his best to look after Fiona when she'd been given to him. It seemed clear to Fenella that Fiona was much happier in her new home than she'd ever been with Mortimer, though.

"How are you?" Harvey asked as they began to walk down the promenade together.

"I'm fine. That's a little upsetting, though," Fenella replied, nodding at the police tape across the road from them.

"Young men with nothing to do with their time but drink and

chase women," Harvey frowned. "I've been talking with young Paul Baldwin about starting some sort of music program for teenagers on the island. He's going back across in the new year, of course, and Todd never stays in one place for very long, but I'm going to try to get something started."

"That's good of you."

"I was lucky. I joined a band when I was fourteen and could only play a few chords on my guitar. One of the older men taught me everything I needed to know, and we very nearly got a big break. When it all fell through, I found I was talented at managing other artists, and that turned out to be rewarding, both emotionally and financially. Maybe I can help a few other young men or women find some success in a tough business."

"I think that's a great idea. If you need any financial support, let me know," Fenella said.

Harvey grinned. "I forgot who you are for a minute there. I may take you up on that offer, though, now that you've reminded me."

"The offer is good," Fenella assured him, "and if you need someone to watch Winston and Fiona while you're having meetings and things, you know where to find me."

Harvey laughed. "I was thinking I would take them with me to meetings," he told her. "I think most teenagers would probably love them."

"And if you have any kids giving you trouble, you can send them out for a run with Winston. If they run him from one end of the promenade to the other they'll be too tired to start a fight when they get back."

"That sounds like a plan," Harvey told her. "Anyway, it's just the very beginnings of an idea now, but I'll keep you informed."

"Excellent."

"Which reminds me, Winston, Fiona, and I would be delighted to join you at your Thanksgiving banquet. Are you sure you want the dogs there, though?"

"I'm quite sure. I made special arrangements with the restaurant and everything. Thanksgiving is all about being thankful for things, and I'm very thankful that Winston and Fiona are part of my life."

Harvey grinned. "So you've only invited me to get to my dogs," he teased.

"I like all three of you a great deal. I'm really pleased you'll all be coming."

They parted ways at Fenella's building. She made her way inside. As the elevator doors opened on the sixth floor, Fenella was surprised to see Shelly pacing in the corridor.

"Are you just walking up and down the hallway?" she asked as she emerged from the elevator car.

"Yes, I am," Shelly replied. "I've been waiting for you to get back. Where were you?"

"I just went for a walk."

"You must have been up very early."

"Katie woke me at seven and I went straight out after my shower and a bit of breakfast," Fenella explained. "I should have stopped to see if you wanted to join me, shouldn't I?"

"I was still in bed," Shelly admitted, blushing. "I overslept for some reason, but now I'm here and I'm ready to go fruit and vegetable shopping."

Fenella nodded. "Let me change my shoes and get my handbag."

She gave Katie a small treat and then grabbed her bag. Her sneakers didn't feel appropriate for talking to witnesses, so she changed into a pair of flats and then headed for the door. Shelly was still walking up and down the corridor.

"What is wrong with you?" Fenella demanded.

Shelly flushed. "Gordon rang last night," she said. "He told me that he really misses me and can't wait to see me again. He may even try to get home for a few days, just to see me."

Fenella frowned. "What did you say?"

"Not much," Shelly sighed. "I stammered something about how nice it would be see him and then pretended that Smokey was tangled up in the curtains."

"I'm going to remember that one the next time Jack calls," Fenella laughed. "Did he give you any idea of when he might be coming home?"

"That's just it," Shelly wailed. "He may be home on Thanksgiving weekend."

"Oh, dear," Fenella exclaimed. "I feel terrible now for not inviting him to the dinner."

"But I've already arranged to go with Tim. What am I going to do?"

"You haven't mentioned Tim to Gordon?"

"No, and, well, I haven't exactly told Tim about Gordon, either," Shelly admitted, hanging her head.

Fenella took a deep breath. "What do you want to do?"

"I don't know. I want Gordon to stay away, mostly. I'm having fun with Tim and I suppose I want to see where that's going for a while longer before I see Gordon again."

"You need to tell Gordon that," Fenella said. "Maybe he truly just wants to be friends. If that's the case, then he should be happy for you."

"Maybe," Shelly said. "I suppose I need to tell Tim about Gordon, too."

"You might mention to Tim that you were spending some time with a male friend before you met him, but I can't see why you need to tell him any more than that."

"You're right, of course. Tim doesn't have to know about the mental anguish I've put myself through trying to work out what Gordon really wanted from me."

"No, he doesn't."

Shelly took a deep breath. "I feel a lot better now. Thank you."

"That's what friends are for."

"Let's go and find Cassie Patton and grill her," Shelly said.

"I don't know about grilling her," Fenella said as they walked toward the elevator. "I was thinking more about asking her a few easy questions and seeing where things went from there."

"Let's see how it goes," Shelly suggested. "I thought we should start with the local ShopFast and go from there. That's the one where the fruit and veg manager asked you out, right? He should be happy to talk to you about Cassie."

"I was sort of hoping we could avoid that store," Fenella said. "He seems like a nice guy. I don't want him to get the wrong idea."

"But he's the only person we know who works for ShopFast, aside from Tim, but he doesn't have anything to do with the shops themselves. I already asked him. He's never even met Cassie."

"Except we don't actually know the fruit and vegetable manager. He only spoke to me once. I've never even seen him again," Fenella told her. That she'd gone out of her way to avoid the man wasn't worth mentioning.

"So I'll strike up a conversation with him. You can just hide behind the apples or something. If he's as friendly as you think, he'll probably be happy to talk to me."

"He probably will be, especially if you talk about vegetables."

"I can do that, and then after we've discussed cauliflower for half an hour, I'll slip in a question about their suppliers and how they decide what to buy and how much to get and things like that. Maybe I'll invent a grandson who wants to be a buyer for a big company one day, or something like that."

Fenella shook her head. "Let's not overcomplicate things," she suggested. "Let's just go and see if we see anyone who might be Cassie anywhere in ShopFast."

They were disappointed, though, as they didn't see either the fruit and vegetable manager that Fenella had met or any women who looked like Cassie in the store. ShopFast was fairly empty, with only a few older men and women and a few frazzled-looking women with babies and toddlers in tow, in the store. Only a handful of staff were in evidence, and most of them were working the registers at the front of the store.

"That was disappointing," Shelly said as she took a bite of her muffin on the way out of the store.

"It would have been more disappointing if we hadn't bought muffins," Fenella pointed out.

"They do make really good muffins," Shelly sighed.

An hour later the pair had visited four different ShopFast locations, and Fenella couldn't face the thought of eating another muffin. "Maybe we should have limited ourselves to a single muffin, rather than having one from every store," she said as she and Shelly climbed back into Mona's car after the fourth store.

"The first one was so good that I had to have the second," Shelly sighed. "I didn't realize that the ShopFast in Onchan did different flavors, though. If I'd known that, I wouldn't have had the second one. Anyway, I've never seen either the double chocolate or the cinnamon crumb cake ones at our ShopFast. I had to try them both."

"Maybe we should have shared one muffin between us at each stop, instead of each getting one every time," Fenella suggested.

"That would have been a better idea," Shelly agreed. She rubbed her tummy. "I won't want any lunch, that's for sure."

"What should we do now? Do we keep visiting ShopFast stores or head for home and come up with a different plan?"

"Maybe we could try one more shop," Shelly said. "Let's try the shop in Ramsey. It's one of their biggest. Maybe they'll have more staff working and we'll find someone in fruit and veg to ask about Cassie."

Fenella nodded. "You know I'm never going to complain about driving Mona's car a little bit further," she smiled.

She'd never taken the racy red car across the mountain road before. Large sections of the road that made up one of the most challenging parts of the TT racecourse had no speed limit. Shelly laughed as Fenella sped up and then slowed down again in rapid succession.

"Mona used to fly along here at crazy speeds," she told Fenella.

"I may get braver once I've driven the road a few more times, but this is the first time I've driven it. I've no idea what's coming."

"There's a nice straight stretch coming up," Shelly said helpfully.

Fenella grinned at her. "Maybe I'll speed up a bit when we get there."

They seemed to get to Ramsey very quickly. Fenella slid the car into an empty space in the large parking lot and smiled at her friend. "That was fun. We should start doing all of our shopping in Ramsey."

Shelly laughed. "You can drive up here just for fun," she pointed out. "I can never find anything in this ShopFast, though."

"I hope we can find the fruits and vegetables," Fenella remarked.

As they walked into the shop, a man was just adding the day's local paper to the racks near the entrance. Shelly grabbed one and held it up to Fenella. "Look, Ronald Sherman's disappearance made the front page."

"You must be kidding me," a strident voice said. A tall blonde woman strode out from one of the aisles and grabbed the paper out of Shelly's hand. "You aren't kidding. I don't believe it."

"I'm sorry?" Shelly made the words a question.

The woman looked at her for a minute and then sighed. "I was the unfortunate woman who was involved with Ronald Sherman when he disappeared," she snapped. "The last thing I want now is to have to talk to the police yet again."

"Surely you'd like to see the man found," Fenella suggested.

The woman looked at her and shrugged. "It's been what, six years? I've moved on and I suspect everyone else that he knew has as well. I can't see why the police are reopening the case, I really can't."

"The article said that they have new leads," Shelly told her.

Fenella tried not to look surprised. Daniel hadn't said anything about new leads.

"Well, it's nothing to do with me," the woman said loudly. "Maybe I'll get lucky and the police won't even bother me this time around."

"Come on, Cassie," another voice said. "You were Ronald's girlfriend. If the police are reopening the investigation, they'll want to talk to you again."

Cassie sighed deeply. "Thanks, Bob. Aren't you just a ray of bloody sunshine for me?"

The man shrugged. "Just trying to be realistic. You may need to take some time off work to deal with the police. If you need someone to help out, you know where to find me."

Cassie nodded. "I do indeed. You'll be here managing the department, not at corporate dealing with suppliers. That's my job and I do it very well, thank you. You worry about your customers and your displays and I'll worry about the suppliers, okay?"

The man frowned but he nodded. "I really was just trying to help," he said as he turned away.

"Of course you were," Cassie said in a saccharine-sweet tone. "Help me right out the door while you take over my job."

"I'm quite happy with my own job," Bob replied. "I'll take customers over suppliers any day."

Cassie tilted her head and then smiled at the man. "I'm sorry," she said in a low voice. "This police investigation thing has me all upset and I'm taking it out on you. I shouldn't do that. I know you were simply trying to help. Anyway, if I did need someone to do my job while I'm talking to the police, you know you'd be the first person I'd ring."

Bob flushed. "Thanks."

"No, thank you," Cassie told him, patting his arm. "You're the best department manager I work with, and I keep telling everyone at corporate that they need to make sure you're properly appreciated. Please ignore me when I blow up. Just thinking about talking to the police terrifies me, even though I haven't done anything wrong, well, not since I was a teenager, anyway." Cassie laughed a low and throaty laugh.

Bob chuckled. "We all have things from our teen years we'd rather forget," he said.

"Yes, don't we," Cassie said. She winked at him. "You get back to work. I'll be over in a minute to help you rearrange the citrus according to the new plan."

"Sounds good," Bob beamed.

As he disappeared deeper into the store, Cassie sighed. "Must put getting rid of him on my short list," she muttered under her breath as she looked again at the newspaper she was still holding.

"He seemed very nice," Fenella ventured.

Cassie glanced at her and then looked back at the paper. "What new information could they possibly have?" she asked.

Shelly and Fenella exchanged glances. "Maybe someone thinks they spotted Ronald somewhere," Fenella guessed.

Cassie raised an eyebrow. "I suppose that's possible. He could put all of us out of our misery by simply letting the police know where he's gone, of course. He's far too selfish and mean to do that, though."

"You think he left voluntarily?" Shelly asked.

"Of course he did. He was talking about it for ages, he was. If we hadn't been fighting at the time, he might have taken me with him. Probably not, though. We fought quite a lot, really. He was boring and dull and not very bright. He also had the ambition of a slug and the sex drive to match."

Fenella swallowed the nervous giggle that bubbled up at the woman's unexpected words. Shelly gasped and then laughed.

"You weren't sorry when he disappeared, then," she suggested to Cassie.

The woman shrugged. "I was incandescent with rage when he first went," she countered. "But I've had a few years to get over it now. What really bothers me is the thought that he's living comfortably somewhere while I'm still here, slaving away for ShopFast, dreaming of an easy life."

"What makes you think he's living comfortably somewhere?" Shelly asked.

"He wouldn't have left all of his money behind unless he had a lot more from somewhere else," Cassie told her. "He left his flat, all of his belongings, his car, and his bank accounts behind and started a new life with nothing, or so he wants us to believe. He must have had funding from somewhere, though."

"Maybe he found himself a rich girlfriend," Shelly suggested.

A ripple of something that looked like anger flashed over Cassie's face before she laughed. "If that were the case, he'd have been back long before now," she said. "There's no way he's managed to keep a woman happy for six or seven years. He and I were only together for six months and I was in no way happy for most of that."

"It seems strange to me that he'd leave all of his things behind," Fenella said. "Even if I'd found a fortune, I'd still take my own money with me, too."

Cassie shrugged. "Not if you were afraid of being tracked," she suggested. "He cleared out one bank account just before he left, but I suppose he didn't have time to clear the others. You want to know what annoys me the most about all of it, though?"

"What?" Shelly asked.

"The banks won't let me have any of the money," Cassie said angrily. "We were living together. Some of the money should have been mine."

Fenella bit her tongue rather than argue with the woman. She'd seen how moody Cassie could be and she didn't want to trigger another outburst.

*"That's a shame," Shelly said after a moment. "I suppose they have to keep track of the funds in case Ronald comes back."

"And he will, I'm sure," Cassie sighed. "One of these days, he'll run out of money and come back to the island. I just hope I'm happily married and super rich before he gets back."

"Well, good luck with that," Shelly told her.

Cassie took a deep breath and then nodded at her. "And now I have work to do," she announced before she spun on her very high heel and strode deeper into the store.

"That was interesting," Shelly said as she picked up another paper from the rack.

"That's one word for it," Fenella chuckled. "I'm ready to go home."

"Me, too," Shelly agreed. "Although I'd like to walk past the bakery and see if they have any different muffins. I'll be buying them for later, not now, if they do," she added quickly.

Fenella felt fortunate that the Ramsey ShopFast bakery didn't seem to do any additional types of muffins to the ones that she and Shelly had already enjoyed. They paid for Shelly's paper and then walked back to the car.

"What new information could they have?" Shelly asked as Fenella started the car.

"I've no idea, but I intend to ask Daniel that very question the next time I speak to him," she replied. "Let me tell you what Donald said when I spoke to him last night, though."

The pair talked about Donald's information and the conversation with Cassie all the way back to Douglas.

"I'm too full to have any lunch," Shelly complained as Fenella parked in the apartment building's garage.

"I could just about manage something small," Fenella admitted sheepishly. "But only something little."

"I have some sandwich meats and bread in my flat. You're welcome to join me for lunch. Then we can plan what we're going to do next."

"That sounds good. I'm having dinner with Todd at his house tonight. I wouldn't want much lunch anyway."

"He's cooking?"

"Yes, he told me he can't cook much, but he has one dish that he always makes to impress people. He said something about chicken and rice. I want to make sure I'm really hungry so that if it isn't good, I'll still eat lots of it."

Shelly laughed. "Good luck. John wasn't much of a cook when we were first married, but over time he learned to make a few things quite well. Gordon has cooked for me once or twice. Never anything too complicated, but he's perfectly competent in the kitchen. Tim hasn't offered yet, but he's been living on his own for years, so I expect him to be capable in the kitchen."

"Jack was hopeless in the kitchen. I'm really looking forward to tonight."

"It's a shame Todd won't be here for Thanksgiving."

"Yes and no. I like Todd a lot, but we're really just friends. He doesn't want to settle down in one place for any length of time and I'm quite content here. I suspect things between us are winding down and I can't see that changing."

"Is that good news for Daniel, then?"

Fenella sighed. "I don't want to talk about Daniel."

8

"What do I need to apply for a credit card?" Fenella asked as the pair ate their sandwiches.

"I don't know. Identification, probably," Shelly told her.

"I'll bring my passport and my driver's license, then. Will they want to know about my monthly income? Because I don't really have a monthly income."

"I suspect once they find out that you're Mona's niece, they won't care. Didn't you say you have an account with them? They should be able to see how much that account is worth, even if they can't see everything you own."

"I have a checking account there and also a savings account. Between the two, they have a fairly large chunk of my money."

"I'm sure if they don't want to give you credit, that someone on the island will. I'm surprised you haven't been flooded with credit card offers since you've been here, really."

"I believe all of that sort of mail goes to Doncan," Fenella told her. "I should probably just call him and ask him to sort out a credit card or two for me."

Shelly laughed. "I can't imagine asking the island's most important advocate to sort out a credit card for me. He'd have his secretary do it, of course, but still."

Fenella flushed. "I didn't think about that," she said. "I don't know what I was thinking, really."

"You were thinking that you're very rich and you don't need to go to the bank and actually apply for a credit card like an ordinary person. That's probably true, but if you have Doncan's office deal with it, we won't get to meet Helen Campbell."

"And that's really what this is all about." Fenella finished her sandwich and washed it down with the last of her soda. She wiped her fingers on a napkin and then stood up. "I'll just go next door and grab my passport," she told Shelly. "Then I'll be ready to go."

Shelly nodded. "I'll be ready by the time you get back," she promised.

Fenella combed her hair and touched up her makeup after she'd given Katie some lunch. "Now be a good kitten this afternoon," Fenella told her. "Don't annoy Mona if she comes by for a visit, okay?"

Katie seemed to sigh before she turned and walked away. A minute later, Fenella spotted her curled up in her favorite chair in front of the windows. That it was also Mona's favorite chair was a constant source of friction between the cat and the ghost. "You're being deliberately difficult," Fenella sighed at Katie.

"She is, rather, but I'll forgive her today," Mona said. "I'm feeling especially kindly towards her as I was just visiting a friend and he has a particularly badly behaved cat."

"Is your friend dead or alive?" Fenella asked.

"He's dead and has been for many years. The cat is dead, too, although he doesn't seem to realize it. Cats are spoiled, of course, with their nine lives, but they aren't always very good at counting. Stan's cat seems to think that he has a few lives left, but he's mistaken."

Fenella considered and then discarded a dozen questions before she gave up on pursuing the matter. There was no way to know if Mona was telling the truth or not, so it probably wasn't worth asking anyway.

She headed into the bedroom and opened the wall safe. Both her US and Manx passports were tucked up inside. After debating as to which one she should take, she dropped them both into her handbag. Better to have more than she needed than not enough.

"Tell me what you learned from Cassie," Mona said as she wandered into the room.

Fenella quickly repeated as much of the conversation as she could remember. "I should probably call Daniel and tell him everything," she added as she finished.

"You should. If you wait until after your visit with Helen, you'll miss out on having two separate occasions to ring him."

Fenella shook her head. "I think I'll wait. We might not even see Helen. Anyway, Shelly is waiting for me. I need to go."

"Don't leave it too late to ring him," Mona warned. "You don't want to be in a rush to get off the phone because of your dinner with Todd."

"I hope things won't take long at the bank," Fenella frowned. "How long can it take to apply for a credit card?"

"That will probably depend on how many other people are already there doing the same thing."

Fenella nodded. "We'd better get going, then."

She gave Katie a quick pat and then let herself out. Shelly opened her door as soon as Fenella knocked.

"We should probably hurry. I've no idea how busy the bank will be today," she said as she locked her door behind herself.

"If it's too busy, we can always leave it for tomorrow," Fenella suggested. "Or maybe we could try to find a different way to meet Helen. Maybe she has a favorite pub or something like that."

"Maybe we should have thought of that earlier. Do you want to forget about the bank?"

"No, let's try that first. I really do need a credit card, after all."

"While I was waiting for you, I read the article in today's paper about the case," Shelly told her as the pair strolled down the promenade toward the bank, which was only a short distance away.

"Was there anything interesting in it?"

"I know where to find Gary now."

"Is he still working for the company that installed your kitchen?"

"No, he's opened his own company. They redo kitchens and bathrooms, and according to Dan Ross, they have some of the most competitive prices on the island."

"What does that mean?"

"I think he was trying to say that they're inexpensive. He may or may not have been hinting that they aren't the best quality."

"Maybe one of us should get a quote for a kitchen remodel."

"I'll do it," Shelly laughed. "You know I'd love a new kitchen. My current kitchen is very high quality, but I don't like the colors at all. I'm not sure I'll ever be able to bring myself to pull out what's there and put in something new, but I wouldn't mind finding out what it would cost to do just that."

"Maybe call Gary and see if he can come around and give you a quote, then," Fenella suggested. "I'm not sure how we'll bring the conversation around to Ronald's disappearance, but we'll think of something."

Shelly nodded and then stopped. They were in front of the bank's entrance. "I hope you've thought of something for doing just that with Helen," she said.

Fenella flushed. "I was hoping maybe you'd have an idea. Was her name in today's paper?"

"Yes, it was, actually. The paper listed her as Ronald's former girlfriend and mentioned where she works, too."

"I suppose we can use that if we have to," Fenella said. "Let's go and get this over with."

Shelly grinned at her. "I'm having a lot more fun with this than you are, aren't I?"

"I'm not sure this is my idea of fun," Fenella muttered as she walked behind her friend into the bank.

"Ms. Woods? This is a surprise," the woman behind the desk right inside the front door said. "What can we do for you today?"

"I need to talk to someone about getting a credit card," Fenella replied, trying to act as if she weren't at all shocked to have been recognized.

"Of course. Let me ring and find out whom you need to see," the woman replied. She picked up the phone at her elbow and pushed a single number on it. "Ms. Woods is here and would like to speak to someone about a credit card," she said in a low voice a moment later. "Very good," followed after another minute.

"Ms. Woods? If you and your friend would like to have a seat, Ms. Campbell, our vice president for lending, will be with you momentarily."

"Thank you," Fenella said. She glanced at Shelly, who looked delighted, and then crossed to the small sitting area just inside the lobby. The chairs were less comfortable than they looked. Fenella hoped they wouldn't have to wait long.

"Ms. Woods?" a cool voice said a minute later. "Good afternoon. I'm Helen Campbell, the vice president for lending. If you'd like to follow me?"

Fenella and Shelly got to their feet and fell into step behind Helen. Fenella studied her as they walked. Helen was blonde with green eyes. She was wearing a dark suit with a bright pink blouse underneath the jacket and her black high-heeled shoes had matching pink bows attached to the ankles. Her hair was in a tight bun and her makeup had been expertly applied.

Helen led them to a small office in a corner. There was a tiny window on the back wall that gave Helen a nice view of the parking lot behind the building. Beyond the parking lot, the huge brick walls of another building prevented most of the natural light from getting to Helen's window.

As they walked into the room, Helen glanced around and then shrugged. "We could meet in one of the conference rooms if you'd rather," she said. "They're larger and have more light and windows."

"This is fine," Fenella said. "I'm hoping this won't take long."

Helen nodded. "It shouldn't, but please have a seat."

Fenella and Shelly sat in chairs that were identical to the ones in the lobby as Helen sat down in the large and comfortable-looking desk chair behind the large wooden desk that took up most of the space in the small room.

"Let me get the right form," Helen said. She pulled open a desk drawer and rummaged around for a moment before pulling out a thick packet of papers. "Here we are," she said brightly. "Let's start with the basics."

It didn't take long for Fenella to give Helen her name, address, and other basic information. Then Helen turned the page over and gave Fenella a curious look. "Will you be adding your, um, friend here to the account?"

Fenella looked surprised. "Shelly just came along because we were out shopping together," she explained. "We're neighbors and friends, but no, I wasn't planning on adding her to my credit card."

Helen nodded. "I wasn't sure if you were partners or not," she said. "It really isn't any of my business, either. You can add her to your accounts if you want to, regardless of your relationship."

Fenella gave Shelly an amused smile. "Sorry, dear friend, but I'm not giving you a credit card."

Shelly laughed. "I have more than enough credit of my own," she replied.

Helen made another note and then turned to the next page of her form. "I'm meant to ask you about income and debts, but I don't think they apply in this case. We all know that you inherited Mona's estate, after all."

"I did wonder if you'd be worried about my lack of an income," Fenella replied.

"In your case, it isn't a factor. There aren't very many people on the island that I can say that for, but you happen to be one of them. I'm not sure exactly what credit limit I'll be able to get for you, but we'll put the whole thing into the computer and see what it says. Once that's done, we can discuss the answer and make any necessary adjustments."

"That sounds good," Fenella told her.

Helen only had a few more questions to finish her paperwork. Once she'd noted all of Fenella's answers, she had Fenella sign the application, and then went to work typing on her computer. Shelly and Fenella exchanged glances as Helen typed. After a few minutes, the woman looked up and smiled at them both.

"Now I send the application up to the magical computer pixies and they send back a reply," she said. "It should only take a few minutes."

"That seems surprisingly quick for computer pixies," Shelly said.

Helen laughed. "Sometimes they need a few extra minutes," she admitted. "This could be one of those times, actually, as Ms. Woods's application is unique."

"Please call me Fenella," Fenella said quickly.

"How are you finding the island, Fenella?" Helen asked.

"I love it," she replied. "It's totally unlike the US and I'm still adjusting to certain things, but I'm really happy here."

"That's good to hear. I love the island, too. I can't imagine living anywhere else," Helen told her.

"Of course, poor Fenella's been caught up in a few murder investigations since she's been here," Shelly interjected. "That's been something of a surprise for her."

"I can't imagine," Helen shivered. "Of course, I've read about all of the cases in the local paper. I'm not sure I'd want to stay on the island if I were in your shoes."

"A few unfortunate events haven't dimmed my appreciation for the island," Fenella told her.

"And from what I read in today's paper, you're caught up in a police investigation yourself," Shelly added, staring at Helen.

Helen blinked a few times and then sighed. "You mean Ronald," she said. "I don't consider myself caught up in his case, not really, but I'm not sure the local press agree with my opinion on the matter."

"According to today's paper, you were involved with him before he disappeared," Shelly said.

Helen shook her head. "We were together for three years, but we split up some six months or more before he disappeared. He was involved with another woman when he vanished."

"I must have misread the article," Shelly waved a hand.

"It's hard to believe that someone could disappear on an island this small," Fenella said.

"I think it would be easy enough to do, if you truly wanted to go," Helen replied.

"Does that mean you think that Ronald left voluntarily?" Shelly asked.

Helen took a deep breath and then shrugged. "Seven years ago I thought that," she said. "He'd often spoken of wanting to leave the island. He thought he'd find fame and fortune, or at least fortune, if he moved to the UK. It was the only thing we ever fought about, really, well, until Cassie Patton came along."

"She's the woman he was seeing when he disappeared?" Shelly asked.

Fenella hid a smile. Shelly actually sounded as if she didn't already know the answer to that question.

"She was the woman that he cheated on me with, and the woman he left me for. She's also probably the person who drove him to run away from the island," Helen replied in a bitter voice.

"You still loved him. I'm sorry," Shelly said softly.

"I still loved him when he left me and I still love him now," Helen said in a low voice. "He was a good man, not the brightest, not the best looking, not the most ambitious, but he was a good man and I loved him dearly. It's been six years and three hundred and forty-three days since I saw him last, and I still can't get him out of my head."

"What do you think happened to him?" Shelly asked after a moment.

"I always thought Cassie drove him into hiding," Helen replied. "They fought constantly. Sometimes he'd come over to my flat to get away from her and he'd tell me how horrible she was to him. Whenever she rang, though, he'd go rushing back to her. I didn't understand it then and I don't understand it now."

"Where would he go? According to the papers, he never touched any of the money in his bank accounts after he left," Shelly said.

"I'm sure he got Gary to help him. Gary is his cousin and the two are close friends, even though they only saw each other occasionally. Gary would have done whatever he could to help Ronald get away."

"Did they have other family somewhere in the UK that Ronald could have gone and stayed with for a while?"

Helen shrugged. "That's a good question. I know Ronald was looking for other family members, but I don't know that he ever found any."

"So where do you think Ronald went?" Fenella asked.

"I wish I knew," Helen replied with tears in her eyes. "When he first left, I was sure he was just running away, and I was furious with him. I told anyone who would listen how much I hated him for how he'd treated me. Now, all these years later, I'm not so sure, though."

"What do you mean?" Shelly wondered.

"If he'd truly gone of his own accord, I feel as if he would have come back by now," Helen told her. "Maybe not to stay, but for a visit, anyway. I can't imagine that he hasn't been in touch with Gary for all of these years, even if he doesn't want to see Cassie or me."

"So what do you think happened to him?" Shelly asked.

"I've no idea. Maybe he went across and got hit by a bus or something," Helen said. "I mean, people die every day. Maybe he left the island and then died, and we just don't know about it yet. That seems the most likely answer, really."

"Eugene Matthews, who used to work with Ronald at Manx Computer Innovations, told the paper that he thought Ronald found a way to get access to a lot of money on one of the computers in their repair shop."

"Ronald wouldn't have done something like that," Helen said firmly. "He was good with computers, and he might have found something like that if he'd gone looking, but he would never have stolen the information. I can see him bragging to his coworkers about the things he'd found, but stealing is a different thing."

The phone on Helen's desk buzzed. She picked up the receiver and had a short conversation with whoever was on the other end. When she put the phone back down, she got to her feet. "I'm very sorry, but I need to go and speak to someone for a moment. Would either of you like tea or coffee while you wait?"

Fenella and Shelly both shook their heads. Helen picked up Fenella's paperwork and left the room.

"That was odd," Fenella said.

"Maybe the computer pixies said no to your application and Helen is going to kick them into submission," Shelly suggested.

"I suppose that's one possibility," Fenella laughed. "She seems really upset about Ronald, even after all these years."

"She does, doesn't she? I'm not sure I'd still be able to love a man who'd broken my heart and then disappeared, not after seven years, anyway."

"She isn't the first person to suggest that Gary must know where Ronald has gone."

"No, she isn't. We really need to talk to Gary."

"Time to get an estimate on your new kitchen, then."

"My only worry is that the quote will be so low that I'll be tempted, even though I know I don't need a new kitchen."

"If you are tempted, make sure you get another quote," Fenella warned her friend. "You said yourself that you weren't sure what Dan Ross was suggesting about Gary's company. If he is giving very low quotes and then performing poor quality remodels, you need to know about it before you agree to anything."

Shelly sighed. "I'm not seriously going to have my kitchen redone. I think I'd probably rather just move to a whole new flat than live through another kitchen remodel."

"Is it that bad?"

"It truly is," Shelly told her. "The noise and the mess were awful. We didn't have a kitchen for months on end, and that was with one of the very best companies on the island. Maybe, if I'm really tempted, I'll try to find some of Gary's customers and hear what they have to say about his work. Their horror stories should be enough to put me off the idea completely."

Fenella chuckled. "You're assuming Gary isn't doing good work. Maybe he's actually very good and reliable."

"I doubt it."

The office door swung open and Helen walked back into the room. "Sorry about that," she said brightly. "The computer couldn't handle the unusual circumstances surrounding your application, so we had to twist its arm a little bit," she said. "You've been approved with a ten thousand pound limit. I appreciate that isn't much, but we can review your limit after a few months. I'm sure we'll be able to raise it from there."

"Ten thousand pounds should be more than enough to cover me for the foreseeable future," Fenella assured her.

"If you find you have an unexpected expense and need a temporary increase, do let us know. Some of our customers request one when they're planning a holiday, for example. They don't want to worry about overspending when they're away from home."

Fenella nodded. "If I ever go on holiday, I'll keep that in mind." She smiled to herself as she used the British word instead of vacation. Maybe she'd learn British English one day.

Helen sighed. "If I had your money, I'd travel almost all the time. Oh, I'd come back to the island a few times each year for a week or so, but otherwise I'd be traveling, seeing the world, experiencing other cultures and trying new things."

"Having all of this money is rather new to me," Fenella told her. "Maybe once I've grown used to the idea, I'll start traveling a little bit. But then, the island is still rather new to me as well. I still feel as if I'm on vacation, just being here."

Helen nodded. "Was there anything else I can help you with today? Other loans or lines of credit you might be interested in, or anything like that?"

Fenella shook her head. "Getting a credit card was a priority, so I can stop using my US cards. I think I'm good otherwise."

Helen turned to Shelly. "Can I help you with anything? Mortgages, lines of credit, credit cards?"

Shelly shook her head and then laughed. "One quick question. If I wanted to take out a loan to remodel my kitchen, would the bank lend me the funds?"

Helen took down Shelly's information and then entered it into the computer. "This one shouldn't take as long," she told the women. "It's a much more straightforward application."

The words were hardly out of her mouth when her computer chimed. "And there's the email from upstairs," she said. "The bank would be prepared to loan you up to fifty thousand pounds for home improvements on your current flat," she told Shelly.

Shelly grinned. "That's a lot more than I was expecting. I'll get back to you if I decide to go ahead."

"You know where to find me," Helen told her. She handed each of them a business card. "Please ring me directly if you need anything at any time. I'm happy to help with things like investments and savings accounts as well. Or rather, I'm happy to talk to you about your problems and then find the right person to solve them for you."

"That's very kind of you," Fenella said. She tucked the woman's card into her handbag and then stood up.

"You should have your card in about two weeks," Helen said as she got to her feet. "If it doesn't arrive, please let me know."

"I will. Thank you so much for your time," Fenella replied.

Helen crossed to the door and then stopped with her hand on the knob. "I'm sorry if I was unprofessional earlier," she said, flushing. "Even after all this time, I can't discuss Ronald without getting emotional. I try to tell myself that some day I'll find another man, but I'm not sure I believe it. Ronald may have been the only man for me. Sadly, I wasn't the only woman for him."

"I'm sorry," Fenella said.

"Perhaps it would be easier for you to find closure if you knew what had happened to Ronald," Shelly suggested.

Helen nodded. "I think you're right. Not knowing is so difficult. I still jump every time my phone rings or I get a text message. I keep thinking that one day Ronald will be on the other end of the line, sounding all sheepish about having been gone for so long. Knowing him, he won't be apologetic, though," she laughed. "I'm sure he'll say something about time just getting away from him. It often did."

"I truly hope you get a happy ending," Fenella told her.

"I'm too old to believe in happy endings," Helen replied. "With the police reopening the case, at least maybe I'll finally find out what really happened to the man I loved. I can understand his running away from Cassie and from the island, I truly can. I just wish he'd have chosen to stay in touch with me."

Fenella stared at the woman for a moment and then pulled her into a hug. When she released her, Helen wiped away a tear. "I'm sorry," Fenella said. "Americans are big on hugs."

Helen smiled. "It's fine. I think I needed that."

Shelly patted the woman's arm. "If you ever need to talk, you have my number," she told her. "My husband and I were married for over thirty years when he passed away suddenly. I know all about grief."

Helen shook her head. "I'm behaving like an idiot," she said. "My mother tells me that all the time. Ronald and I were only together for three years, and we didn't even live together. He wasn't ready for that level of commitment, he always said. Of course, Cassie moved into his flat the day after I found out about her, but that's another matter." She sighed. "I have a lot of unresolved bitterness."

"As I said, if you want to talk, ring me," Shelly repeated. "We can open a bottle of wine and a tub of ice cream and really talk."

"Am I invited?" Fenella asked.

Shelly laughed. "You should hear Fenella's stories about her ex-boyfriend. They'll make you glad you're single."

Helen laughed. "I appreciate the offer. I may just take you up on it, actually. I have a feeling this police investigation is going to be stressful for me."

She pulled open her office door and then escorted the women out of the building. "Thank you both, for everything," she said before Shelly and Fenella turned and headed for home.

"She's a mess," Fenella said once they were far enough away that she was sure Helen couldn't hear them.

"She is, at that," Shelly agreed. "It sounds as if she truly loved the man, but she's awfully bitter about the way he treated her."

"I hope Daniel can work out what happened to Ronald. I think Helen needs to know in order to get on with her life."

"I think you're right. I don't understand men. Helen was clearly madly in love with Ronald and he dumped her in favor of Cassie, who doesn't seem to care about anyone."

"I suspect Helen was too nice," Fenella suggested. "Presumably Cassie was a challenge."

"I suppose I'm lucky that John preferred nice women," Shelly said.

They walked back to their building and boarded the elevator. "What now?" Shelly asked as the doors slid open on the sixth floor.

"Now I suppose I should ring Daniel," Fenella sighed.

"I wonder if Tiffany was a challenge," Shelly said dryly.

"Tiffany was young and gorgeous. I'm sure that was more than enough of a temptation for Daniel."

"We still don't know that they were anything more than friends," Shelly pointed out.

"And we may never know, as Daniel seems to be avoiding talking about her."

"You need to get him alone and demand answers," Mona suggested as Fenella let herself and Shelly into her apartment.

"I can't do that," Fenella replied without thinking.

"You can't do what?" Shelly asked, looking confused.

"Oh, sorry, I was just having a conversation in my head and only said some of it out loud," Fenella replied, glaring at Mona, who was laughing in her chair.

"Are you going to ring Daniel now, then?" Shelly asked.

"After I have a cold drink," Fenella decided. "I need a minute to gather my thoughts before I speak to him."

"Do you mind if I go and get Smokey? I'm sure she'd like a play date with Katie."

"Go get her. When you're back, I'll ring Daniel and put him on speakerphone."

Shelly nodded and then let herself out.

"Did you get to speak to Helen?" Mona demanded as soon as the door shut behind Shelly.

"Yes, but I'm not going to go into all of that right now. You'll be able to hear it as I tell Daniel, and I won't have to repeat myself."

Mona frowned but didn't object. Fenella pulled a soda out of the refrigerator and took a long drink. "That's better," she sighed.

A moment later Shelly was back. Fenella couldn't think of any more excuses to avoid ringing Daniel.

9

"Ring his mobile," Mona suggested.

"I think I'll just call the station," Fenella said. "He might be busy. I can leave a message."

Shelly grinned at her. "You mean, you hope he's busy so you can just leave a message," she teased. "At least this way you're choosing when to speak to him. If you leave a message, he could ring back any time."

"Yeah, but I don't have to answer," Fenella muttered as she picked up the phone. She dialed the non-emergency number for the Douglas police station.

"May I speak to Inspector Daniel Robinson, please?" she said when the call was answered.

"May I have your name, please?"

"Fenella Woods."

"Please hold, Ms. Woods."

Fenella switched the call onto speakerphone and then settled in on the couch next to it. Shelly sat in the chair on the opposite side. Mona quickly crossed the room and sat down next to Fenella.

"Ms. Woods? I'm sorry, but Inspector Robinson is not at his desk at the moment. Would you like me to put you through to his voicemail?"

"Yes, that would be good," Fenella replied, feeling flustered. They'd never given her that option when she'd called before.

"Is that new?" Shelly demanded. "I've rung Daniel a few times and they've never suggested that to me."

"It's the first time I've been offered it, as well," Fenella told her.

A few clicks on the line later, Fenella heard Daniel's voice. "This is Inspector Daniel Robinson with the Isle of Man Constabulary. Please leave a message after the tone."

"Hi, it's Fenella," she said in a perky voice that immediately made her wince. "Shelly and I talked to both Helen and Cassie today, and I thought I should let you know about the conversations. Call me back when you have time. Um, bye."

She put the phone down and covered her face with her hands. "That sounded dumb," she groaned.

"On the plus side, Daniel probably won't even notice," Shelly said soothingly. "I think it's only women who play and replay messages to overanalyze every word."

Fenella laughed and then shook her head. "I always sound like an idiot on answering machines. I should have just left a message with the woman who answered the phone."

"What are you going to wear tonight?" Shelly asked.

"I've no idea. What do you think?"

"I think it's time to raid Mona's wardrobe," Shelly laughed.

Half an hour later, Fenella was debating between two different dresses, both of which she loved, when the phone rang.

"That will be Daniel," Mona said.

"Do you think that's Daniel?" Shelly asked.

"Probably," Fenella replied. "I don't get a lot of phone calls. It could be an insurance salesman, I suppose."

She picked up the nearest phone. "Hello?"

"Good afternoon. I got your message," Daniel said.

"Let me put you on speaker," Fenella said quickly. "That way Shelly can contribute as well." She put the phone down and then she and Shelly settled on the bed next to it. Mona came and stood nearby.

"Tell me everything that you did today, then," Daniel said once Fenella told him she was ready. "Start with breakfast."

Fenella did her best to give the man a complete rundown of her day. Shelly chimed in once or twice when Fenella missed out a bit of conversation, but Daniel didn't say a word until Fenella was done.

"Interesting," was the first thing he said.

"What's interesting?" Shelly demanded.

"People are telling you slightly different things to what they told the police and the papers seven years ago. It may just be that time has colored their memories, but I find it interesting to hear the differences. I'm eager to start talking to everyone myself, of course, but I'm going to be tied up with last night's incident for another day or two. I wish we could have held the newspaper article for next week, though."

"Why?" Fenella asked.

"It's causing all sorts of grief for the poor men and women who answer the phones," Daniel told her. "Apparently, half of the island's residents seem to think they know what happened to Ronald Sherman. They've all just waited until now to share their thoughts."

"Have you learned anything valuable?" Shelly wondered.

"I've learned that there's a small but vocal minority of islanders who believe that alien abduction is a real threat to all of us. I've learned that there are more conspiracy theory obsessives out there than I'd ever realized, and I've learned that there are a handful of people on the island who live in fear of spontaneous natural combustion."

Shelly laughed. "Oh, dear, none of that seems especially helpful."

"I don't think it is," Daniel agreed. "We've also had a few phone calls from various people who knew Ronald. Most of them seem happy to hear that the case is being reinvestigated. As I said, I'm looking forward to speaking with all of them."

"Have any of the people we spoke with rung?" Shelly asked.

"I can't answer that," Daniel told her. "In part because that information is confidential, and in part because I've really no idea. I haven't had time to go through my messages yet today. Reception has been given a very short list of people who are to be put through to my voicemail. Otherwise, they're taking paper messages for me and I'll go through them later."

"We're going to try to get Gary around to give me a quote on a new kitchen," Shelly told him.

"I'm not sure I like that idea," Daniel replied. "It's one thing meeting people in public places, but I don't like the idea of you having someone in your flat, not even if Fenella is there too."

"What if I have Tim join us?" Shelly asked.

"I'd rather you met the man at his showroom," Daniel replied.

"He has a showroom?" Shelly sounded surprised.

"As I understand it, it isn't much of a showroom, but it's more public than your flat. I still want you to take Tim and Fenella with you, and maybe a dozen other people as well, if possible."

"I don't know if I can find a dozen people, but I'll try to arrange for a small crowd," Shelly promised. "Where is he?"

"In Peel, just off the high street," Daniel told her. He gave her the exact address.

"I'm sure we can arrange something for tomorrow," Shelly said thoughtfully. "It probably never gets very busy in his showroom, so maybe I shouldn't have lots of people show up there, but there's a small café in that area. Maybe I could have some friends stationed there."

Daniel sighed. "I said I didn't mind if you tried to meet a few witnesses. I wasn't expecting you to plan these things like a police operation."

Shelly laughed. "Hardly a police operation. This is definitely amateur hour."

"That's what worries me," Daniel replied.

"We may not even get to see Gary," Shelly told him. "Just because it's his showroom doesn't mean he'll be there."

"You've done surprisingly well with everyone else," he pointed out.

"We've been lucky," Shelly said. "Our luck will probably run out tomorrow."

"You're having better luck than I am, anyway," Daniel retorted. "I'm stuck dealing with other things for the moment."

"Can you think of anyone else we might want to try to find?" Shelly asked. "Gary is the last person on our list, unless you have any other ideas."

"I think once you've spoken to Gary, that will be quite enough," Daniel replied. "We'll have to see how things go once I'm actually investigating the case myself."

Fenella looked at Shelly and shrugged. "Thus far I don't feel as if I've gained any new insights into what happened to Ronald," she told Daniel.

"At least people are talking about the case again," Daniel said. "I keep hoping that someone will come forward with new information now."

"Good luck," Shelly said.

"Thanks. I'm afraid I'm going to need it," Daniel chuckled. "Now I mostly need to get through this paperwork and then get some dinner. I don't suppose either of you are free to join me for a meal later?"

Fenella swallowed a sigh. "Sorry, I have plans for tonight," she said, suddenly wishing she hadn't agreed to see Todd that evening.

"I do, too," Shelly said apologetically, "and I have to arrange everything for tomorrow, as well."

"Perhaps one or both of you will be at the pub later," was Daniel's reply.

"Maybe," Shelly said. "It sounds like a good idea right now, anyway."

"I'm not sure how my evening is going to go," Fenella told him. "If I do drop into the pub, I'll look for you."

"I'll be upstairs, curled up with a cat and a book," Daniel told her. "Assuming it's nice and quiet, that is."

"The band isn't playing, anyway," Shelly said. "It gets busy when they perform, but otherwise it's usually reasonably quiet."

When Daniel disconnected a moment later, Fenella buried her head in her hands. "I'm still angry at him about Tiffany," she said, "but I wish I didn't have plans for tonight."

"You need to get him alone and have a long talk with him," Shelly told her. "You need to find out exactly what went on with Tiffany and ask him how he truly feels about you."

"And I could have done both of those things if I didn't have plans tonight," Fenella sighed. "It wouldn't be fair to Todd to cancel on him. He's been planning tonight for a while. He even texted me earlier to ask me which dessert sounded better."

"What were your options?" Shelly asked.

"Triple chocolate mousse cake or chocolate brownie trifle," Fenella replied. "He wasn't planning on making either himself. He was in that specialty bakery in Onchan."

"Which one did you pick?"

"Chocolate mousse cake. I can't remember them now, but he read me full descriptions of both items and that was definitely the one that sounded better."

"I think I'd choose that one, too," Shelly mused. "Or maybe I'd just have told him to get both."

Fenella laughed. "Now why didn't I think of that?"

As the conversation with Daniel was out of the way, Fenella could focus on working out what to wear for the evening ahead. "I still like the black one better," she told Shelly as she twirled slowly in front of her mirror. "I don't know about wearing red tonight."

"Wear the red one," Mona said from where she'd settled on the bed.

"I really like the red one," Shelly told her. "The black one is pretty, but the red one is gorgeous."

Fenella slipped the red dress off and put the black one back on. "There's just something I really like about this one."

"I'm sorry to say it, but it's boring," Shelly replied. "If you really don't like the red one, look through the wardrobe again. I'm sure you'll be able to find something better than that black dress."

"It's not boring," Fenella argued. "None of Mona's clothes are ever boring."

"I got that one for funerals and memorial services," Mona told her. "It's deliberately unspectacular. Wear the red one. It's perfect for tonight."

Fenella opened the wardrobe and flipped through the dresses. Unusually, nothing seemed to catch her eye. Eventually she pulled a dark purple sheath out. "What do you think?"

"It's pretty, but not for tonight," Shelly said.

"Wear the red one," Mona yawned. "Why do I have to keep repeating myself? Can you still hear me? If you can hear me, wink your left eye."

Fenella winked.

"That was your right eye," Mona sighed, "but at least I know you can hear me. Wear the red dress."

Fenella took the black dress off and hung it back in the wardrobe. As she tried to slide the purple dress over her head, she found herself stuck. "I must have missed a zipper somewhere," she exclaimed as she pulled the dress off. As far as she could tell, the zipper was open as far as it would go and there weren't any other fastenings that were stopping the dress from going on.

"Maybe Mona bought that one when she was much thinner?" Shelly suggested as Fenella tried the dress a second time.

No matter what she did, she simply couldn't get into the dress. It was at least two sizes too small.

"Wear the red one," Mona said.

"Maybe I'll just wear the red one," Fenella sighed. She hung the purple dress back in the wardrobe and then slipped the red dress back over her head. As she turned in front of the mirror she had to admit that the dress was flattering and beautiful.

"I'm glad that's settled," Shelly laughed. "What time are you meant to be at Todd's?"

"He's meeting me here in about half an hour," Fenella replied. "He said his house is difficult to find."

"What does that mean?" Shelly wondered.

"I've no idea. What are you doing tonight?"

"Tim and I are having dinner together, but not until later. While I wait for him, I'm going to ring a few people, though. I really do want some of my friends scattered around Peel tomorrow morning."

The pair had a brief discussion about their plans for the next day before Shelly headed for home. Fenella gave Katie her dinner and then fixed her hair and makeup. She was ready with one minute to spare before Todd knocked on the door.

"You look fabulous," he greeted her. The huge bouquet of roses went into a vase in the kitchen.

"I hope you don't mind walking from here," Todd said as they boarded the elevator a moment later. "It isn't far, but those are awfully high heels."

"All of Mona's shoes are incredibly comfortable," Fenella assured him. "If I need to, I can always kick them off once we get to your house."

"That sounds like a plan," he laughed.

They walked down the promenade for a short distance, and then Todd turned down a small alley. The alley was lined on both sides with huge Victorian row houses. Todd stopped at the very first one and led Fenella up the stairs to the door.

"This is it," he said, stepping back to let her walk into the house in front of him.

Fenella stepped inside and felt as if she'd stepped back in time. "It's amazing," she gasped as she looked around the spacious foyer.

"I had it fully restored when I bought it," he told her as he shut the door behind them. "A previous owner turned it into a bed and breakfast. In doing so, he stripped out a lot of the period features. It took time and money, but I brought them all back. Would you like a tour?"

"Oh, yes, please," Fenella exclaimed.

The ground floor had several rooms, each decorated in Victorian splendor. The kitchen was something of a surprise, though.

"It's huge," Fenella gasped as she looked around the room.

"This was an addition," Todd explained. "I've done less here than elsewhere, so it doesn't fit in with the rest of the house as much as I'd like, but I've added a few touches where I can. I'm afraid I'm too fond of my modern conveniences to redo the kitchen to Victorian standards."

Fenella laughed. "I wouldn't want to change a thing in this room, either," she said. "It's lovely."

"It's all very functional, which is great on the very rare occasions when I actually try to cook anything," Todd told her.

The rest of the house was equally stunning. There were several bedrooms on the next two floors, but the top floor contained only the master bedroom and its huge en-suite bathroom and walk-in closet.

"What amazing views," Fenella said as she looked out the master bedroom window. The window was on the side of the property, which meant it looked out onto the promenade and to the sea beyond it. It was a similar view to the one from Fenella's living room.

"Yes, the views are one of the best parts," Todd agreed. "You're welcome to stay and admire them for as long as you'd like, but I need to get back down to the kitchen to check on dinner. I'd hate to burn anything."

After one last glance out the window, Fenella followed Todd back down to the kitchen. She settled at the small dining table there while Todd dashed around, crashing pots and pans together and muttering to himself.

"Sorry, let me get you a glass of wine," he said after a few minutes. "Red or white?"

"I'd rather have a soft drink, if you don't mind," Fenella told him. "That migraine the other night has put me off the idea of drinking for a while."

Todd handed her a drink and then poured himself a glass of wine. "I hope you don't mind," he said.

"Not at all," she assured him.

A short while later, he began piling food onto plates. Fenella was relieved to find that everything was delicious.

"I'm glad you're enjoying it," Todd said when she told him so. "Save room for pudding, though."

After dinner they settled in one of the ground floor rooms, snuggled up together on a couch, looking out the window at the sea.

"I'm glad we could do this tonight. My plans have changed again. I'm leaving tomorrow," Todd told her.

"Tomorrow? My goodness, that's sudden."

"An old friend is having some medical issues and she asked me to come to see her. She reckons she's dying, and I'm afraid she might be right."

"I am sorry."

"Thank you. She's something of a hypochondriac who nearly always thinks she dying, but, as she'd no doubt say, she was bound to be right sooner or later. I'm going to spend a few days with her before I head to Hawaii. If I hadn't already promised to go, I'd probably skip Hawaii and stay with her until the end. As it is, if she holds on until after Thanksgiving, I'll probably go back and stay with her again."

"That's good of you."

Todd shrugged. "She was a good friend in the early days when I was struggling and she was successful. Now she's been more or less forgotten by the public and the industry. I don't want her to die alone if I can help it."

Fenella sighed. "This isn't going to work," she blurted out.

Todd gave her a surprised look. "What do you mean?"

"I mean our relationship isn't going to work. You're never going to settle down in one place, which is fine for you, but not for me."

"You know that you're welcome to join me on my travels. I already invited you to come to Hawaii with me, but you're welcome to come with me tomorrow as well. Miriam won't mind the extra company. In fact, she'd probably love it."

Fenella shook her head. "I don't feel ready to start traveling the world with you."

"You have plenty of your own money, I believe. Perhaps you could travel the world on your own, but to some of the same places I'm going?"

"That's just it. I do plan to travel more, probably in the new year, even, but not just yet. I'm still settling in and finding my way here. The island still feels new and exciting to me. I'm not in any hurry to leave."

Todd sighed. "I was hoping we could find a way to make this work, in spite of our differences. I really like you."

"I really like you, too. I just can't see this working in the long term. It seems sensible to end things now before either of us gets really hurt."

Todd hesitated and then nodded. "Thank you for not asking me to change," he told her. "My wife could never understand why I felt as if I needed to travel all the time, but she never complained or asked me to stop. After she died, the woman I became involved with next complained constantly. I moved to London to be closer to her, but my traveling was always a problem. She was bored when she came with me, but she didn't want to be left behind. It was a very difficult relationship and we only continued with it because we loved one another deeply. I stayed with her for three months when I knew she was dying. They were the longest three months of my life and I suspect they're part of the reason why I feel the need to travel now more than ever."

"I've really enjoyed your company this last month or so," Fenella told him. When you were on the island, anyway, she added to herself.

"It's been fun," he agreed. "Maybe we're both too old and set in our ways to make it work, but at least we had some fun."

They chatted for a few more minutes before Todd glanced at the clock. "Will you hate me if I suggest that we call it a night?" he asked. "I have a very early flight in the morning, otherwise I'd never suggest such a thing."

Fenella got to her feet, feeling sad but relieved. "It's fine. I hope you and your friend enjoy your time together."

"I'll walk you home," Todd insisted.

As they walked past the Tale and Tail, Fenella thought about going inside for a drink. Todd would probably be happy to leave her there and it might give her a chance to talk to Daniel. Somehow it didn't feel right, though, not after the difficult discussion with Todd.

He left her at her door, giving her a very gentle kiss before he went. "As I said, it's been fun. If you ever change your mind and want to try again, let me know."

Fenella nodded. "Thank you for everything," she told him.

"You're home early," Mona said, looking surprised as Fenella entered the apartment.

"I ended things with Todd."

"Because he wants to do nothing but travel and see the world and you feel the need to put down roots," Mona suggested.

"Yes, exactly that."

Mona nodded. "Perhaps we are related, then," she said. "Max loved to travel. He and Bryan, his partner, used to go away at least once a month for a few days or even a week at a time. I was always invited, of course, but I rarely went. Sometimes, if Bryan's wife was going along, I'd go, but mostly I was quite content to stay here. I always felt as if the island was where I belonged, and I never felt quite right anywhere else in the world."

"It's a very special place. I'm not in any hurry to leave, even though I know I could afford to go anywhere I'd like."

"I'm sure, once you're feeling more settled, that you'll start traveling more," Mona said. "For now, I'm glad you're happy here. I'd hoped that you'd come to love the island as I did, but I did worry that you'd simply take the money and run."

"If Doncan had told me how much money there was at the very beginning, I may have. It was good that he was vague at that point and I was afraid to go any further than that fortnight I spent in London."

A knock on the door startled both women.

"It's awful late for visitors," Fenella said as she walked toward the door.

"It's only Shelly," Mona assured her.

Fenella opened the door to her friend.

"Are you okay?" Shelly asked, giving her a hug.

"I'm fine, why?"

"Todd rang Tim while we were eating and told him that you and he had ended things. He insisted that you were fine, but Tim and I agreed that I should come home and see for myself."

"I'm fine," Fenella said firmly. "It was my idea. I simply don't want to keep stopping and starting things every time the man goes away and then comes back. He wants to travel and I want to stay here. It seemed easier to end things now, before either of us gets too involved."

"That makes sense," Shelly said slowly. "Are you sure you're okay?"

"I'm positive. I've been rushing about, dating anyone and everyone since I've been here, and it's been fun, but I suppose I've just decided that I've had enough. I may just dump Donald the next time he calls, too."

Shelly frowned. "I hope you aren't doing all of this in an effort to win Daniel back," she said softly.

Fenella shook her head. "I just think it's time to take more control over my life. Moving and changing everything was overwhelming, and I've been sort of drifting along ever since. It's time to stop drifting and start focusing on what I want to do with what's left of my life."

Shelly nodded slowly. "Great."

Mona chuckled. "When do you turn fifty?" she asked.

Fenella opened her mouth to reply and then quickly shut it again. "Anyway, I'm fine. Did you manage to arrange anything for tomorrow?"

"Yes, everything is set," Shelly replied. "There's a group of retired teachers from all over the island who meet at least once a week for coffee. A few of them are going to be at the café near Gary's shop tomorrow morning from around half nine. I told them we'd be there around ten. They're going to watch for us and then make sure we come out in a timely fashion."

"That sounds good," Fenella said.

"Tim will be here around nine to collect us both," Shelly added. "We've decided that he'll pretend to want the new kitchen. He doesn't mind giving Gary his address, and he truly does need a remodel. His house was built in the forties and it still has the original kitchen."

"I can't imagine," Fenella shuddered.

"Luckily for him, Tim doesn't really like to cook. We talked about it tonight when I mentioned that Todd was cooking for you. Tim told me that he has a microwave on his counter and he uses that to heat ready meals. Otherwise, he eats a lot of takeaway and pub food."

"Maybe a new kitchen would inspire him," Fenella suggested.

"Maybe, or maybe it would be a huge waste of money," Shelly said. "Anyway, for the moment it's all pretend, anyway. It should get us into Gary's shop, which is what matters."

"Have you worked out how you're going to bring the conversation around to Ronald?" Fenella asked.

"Not exactly, but Tim has some ideas. He suggested that he might tell Gary that he knew Ronald or even that he used to work with him somewhere."

"He'd have to be very careful if he tried that," Fenella remarked. "Gary must have known Ronald better than anyone else. It seems likely that Tim will get caught in his lie."

"We can talk about it while we drive to Peel tomorrow," Shelly suggested. "I've promised Tim breakfast before we go, so we'll be over to get you around quarter past nine, I suppose."

"I'll make sure I'm ready," Fenella promised. She let Shelly out and then gave Katie a snack and refilled her water bowl.

"I don't mind being on my own," she told the animal.

"Really?" Mona asked. "You've been getting involved with men as if you were terrified of the idea."

Fenella frowned. "It wasn't like that. I was with Jack for such a long time that I sort of forgot what it was like to be, I don't know, chased, I suppose, is the right word. It felt good to suddenly have men wanting to take me out and buy me dinner or spend the day with me. Jack and I were in a routine that didn't include very many romantic evenings."

"When was the last romantic evening you had with Jack?" Mona asked.

Fenella thought for a minute and then sighed. "It was probably in the first few months when we first started dating," she admitted. "Even then, it wasn't very romantic, not the night I'm thinking of, anyway."

"Seeing the look on your face as you remember that evening makes me want to know more."

"When we first started dating, we went out to dinner at least once a week," Fenella told Mona. "Jack didn't really like restaurants, but he tried to pretend that he didn't mind in those early days."

"I suppose that's something," Mona sighed.

"Anyway, we went to this fancy restaurant right in downtown Buffalo, near the water. It was really romantic, actually, with tables on a deck outside. I'm not a huge fan of eating outside. I'd rather not dine with bugs, but Jack insisted that we sit on the deck, right on the water's edge. There were dozens of those electronic bug killers all around the deck, which kept the bug population down, but sort of spoiled the mood a little bit. There's nothing romantic about hearing a bug get electrocuted."

Mona grinned. "I almost wish I'd been there," she said.

"We'd finished dinner and we were sipping the last of our wine. Jack had this weird look on his face. At the time I was afraid he was going to propose, actually. Anyway, he took a deep breath and then leaned forward to say something at the same time, we heard a huge zap. A giant beetle or grasshopper or something plummeted down from the nearest zapper and landed right on Jack's head. He jumped up, screaming this really high-pitched scream, and then tripped over his chair and fell over backwards, over the railing and into the lake."

It was several minutes before Mona stopped laughing. When she finally did, she stared at Fenella for a minute before she spoke. "And you stayed with him for another ten years?" she asked eventually.

Fenella sighed. "I felt sorry for him that night, and for some weeks afterwards. It was September or October and the water was already really cold. He came down with a horrible virus and needed quite a lot of looking after for months."

"You mean years."

"Yes, I suppose I do," Fenella sighed. "On that note, I'm off to bed."

Katie was already fast asleep in bed when Fenella slid under the covers. She worried briefly about nightmares, but fell asleep before the thought could keep her awake.

When Katie woke her at seven, she was happy to find that she couldn't remember any of her dreams from the previous evening.

✻ 10 ✻

"We'll work out a way to bring it up," Tim said confidently as he drove across the island. "Maybe I'll mention that I read about it in the paper or something. That would work, right?"

"Maybe," Shelly said. "I mean, Gary's name was given in the paper, but it didn't specifically say where the man worked. There could be more than one Gary Mack on the island."

"Let's just see what happens," Tim suggested. "I'm sure we'll think of something."

"I wish I had your confidence," Fenella muttered from the backseat. She was starting to regret her involvement in the Ronald Sherman case entirely. After last night, she was wondering if she might be better off staying well away from Daniel Robinson. He was a complication she didn't really need in her life.

"Gary may not even be at the shop," Shelly reminded everyone. "If he isn't, we'll just chat politely with whoever is there and then leave without giving our names."

"I'm not sure they'll let Tim get away without leaving a name," Fenella said. "Not if they think he's serious about wanting a new kitchen."

"I'll give them Todd's name," Tim teased. "They'll struggle to track him down."

Shelly gave Tim a look that made him grimace. "Sorry about that," he said to Fenella.

"It's fine. Todd and I parted friends and I'm perfectly okay," she said quickly.

They reached Peel with a few minutes to spare. Tim found a parking space on the street and they sat in the car for a while.

"Which one is it?" Fenella asked, looking up and down the road.

"The one next to the estate agents," Shelly told her. "The sign on the door says 'Great Kitchens and Better Baths.' It sounds very much like he's suggesting that he's better at bathrooms than kitchens, doesn't it?"

"Maybe he is," Tim said. "I could tell him I need a new bathroom if you think that would be better."

"Let's just stick to the original plan," Shelly said, patting his arm. "We don't really care which he's better at doing, do we?"

"I suppose not, unless I really do decide to get a new kitchen."

"We'll worry about that later," Shelly said. "For now, let's go and see if Gary is actually working today."

On the way to the shop they had to walk past the small café where Shelly's teacher friends were meeting. Shelly waved, making Fenella laugh.

"There are about twenty-five women in there," she said to Shelly.

"I wasn't sure how many were going to actually come," Shelly replied. "It seems as if nearly everyone made it. They do love a nice day out, and I'm sure the chance to feel as if they're helping with a police investigation excited some of them."

"I hope you didn't tell them that this was a police investigation," Fenella said.

"Oh, no, not at all," Shelly assured her. "I may have hinted at it, but only a little bit."

Fenella frowned but didn't reply. They were only steps away from the kitchen shop now. The sign on the door said "Open" and it was flashing on and off. Fenella didn't think that was deliberate. It seemed more likely that there was a problem with the sign.

"Here goes nothing," she said as she reached for the handle.

"Allow me," Tim said, reaching around her to pull the door open. A loud buzzing noise greeted them as they walked into the showroom.

Fenella looked around. One entire wall was filled with cupboards in various shapes and sizes. Every single cupboard door was different, and Fenella might have been intrigued by the possibilities, but she noticed that nearly every door was slightly crooked. A few didn't appear to shut properly and one had a nasty crack running through it.

The back wall of the shop seemed to showcase countertops. There were several different ones mounted at the appropriate height along the wall. Above the counters were blocks that presumably were samples of the options. Each counter sample was only about a foot wide and three feet deep, but some of them seemed to sag somehow, and there were cracks in a few that were noticeable even from a distance.

The third wall was devoted to bathroom fixtures, mostly sinks. There were several of the pedestal variety, along with a few stuck into a single long counter that looked to be made out of plywood. There were a few model kitchens dotted around the room, and Fenella and Shelly both headed toward one of them while Tim walked in the opposite direction.

"I don't like the counters," Shelly whispered as they inspected the model.

"They look as if they're made out of cardboard," Fenella whispered back.

"Ah, good morning," a loud voice said from the back of the room. Fenella recognized Gary Mack from the seven-year-old photo that had been in the local paper. He hadn't changed much. He probably had a few more grey hairs scattered through his dark brown hair, but the photo had been in black and white so it was impossible to be sure.

"What can I do for you today?" he asked, looking from Shelly to Fenella to Tim and then back again.

"I need a new kitchen," Tim said. "Or, at least, my girlfriend thinks I need a new kitchen."

Shelly blushed at the word girlfriend. "You definitely need a new kitchen," she said firmly.

"Right, well, I'm your man," Gary replied. "Do you have any ideas about what you want, or are you open to anything?"

"I suppose I'm open to anything," Tim told him. "I don't want to spend too much money. I've been doing the house up slowly, and I'll need a new bathroom, too, at some point. I can't spend all of my savings on the kitchen."

Gary nodded. "Everyone is watching their pennies these days. We have a lot of very affordable options. I can get you started, but my sales assistant, Bunny, should be here soon. She's better at helping with the design stages."

"Bunny?" Shelly echoed softly.

"Just a nickname," Gary told her. "Anyway, let's start with the dimensions of the room. I hope you measured before you came in."

"I did," Tim replied. He pulled a slip of paper out of his pocket and read some numbers off of it.

Gary grabbed a tablet of paper and began to make notes. "Right, that isn't the biggest kitchen in the world. Were you thinking about expanding it at all? Do you have other rooms around it that you could borrow some space from?"

Tim frowned. "I don't know. I never really thought about it. Wouldn't that be a lot more work, though?"

"Maybe," Gary shrugged. "It could be well worth the extra time and money, though. A few extra square feet in the kitchen could really make a difference in the resale value of your home."

"I'm not sure I can afford to start taking down walls," Tim replied.

"And you've just finished decorating the rest of the ground floor," Shelly added. "It would be shame to start taking down walls that you just painted and decorated."

Tim looked confused for a minute and then grinned. "Yeah, that's true," he said. "I think we'll have to keep the walls where they are."

"Right, so let's talk about cabinets," Gary said. He led them over to the wall of cabinets. "What were you thinking about?" he asked Tim.

Tim looked at the wall and then gave Shelly a slightly desperate look. "I didn't realize there would be so many options," he said.

"I think we want solid wood," Shelly said, opening and closing a few cabinets. "I'm not sure that any of these are appropriate."

"We can get you anything you want," Gary assured her. "Light or dark wood? Stain or paint?"

Shelly sighed. "Those would be easier choices if we could see examples."

Gary nodded. "I'm getting ready to open another showroom with, well, higher-end options. This one works for the average customer in this part of the island, but I'm planning a bigger and better shop in Onchan. That's where I'll have the solid wood cabinetry and the granite and solid surface countertops."

"When will that showroom open?" Shelly asked.

"I'm hoping to have it open by the first of the year," Gary told her.

"So maybe we should wait and start planning then," Shelly sighed.

"I couldn't do anything for you before the first of the year anyway," Gary said. "What we can do is book you a space in our schedule now for some time in January, and then once the showroom is open, you can come in and select what you want us to install."

"What if we don't like anything in the new showroom?" Shelly asked.

Gary laughed. "That's not going to happen. I'm going to have the very best of everything. Your boyfriend said he wanted to work within a budget, though. There may have to be some compromises between what you want and what he can afford," he said with a wink.

Shelly frowned. "I don't think we want to book anything until we've had a chance to see what you actually have to offer."

"That's your choice," Gary shrugged. "I was just trying to save you some time. If you wait until January to get on the schedule, you'll be looking at March or April before we can actually get started."

Tim glanced at Shelly and then shrugged. "I'm not in any hurry," he said.

Shelly laughed. "And I have a perfectly good kitchen in my flat, so I suppose there's no rush. Where will your new showroom be?"

When Gary mentioned the strip plaza where Manx Computer Innovations was located, Shelly and Fenella exchanged glances.

"We were just there last week," Shelly exclaimed. "We were at the computer shop, looking at laptops."

"The guys there are good friends of mine," Gary said. "My cousin used to work there. They're really good guys."

"Your cousin?" Shelly echoed. "You aren't talking about Ronald Sherman, are you?"

"I am, actually," Gary replied.

"The men at the computer shop were telling us about him. I'm sure the manager said Ronald's cousin knew where he was but won't tell anyone else. That would be you, then, right? Do you know where Ronald is?" Shelly asked.

Fenella hoped her surprise didn't show on her face. Shelly hadn't mentioned saying anything like that when they'd talked about how they'd approach Gary.

"Eugene is sadly mistaken," Gary said. "I've no idea where Ronald is, and I'm delighted that the police have chosen to reopen the investigation into his disappearance."

"Really? Eugene, was that his name? He said you were Ronald's only family and that he couldn't imagine Ronald not staying in touch with you, no matter what happened," Shelly pushed him.

"I was Ronald's only family. Or rather, I am Ronald's only family. I refuse to talk about him in the past tense. Unfortunately, it seems I felt more strongly about that relationship than Ronald did. He hasn't made any effort to contact me since the night he vanished."

"That's really sad. Eugene seemed to think that he'd gone to get away from his girlfriend. He said she was horrible."

Gary smiled. "Horrible is a strong word, but Ronald and Cassie had a very volatile relationship. Getting away from her may well have been the motive behind his decision to leave without any warning, and it could be part of why he hasn't been in contact with me since."

"Surely you wouldn't tell Cassie where he was, if he did get in touch," Shelly suggested.

"Of course I wouldn't, but Ronald may be afraid to trust anyone, least of all himself. He and Cassie split up just about every week, but he always went back to her for one reason or another. Perhaps he's afraid that contacting anyone on the island will ultimately send him back to Cassie."

"It's been seven years," Shelly argued. "He must be over Cassie by now."

"I lost my first love in a tragic accident while we were planning our wedding," Gary said solemnly. "I've never recovered from my loss. I still love her and I miss her every day."

"Oh, I am sorry," Shelly said.

"But you didn't come in to talk about me," Gary laughed. "Do you want to look at countertops here or wait until the showroom in Onchan opens?"

"Do you have anything solid-surface here?" Shelly asked.

"I have some very low-end granite tiles," Gary told her. "We'll have slab granite in Onchan."

"I think we'll wait, then," Shelly said.

"Eugene said that Ronald was looking for other relatives," Fenella said. "Maybe he found another cousin or something and went to find him or her."

Gary looked surprised by the sudden change in subject. "Ronald never told me anything about that," he said, waving a dismissive hand. "What about bathrooms?" he asked Shelly.

"I think we need to focus on the kitchen for now," Shelly said. "Did you ever look for other family? I think I would if I were you, especially after Ronald left."

"Ronald and I may well have some very distant relatives out there somewhere, but the family has been on the island for many generations. I'm not especially interested in finding a twenty-third cousin twice removed who's lived his entire life in Birmingham and has nothing in common with me."

"Did Ronald feel the same way?" Shelly asked.

"As far as I know, yes. As I said, he never mentioned anything about looking for family to me. And he told me everything that was going on in his life, I must add. If he were looking for his family, well, he would have been looking for my family, too. He would have told me about it."

"Eugene also suggested that he talked about finding a fortune on one of the computers he was meant to be repairing. Eugene seemed to be suggesting that Ronald might have stolen the money and used that to disappear," Shelly told him.

Gary frowned. "I'd like to say that Ronald would never have done such a thing, but I can see him doing it, under certain circumstances, anyway."

"What sort of circumstances?" Shelly asked.

"Ronald has his own moral compass. If he found money hidden on someone's computer that he knew had been stolen in some way, well, I can see him taking it away from the thief," Gary explained.

"And then keeping it for himself?" Fenella tried not to sound judgmental.

"Knowing Ronald, he'd probably have tried to work out who the money actually belonged to and then return it to them," Gary said quickly. "Maybe that's where he's been for the past seven years. Traveling all over the world returning stolen property to its rightful owners."

Fenella and Shelly exchanged glances. It was a theory that they hadn't considered, but it seemed so unlikely that Fenella nearly laughed out loud.

"Maybe the police will finally be able to work out what happened this time," Shelly said. "The inspector who's working on the case is excellent."

"Is he? That's good to hear," Gary said. He glanced at his watch and then smiled at them. "We seem to have wandered rather far off topic. What about that kitchen, then?"

Shelly looked at Tim. "I think we'll visit you in Onchan in January," she said. "It sounds very much as if things there will be more to my style."

"And less to my budget," Tim muttered good-naturedly.

Gary laughed, but it sounded forced. "Right, let's make you an appointment for January, then," he said. "Wait here. I'll be right back."

As Gary disappeared into the back room, the front door of the shop swung open. "Everything okay?" a tall, grey-haired lady called to Shelly from the doorway.

"It's fine," Shelly assured her. "We won't be much longer."

The woman nodded and then turned and walked away.

"Did I miss a customer?" Gary asked as he walked back into the room.

"It was a friend of mine," Shelly told him. "I promised that we'd meet her for coffee since we're on this side of the island. She was just checking to see how much longer we'd be."

"Right, well, let me see what I have open," the man said. He opened an appointment book for the new year and flipped through the pages. "We open on Monday the ninth, but I'm already booked solid for that day. Can you manage Tuesday at one?"

Fenella was standing close enough to see the pages in front of the man. To her eyes it looked very much as if a bunch of names had been scribbled into the book in random places. She couldn't help but suspect that the man had just added them all himself two minutes earlier.

"I'm not sure if I'll be on the island or not," Tim said apologetically. "I travel a lot for work and I don't know where I'll be in January. If we take our chances and just turn up at the showroom, can we have a look around, at least?"

"Of course you can, but I can't promise that there will be anyone available to help you," Gary replied "We're planning on operating that location mostly by appointment, unlike here."

Tim nodded. "I think we'll have to see how it goes. Maybe I can book something in a few weeks. I should have a better idea of my schedule by then."

"Excellent. Let me give you my card," Gary said. He reached into a pocket and pulled out a slightly bent business card. "I'm having new ones printed with the new address on them," he explained. "This is one of the last of the old ones. My mobile number won't change, anyway."

"Great, thanks," Tim said. He put the card into his pocket and then grinned at Shelly. "Are we done?"

"I suppose so," she sighed. "I was hoping we might actually make some progress today, but I suppose I should be happy you were willing to at least talk about a new kitchen."

"I'll buy you a slice of cake to go with your coffee or tea," Tim said, "and while we wait for January, you can show me as many pictures of kitchens in your magazines as you like."

Shelly laughed. "Now I really can't complain," she said.

"How's your kitchen?" Gary asked Fenella.

"It's pretty much perfect," Fenella told him. "I hope they find your cousin for you."

Gary nodded. "Thank you. I have mixed emotions about it, really. I keep telling myself that Ronald is out there somewhere, absolutely fine and just staying away for his own reasons. If he really doesn't want to be found, then I don't want him to be found, even though I know I'll sleep better at night once I know what happened to him."

"You think he left voluntarily?" Fenella asked.

"He must have, mustn't he? It's too painful to think of anything else."

✒"If he did find a lot of money on someone's computer, perhaps the computer's owner worked out what happened and tracked him down," Fenella suggested.

Gary looked at her for a minute and then sighed. "I wouldn't have given that idea a moment's thought seven years ago," he told her. "When Ronald first disappeared, I was sure he'd be in touch within a few days, though."

"So why did you report him missing?" Fenella asked.

"Why did I, well, I mean, what else was I meant to do? He was missing, after all," Gary stammered.

Fenella nodded. "I hope he hears that the police are looking for him and gets in touch," she said. "Thank you for your time today."

The door to the shop swung open, and a short and slightly overweight woman walked in. "Hey, I'm here," she announced.

"Bunny, it's about time," Gary snapped.

Fenella stared at the woman's short hair, which was over half grey. Bunny was wearing thick glasses, and when she smiled back at Gary, Fenella noted that she was missing a few teeth. She was not at all what Fenella had been picturing when Gary had mentioned "Bunny" earlier.

"I slept late," Bunny shrugged. "Fire me if you want."

Gary opened his mouth and then shut it again. "Of course I don't want to fire you," he said tightly, "but I have a job to get to and I'm already late."

"Eh, they'll wait," Bunny replied. "They don't have a choice, do they? Knowing you, you've demolished their entire kitchen and left them with gaping holes everywhere."

Gary laughed nervously. "Bunny does like to exaggerate," he said. "Let me show you out and then we can all be on our way."

"Show them out? What are they having done? I haven't had a chance to talk them into unnecessary upgrades yet. What about my commission?" Bunny demanded.

"They aren't having anything done yet," Gary told her. "They're going to visit my Onchan showroom in January."

Bunny rolled her eyes. "I should have guessed. They look like granite countertop kind of people."

Fenella wasn't sure if that was meant to be an insult or not, but she'd had quite enough of both Gary and Bunny, regardless. "We should get going," she said to Shelly.

"Yes, I know," Shelly replied. "Thanks again," she told Gary as she turned and headed for the door.

Tim beat her to the door by half a step and held it open as both Shelly and Fenella walked through it. As the door swung shut behind the trio, Fenella could hear Gary shouting at Bunny about the time.

"That was awful," Shelly said as they walked into the coffee shop a minute later.

"Let's talk about it when we get home," Fenella suggested, as a dozen different women seemed to descend on Shelly at the same time. She shot Fenella and Tim an apologetic look and then let herself be pulled into the middle of a crowd of retired teachers.

"This is fun," Tim said a few minutes later. He and Fenella were together at a tiny table for two in the corner of the room. Teachers occupied every other seat in the room. Shelly seemed to be trying to talk to everyone at once as a very flustered-looking waitress made her way around the room.

"Can I get you anything?" she asked Fenella and Tim.

As soon as the words were out of her mouth, someone shouted from behind her. "'May I get you anything,' dear. We just went over this."

The waitress frowned. "Yeah, whatever. Do you want anything or not?" she snarled.

They both ordered coffee before the woman walked away. "I wanted a piece of cake," Tim whispered as the door to the kitchen swung shut behind the waitress. "But I was afraid to ask her for one."

"I don't think she's having a good day," Fenella replied.

The pair chatted about nothing much over their coffee. Eventually Shelly crossed to them. "I'm so sorry," she said. "I wasn't expecting this large of a turnout."

"It's fine," Fenella assured her. "I'm grateful they were here keeping an eye on us."

"Yes, well, I think I've spoken to them all now, so we can go," Shelly said. "Let's do it quickly, in case I missed anyone."

Tim laughed and then offered Shelly his arm. "Let's go, my very popular darling," he said.

Fenella followed the couple out of the café and back down the street to Tim's car. They'd only just pulled away from the curb when Shelly spoke.

"I didn't like Gary," she said. "He seemed to contradict himself, too. He said he didn't want Ronald found if Ronald didn't want to be found, but he was the one who filed the police report about his disappearance."

"He also claimed not to know anything about Ronald's search for other family," Fenella said thoughtfully. "He may be telling the truth, but I think I believe Helen."

"Maybe Ronald didn't tell Gary what he was doing because he was afraid of hurting his feelings," Tim suggested.

"Or maybe he was waiting to surprise Gary with what he'd found. If I thought I only had one living relative and then someone told me that I had a whole host of other family, I'd be thrilled," Shelly said.

"I can't see Gary being thrilled about anything," Fenella muttered.

Shelly laughed. "Okay, there is that," she admitted. "Still, maybe Ronald thought he'd be thrilled."

"Maybe. We need to call Daniel when we get home," Fenella said.

Shelly looked back at her. "Can you do that on your own?" she asked. "Tim took the day off to help us out. I thought maybe I could spend the rest of the day with him, doing something fun to thank him."

"Sure, no problem," Fenella said, even as her brain was screaming no. She really didn't want to call Daniel by herself, but she couldn't very well ruin Shelly's plans just because she was afraid to talk to the man.

"Are you sure?" Shelly asked, staring hard at Fenella.

"I'm very sure," Fenella said in a firm voice. "Knowing him, he'll be too busy to talk, anyway."

Shelly looked as if she wanted to discuss the matter further, but Tim said something that caught her attention. Fenella couldn't quite hear what he was saying, but whatever it was, Shelly replied in a low voice and the pair chatted very quietly for the rest of the journey. Fenella looked out the window and enjoyed the scenery while she tried to pretend that she didn't mind being ignored.

Tim dropped Fenella off in front of her building, and then he and Shelly drove away for their afternoon together. She'd offered to feed Smokey, so Fenella stopped in Shelly's apartment first and gave Smokey a pat and some lunch. "I'm happy that Shelly's found someone," she told the cat. "I'm just annoyed that I have to be a big girl and call Daniel all by myself."

"Meerow," Smokey told her.

Fenella nodded and then gave her another pat before she headed for the door. "Shelly has promised to be back in time to give you your dinner," she told Smokey. "I did tell her that she could call me if she couldn't make it, though. Don't be surprised if you see me again in a few hours. I think she and Tim have a busy afternoon planned."

Katie seemed happy to see her, but happier to see her lunch as Fenella put it out for her. Lunch for Fenella was a sandwich. She ate it over the sink.

"Now you're going to go and take a nap, aren't you?" Fenella asked as Katie finished her meal and headed out of the kitchen.

"It sounds as if you could use a nap, too," Mona said as she walked into the kitchen.

Fenella jumped and then sighed. "I'm just out of sorts because I have to call Daniel, that's all. Shelly wanted to spend the afternoon with Tim, rather than come back here and call Daniel with me."

"I don't blame her," Mona laughed.

"I don't either, really, but I also don't want to talk to Daniel."

"Just ring him and get it over with. I'm sure he'll be strictly profes-sional. He doesn't know what to do about your relationship, either, you know."

"I suspect he doesn't want a relationship with me at all."

"If he didn't, he wouldn't have asked for your help with this case."

"Maybe," Fenella sighed. She picked up the phone and dialed the number for the station. A few minutes later she was put through to Daniel's voicemail.

"Hey, it's Fenella. Shelly and Tim and I had a chat with Gary this morning. I didn't like him, but I haven't really liked anyone involved in this case except for Helen. Anyway, if you want to hear all about it, call me back. Shelly is out with Tim for the rest of the day, but I should be home."

She put the phone down and then hunted on Mona's bookshelves for something to distract her. She found the first in a series of cozy mysteries by an author she'd never heard of before. "Are these any good?" she asked Mona.

"They aren't bad," Mona replied. "I bought the first twenty or so books in the series and then stopped. They started to get a bit too formulaic after that, but the first twenty were very readable."

Fenella nodded and then curled up in a chair. She was lost in another world when the phone rang.

"Hello?"

"It's Daniel. I have about six minutes before I have to be some-where else. Can you tell me everything from this morning in six minutes?"

"I can try," Fenella replied. She did her best, speeding through a lot of the conversation that was primarily about kitchens, focusing on the times when Ronald was mentioned. The whole recitation took about ten minutes.

"I have about a dozen questions for you, but they'll have to wait for another day," Daniel sighed. "I'll try to ring you tomorrow. Try not to forget anything, okay?"

"How am I supposed to do that?" Fenella demanded. She frowned when she realized that Daniel had already hung up.

"That was pointless," she grumbled as she put the phone down.

"You should be relieved it's over," Mona suggested.

"He's going to call me back tomorrow," Fenella told her.

"But maybe Shelly will be here when he does," Mona suggested.

The idea cheered Fenella up so much that she didn't even mind when Shelly called and asked her to give Smokey her dinner.

"I'll bring her over to play with Katie for a while after," Fenella told her. "You can collect her from me when you get back."

"It might be really late," Shelly warned her.

"If it gets to my bedtime and you aren't back, I'll take Smokey home and leave you a note on your door," Fenella offered.

"That sounds good."

Fenella wondered, some time after eleven o'clock as she returned Smokey to Shelly's apartment and left Shelly her note, exactly what Shelly and Tim were doing. She could only hope that they were having fun.

The sun was shining on Saturday morning when Katie woke Fenella. After getting breakfast for her pet, Fenella took a shower and then made herself some toast. "What should I do today?" she asked Katie as she ate.

Katie shook her head and left the kitchen, leaving Fenella on her own.

"Thanks," Fenella muttered after her. Thinking that maybe a dog would have been a better choice, Fenella decided to take a walk before she did anything else. It was a perfect day for a long walk along the promenade. Hoping she'd run into Harvey with the dogs, Fenella walked from one end of the walkway to the other. There were a few other people around, even one or two walking dogs, but Fenella didn't see anyone she knew.

While she was tempted to walk the whole length a second time, she was starting to feel chilled. The wind had been picking up steadily all morning, and it was a cold wind that seemed to go right through her. As clouds covered the sun, Fenella headed for home.

It was far too early to bother Shelly, especially after her late night, so Fenella found things to do in her apartment. She rearranged a few shelves of books in the spare bedroom and then ran the vacuum around every room. She was returning the vacuum cleaner to its cupboard when the phone rang.

"Hello?"

"Maggie, darling, please tell me that you were kidding," Jack's voice came down the phone line to her.

"Kidding? About what?" Fenella asked, frowning at the "Maggie." She'd gone by Margaret, her middle name, in the US because it was easier for people to spell and pronounce than the Manx "Fenella." Jack was the only one who ever called her Maggie, and she'd always hated it.

"I've just finally found time to read through the list you sent me. It's much longer than I was expecting, I have to say. I truly hope you're kidding, at least for some of the items on the list."

Fenella frowned. Jack, her former boyfriend, was incredibly smart when it came to US military history. His skills in dealing with the real world were somewhat less impressive. His mother had still been doing his laundry and grocery shopping, paying his bills, and balancing his checkbook each month when Jack and Fenella had started dating. When she'd decided to retire to Florida, Fenella had taken over many of those jobs. When she decided to move to the island, Fenella had done her best to help prepare Jack for her departure, but when he'd started missing payments on his credit card, she'd agreed to make him a list of all of the things that he needed to do each month so that he could check to make sure he hadn't missed anything.

She'd done her best, writing down everything she could remember that she used to do for the man. The long list had gone in the mail to him several weeks ago. For a moment she was annoyed that he'd only just found time to look at it now.

"What do you think I'm kidding about?" she asked, reminding herself to breathe deeply and not shout at the man.

"I don't know. It's just a long list. Surely there must be a way I can pay all of my bills in one big lump, rather than paying them all individually, for example."

"I don't know about that, but you can set up automatic payments, if you'd rather. We did talk about that before I left. You told me that you didn't want to do that."

"And I still don't. I don't like the sound of automatic payments."

"Fine, then you'll have to make each payment every month."

"What if I skip a month? Do they charge a lot if you miss a payment?"

"I've no idea what they charge, but I don't think it's a good idea," Fenella said, trying to be patient.

"I just thought, if I could skip a month on each of them, I could halve my workload. I could pay the electricity bill one month and the gas bill the next, for example."

"You'll pay late fees or penalties of some sort if you do that," Fenella warned him. "Paying online only takes a few minutes, anyway."

Jack sighed. "Yes, I know, but it's still annoying. What about balancing my checkbook? Surely I can do that every other month."

"Sure, why not," Fenella decided not to argue.

"And I can wash my bedding every other month. That should be often enough."

"You're really meant to wash it weekly," Fenella told him. "I read that in a magazine the other day."

"Weekly? My goodness. I don't have time for that."

"It doesn't take long, though, really. You just have to get into the habit of it."

"All of my white sheets have turned pink since you were here," Jack complained, "and that red blanket that I used to have on the bed has shrunk down to almost nothing."

"You washed the blanket with the sheets," Fenella sighed.

"Of course I did. They go together on the bed, so they should go together in the washing machine and dryer."

"What temperature did you wash them on?"

"Temperature? I've no idea. I pushed the button that said bedding. The machine should know what to do from there."

Fenella swallowed another sigh. "It probably washed them in hot water, which is good for plain white sheets, but not so good for bright red blankets," she told the man.

"Well, then it should say that somewhere."

"I believe the blanket care tag probably says something about washing colors separately."

"Does it? I don't have time to read those tags, though. The print is too small and they're full of symbols that don't make any sense."

"Perhaps you should find a laundry service," Fenella suggested.

"I'm not paying someone to do my laundry, not when I've just spent two hundred dollars getting my washing machine repaired."

"What was wrong with the washing machine?"

"The repair man thinks that I might have used too much of the wrong sort of detergent. The bottle said it was for washing machines, and I just filled the cup thingy in the door, but it ended up making far too many bubbles and leaked all over the kitchen."

Fenella turned her laugh into a cough. "Oh, dear," she gasped out. "I am sorry."

"Yes, well, it cost a small fortune to repair, but it's working again now. The man who fixed it suggested that I buy pre-measured detergent from now on. He even left me a few samples. They seem much easier."

"Yes, I'm sure they are. Was that all that concerned you from the list?" Fenella was sure she was opening a can of worms, but there was still a small part of her that cared for Jack and she did worry about him.

"You've put garbage night on here and noted that they come once a week. Last month it was windy and my special container for recyclables blew away. Actually, I'm pretty sure the woman next door found it in her yard and simply kept it. She's like that. Anyway, now I can't put out my recyclables any more. I have a huge bag of them in the kitchen and I don't know what to do with them."

"Call the garbage company and request a new container," Fenella told him. "They may charge you a little something for it, but at least you'll be able to get rid of everything."

"You know I hate calling people."

Everyone except me, apparently, Fenella said silently. "You could try looking online to see if you can request a replacement through their website," she suggested.

"That's a good idea. Right, what about grocery shopping?"

"What about it?"

"You didn't put anything about grocery shopping on my list."

"I just assumed you wouldn't forget to go shopping."

"I try to remember, but I usually only think of it when I get home from work and go into the kitchen and discover that I don't have anything to eat. I always worry that the grocery stores will be shut if I go back out to go shopping."

"I believe a number of the larger stores around you are open twenty-four hours a day," Fenella told him. "You could always start going shopping every Saturday or Sunday. That's what I used to do."

"Did you? I don't recall."

"I used to get up on Saturday morning and go grocery shopping while you slept in," Fenella said dryly. "Did you never notice that your cupboards and refrigerator were magically refilled every Saturday morning?"

"Yes, well, maybe I could go on a Saturday afternoon," Jack said. "What about my prescription refills? They keep calling me and reminding me to pick them up, but I'm not sure where to go."

"You haven't been taking your medications?" Fenella asked worriedly. There wasn't anything seriously wrong with Jack, but he was supposed to take a tablet every day to keep his blood pressure under control, and another for his cholesterol.

"Of course I'm taking my medications. I'm nearly out, though," Jack retorted. "Where do I go to get more?"

Fenella took a deep breath and then recited the name and address of the pharmacy where the man's prescriptions had been being filled for the last twenty years or more. "You had a physical recently, so you should schedule another one for March or April next year," she added. "Assuming everything is the same, your doctor should give new prescriptions, good for another year."

"When my mother was here recently, she picked everything up for me, and before that Hazel was getting them for me when she was getting her own things. Now I shall have to make an effort to get to the pharmacy, I suppose."

"You should make it a priority. It's important that you keep taking your medications."

"You sound concerned," Jack said. "I knew you still cared about me."

"Of course I still care about you," Fenella replied. "We were together for ten years. You'll always hold a very special place in my heart."

"Really? I feel the same way. I still care deeply for you. I still think we should give our relationship another go."

"I'm sorry, Jack, but I don't think that's a good idea. I've moved on with my life. It's time for you to do the same."

"Or maybe it's time for me to move to the Isle of Man," he suggested. "Then I wouldn't have to worry about this list any longer. You would be there to remind of all of the things that I need to do."

"You can't simply move to the Isle of Man. You would need a visa, and before that you would need a passport."

"Yes, I'm going to add that to my list of things to do," Jack said. "I have to go to the post office anyway. I seem to have run out of stamps, which means I can't pay my bills."

That he'd worked out where to go to apply for a passport was slightly worrying. Fenella decided not to mention it. "You can pay them all online, remember? I gave you all of the login details for all of the accounts."

"Did you? I wonder where I put it. It doesn't matter. I don't mind writing checks and mailing them, although I seem to be almost out of checks, now that I think of it. How do I get more?"

"There should be a reorder form on the front of the last book of checks. It should tell you how to get more. I believe you can order them from your bank, or you can order them from other places. Other places are usually cheaper."

"I'm more worried about faster, rather than cheaper. I may only have one or two checks left and I haven't paid any bills yet this month."

Fenella sighed. "You should have ordered more as soon as you started that last book of checks."

"Yes, well, I didn't know that at the time. What are you doing for Thanksgiving? They don't celebrate it there, do they?"

The change of subject left Fenella momentarily confused. "Er, no, they don't celebrate it here," she said after a moment. "I'm hosting a dinner at a restaurant near my apartment for all of my new friends on the appropriate evening, though."

"All of your new friends? It seems as if every time I call you've found a new male friend, anyway. How many of your boyfriends will be at your dinner, then?"

Fenella frowned at the bitterness she could hear in the man's voice. "I have many new friends, both male and female. I don't have a final count yet for how many people are coming, though." Which reminded her, she still hadn't heard back from many of the people that she'd invited. She hated the idea of calling them all, but she needed to get a final count to the restaurant on Monday.

"Yes, well, my mother is not coming to visit, since she was just here. I suppose I shall spend the day alone," Jack told her.

"Why don't you go to Florida to see her instead? That's what you used to do," Fenella suggested.

"I don't like Florida. It's too hot and sunny."

"It isn't all that hot in late November," Fenella countered. "I thought you liked spending time there with your mother."

"Well, I don't feel like doing that this year."

Fenella thought about arguing further, but Jack was probably right. He probably wouldn't enjoy Florida. "You should mention around the department that you don't have plans. I'm sure someone would be happy to have you at his or her house for dinner."

"I may, but I don't want to start another fight between Sue and Hazel."

The two women had worked with Jack and Fenella for many years. Fenella had always suspected that both women were interested in Jack, and from what she'd heard, they'd both made a play for him after she'd left. The last she knew, however, they'd both given up and moved on with their lives.

"I hate the thought of you spending Thanksgiving alone," Fenella said, feeling a small pang of guilt for leaving the man, something she hadn't been expecting.

"I'll be fine," Jack told her. "I'll buy myself a TV dinner and eat while I watch some television or something."

"I'm sure someone from work will welcome you into his or her home," Fenella repeated herself.

"We'll see. Anyway, as you keep telling me, I'm no longer your concern. You have your own life now, with tons of new friends."

Stop trying to make me feel guilty, Fenella thought. "I'm sure, if you tried, you could make new friends," she said.

"Perhaps I should add that to my list of jobs to do," Jack mused.

"That isn't a bad idea."

"Anyway, I must go. I have a class to teach soon."

Jack hung up before Fenella could reply. "Okay, bye," she said into the dead receiver. "You're welcome for the list that took me ages to make, by the way. I hope it makes your life easier, I truly do."

"I don't know why you care," Mona said as she appeared next to Fenella on the couch.

"We were together for a long time. I'll always care about him."

"He's going to use that against you, just wait. Before long you'll be paying his bills online for him, and flying back to Buffalo once a month to collect his prescriptions and do his laundry."

"That's not going to happen," Fenella said firmly.

Mona shrugged. "I don't think he's anywhere near as helpless as he pretends. I think he's just trying to guilt you into moving back to look after him."

"That isn't going to happen either. I'm happy here, and I've no interest in moving back to Buffalo."

"It's a shame you can't seem to convince Jack of that."

When the phone rang again a short time later, Fenella let the answering machine answer it. It was the first in a sudden flurry of phone calls, all confirming that people would be coming to the Thanksgiving banquet. Fenella let the calls go to the answering machine, making notes as they did so.

"That's a dozen more people for Thursday," she told Mona during a lull. "It's going to be a proper party now."

As the phone rang again, it occurred to her that she hadn't checked her emails in a few days. Some of her friends might have emailed their replies. She fired up her laptop and then waited while several hundred messages downloaded. She'd forgotten that the busy holiday shopping season was rapidly approaching. Deleting page after page of emails about amazing sales at stores in the US to which she no longer had access took far longer than Fenella liked.

When she was done, she was left with two replies to her Thanksgiving invitations and an email from Hazel, her former work colleague. It was the first time the woman had emailed her since she'd moved to the island, and Fenella was incredibly curious as she clicked on the message.

Dear Margaret,

I hope all is well with you and that you are enjoying your new life on the Island of Mann. I apologize for reaching out to you like this, but it seemed the easiest way to get the information that I need.

So many of the professors in our department are on their own this Thanksgiving that I've invited everyone to dinner at my home. Everyone is supposed to be bringing something to add to the table, and I have concerns about what to ask Jack to bring.

I don't believe that he is much of a cook, but you were with him for many years. Does he have any dish that he can reliably prepare for a dinner for ten to twelve people? I don't want to ask him because I'm sure he'd find the question confusing.

Please let me know your thoughts at your convenience. Jack mentioned that you might be coming back to Buffalo for the holidays. If you are going to be here for Thanksgiving, you are, of course, welcome to join us as well.

Sincerely,

Hazel

Fenella sat frowning at the message for several minutes. "He lied to me," she said eventually.

"Who lied to you, darling?" Mona asked.

"Jack. He said he was going to stay home alone and eat a TV dinner in front of the television on Thanksgiving, but I've had an email from Hazel. She's having a big dinner for everyone from the department at the university."

"Why are you so surprised? I told you Jack isn't nearly as helpless as he acts. He was probably hoping you'd feel guilty enough to fly home and have dinner with him."

"I might have, as well, if I weren't planning for the dinner here,"

Fenella sighed. "I can't believe he lied to me, though. He never used to lie to me. Okay, he would sometimes bend the truth a little bit to manipulate me, but flat-out lying? That's new."

"Stop answering when he rings," Mona suggested.

"I may just have to do that. But what should I tell Hazel? There's a little bit of me that's tempted to tell her that he can make something incredibly complicated. As I can't be a fly on the wall when she asks him to supply it, though, it's probably not worth it."

"It would be funny, though."

Fenella nodded and then sighed before she typed her reply.

Dear Hazel,

Thank you for the kind wishes. I'm very happy on the island and am enjoying my new life very much. At the moment I don't have any plans to visit Buffalo, but I do appreciate the invitation.

As for Jack, I suggest you would do best with having him bring something that he can purchase already prepared. Perhaps he could bring drinks or napkins or something like that? Or maybe he could be trusted to bring rolls from a local bakery, if you tell him exactly what to order and then remind him to actually place the order and then pick it up. Otherwise, I'm afraid he's rather hopeless.

Good luck to you,

Fenella Margaret.

She pressed send before she could go back and edit her words. They were probably a bit cruel, but she was still upset that Jack had lied to her. When someone knocked on her door a short while later, Fenella was pacing around the kitchen, feeling as if she should be doing something useful, but unable to settle to anything.

"Hello," Shelly said brightly when Fenella opened the door. "How are you today?"

"I'm in a bad mood," Fenella warned her, "and I don't want to talk about it."

Shelly raised an eyebrow. "Okay, then. Should I go away and come back tomorrow?"

Fenella thought for a minute and then shook her head. "I could probably use some company, if I'm honest."

"I just wanted to see how things went with Daniel last night,"

Shelly explained as she sat down next to Fenella. "What did he think of our conversation with Gary?"

"He didn't really say, actually. He was in a big hurry to get somewhere, so we only talked for a few minutes. He told me he was going to call me back today, but he hasn't, at least not yet."

"So what have you been doing all day?"

"Nothing much. Several people have finally called to let me know that they're coming for Thanksgiving, at least."

"That is good news. Who's coming?"

Fenella went through the list with Shelly. While they were talking, another friend left a message on Fenella's machine to say she was coming, too.

"It's going to be a real party, then," Shelly said happily. "I wasn't worried, once I knew that Harvey and the dogs were going to be there, but now I'm quite excited. Even better, Gordon isn't going to be here. He rang last night while I was out with Tim to let me know that he won't be back on the island after all."

"How was your evening, then?" Fenella asked, watching her friend closely.

Shelly blushed bright red. "It was good," she said, looking at the ground.

"What does that mean?"

"We had a lovely lunch in Onchan and then wandered around the shops in Douglas for a few hours. Then we had dinner at the really fancy place on the promenade. Tim got almost the same level of VIP service that you get. Our waiter is a huge fan of The Islanders."

Fenella smiled. "I'm sure you enjoyed that."

"Oh, I did. Then we went back to Tim's house and started talking about remodeling his kitchen. It really does need it, but so does the bathroom. Anyway, after a while I realized how late it was and made him bring me home."

Fenella thought that Shelly was leaving a few things out of the story, but she didn't need every detail, especially since the ones she thought Shelly was leaving out were probably very private details. "I'm glad you had a good time with Tim. He seems very nice."

"He is very nice, but we should talk about Ronald Sherman," Shelly said.

"I'm here," Mona called as she appeared near the window. "I don't want to miss a chance to discuss the case."

"I don't know that we have that much to discuss," Fenella said. "I don't have any idea what happened to the man."

"There was something I didn't like about Gary," Shelly replied. "I think whoever said it was right. I think if Ronald had gone voluntarily, he would have stayed in touch with Gary."

"I agree with Shelly," Mona said firmly.

"If he didn't leave voluntarily, what do you think happened to him?" Fenella asked.

"He was murdered," Mona replied.

"I hate to think," was Shelly's less dramatic answer.

"I know I've been involved in far too many murder investigations since I've been on the island, but is it possible he was murdered?" Fenella asked.

Mona nodded. "Of course he was. That's the only solution that makes any sense."

"I suppose it's possible," Shelly said in a doubtful tone. "I don't know that we've uncovered any reason why anyone would have murdered the poor man, though."

"He and Cassie were arguing a lot. Maybe she finally got fed up and bashed him over the head," Fenella suggested.

Mona laughed. "Highly unlikely," she pronounced.

"I suppose that's one possibility," Shelly said, looking as doubtful as Mona clearly was.

"Maybe it was something to do with work," was Fenella's next suggestion. "Maybe Ronald really did find something on someone's computer. If the computer's owner didn't kill him, maybe Eugene did it so that he could get his hands on the money."

"Except Eugene clearly isn't rich," Shelly objected.

"Maybe he's hoarding the money until he feels he can safely start spending it. Or maybe he has a double life and spends half of his time in a luxury home in France or something," Fenella imagined.

"Maybe we should pay the man another visit," Shelly suggested.

"I'd rather not," Fenella replied with a small shudder.

"But he could be the key to solving the whole case," Shelly argued.

"Let's not plan to visit anyone else until Daniel has started doing his investigation," Fenella told her. "He'll be able to ask Eugene direct questions. That's probably smarter than us going and trying to work our way around to finding out anything."

"Since we're talking about suspects, what about Lucas?" Shelly wondered. "Maybe he was the one who found out what Ronald was doing. Can you see him killing Ronald?"

"I don't know. We barely spoke to him, really. Once Eugene arrived, he rather dominated the conversation. I didn't form much of an opinion about Lucas," Fenella replied.

"You need to go and talk to him again," Mona said. "Maybe you can find a way to get Lucas alone. That would probably be best."

"Maybe we should go and talk to him again. We'd just have to try to go when Eugene isn't there," Shelly said.

"Or maybe one of us could talk to Eugene while the other talks to Lucas," Fenella said thoughtfully. "Only after Daniel has spoken to everyone, though. I feel as if we're in danger of getting in his way if we keep being nosy."

Shelly laughed. "Daniel needs to get on with it, then. Any thoughts on Helen?"

"Helen? She seems to be struggling to get over Ronald, which is unfortunate after all these years," Fenella said.

"Unfortunate or odd?" Mona asked.

"Is it unfortunate? Or is there something else going on there? Maybe she killed him and she's just acting sad to try to deflect suspicion," Shelly said.

"She didn't seem like a murderer," Fenella replied.

"And yet you should know better than anyone that wives can kill their husbands and pretend to be devastated afterwards," Shelly reminded her. "Helen admitted she's still angry with the man and that she felt as if he treated her badly. It may not be a strong motive, but it's something."

Fenella nodded. "So we have motives for Lucas and Eugene to do with work in some way, and a motive for Helen, even if it seems a slim one. Ronald and Cassie were fighting a lot, so maybe we can use that as a motive for her. The only person we don't have any motive for is Gary, and he's the one I think I disliked the most."

"I thought Eugene was worse, but I certainly didn't like Gary," Shelly told her. "Anyway, maybe they had a fight about something stupid and Gary just bashed him over the head or stabbed him in anger. It might have been impulsive, almost."

"But what could they have fought over?" Fenella asked. "They were cousins who met for a meal once a month. I can't believe they disagreed over where to eat the next time. That couldn't have been enough to drive Gary to murder, surely."

"The only thing I can think of that might be odd is that Helen said Ronald was looking for other relatives and Gary said he wasn't," Shelly replied after a moment. "If Ronald discussed it with Helen, then he must have been looking for them for a while before he disappeared. Ronald and Cassie had been together for six months before Ronald vanished, right?"

"I believe that's right, but didn't Helen say something about Ronald coming to her apartment to complain about Cassie? She said something that made me think that they were still seeing one another, at least occasionally, after they split up," Fenella said.

"We really need to talk to Helen again," Shelly suggested. "If it weren't Saturday, I'd ring the bank and suggest that she meet us for a drink or something."

"Let's see how Daniel does once he starts talking to everyone," Fenella told her. "If he doesn't make any progress after a few days, maybe we can meet up with Helen again. I may even consider going back to Manx Computer Innovations again, but only if we get desperate."

Shelly laughed. "Let's hope Daniel solves the case before you get desperate, then."

The pair chatted for a while longer and then went out for a meal together. A glass of wine at the pub on the way home was all that Fenella needed to get her talking. She told Shelly all about Jack and his efforts to make her feel guilty for not going back to him.

"Change your number," Shelly suggested when she was done.

"That's an idea," Fenella replied.

When she was getting ready for bed a short while later, she gave the idea some thought. While it was tempting, she wasn't sure she was ready to completely cut the man out of her life. Even though he wasn't her problem anymore, she knew she'd worry about him if she changed her number.

As she crawled into bed, she remembered that Daniel had never called her back to discuss Gary Mack. Maybe it no longer mattered for some reason, she told herself as she curled up next to Katie. Or maybe the man was avoiding her.

❦ 12 ❦

Fenella was having a lazy Sunday morning when Shelly knocked on her door.

"I know you said you wanted to wait until Daniel had spoken to everyone before we did anything else, but Helen's just rung me. She wants to meet for a chat today, if possible."

"I'm going to guess that you've already told her yes," Fenella replied.

Shelly blushed. "She was upset and needed to talk to someone. We don't have to talk about Ronald if you'd rather not, but I couldn't tell her no."

Fenella nodded. "What time are we meeting her and where?" she asked.

"Helen lives and works in Douglas, so she thought it might be nice to go somewhere else. I suggested a little café in Port St. Mary that I quite like. It's just a little bit out of the way and should be quiet on a Sunday afternoon."

"Shall I drive?"

"You want to take Mona's car, don't you?"

"I love that car," Fenella sighed. "I'll take any excuse to drive it."

"That's fine with me. I'm happy to simply navigate if you need it."

"I will. I haven't been to Port St. Mary more than once or twice."

"I'm sure you've not been to the café I mean, either. An old school friend of mine owns it and she doesn't do much in the way of advertising or anything. It's really just locals who eat there, mostly."

"Does she have nice cakes?" Fenella wanted to know.

Shelly laughed. "She does wonderful cakes. That's one of the reasons why she doesn't advertise the café much. She bakes cakes for several of the restaurants in the south of the island. I believe that provides most of her income. The café is just something that gets her out of the house, or at least that's how she's always described it to me."

"Are you thinking of having a late lunch there or just cake? Did you tell me what time we're going?"

"I don't think I did. We're meeting Helen there around two, so just cake, I think. I don't want to wait until two for my lunch."

Fenella nodded. "I haven't done anything today except sit around and watch the sea. Now that I know I'm going out later, I probably should do something. I really need a trip to the grocery store before lunch."

"You go and do your shopping," Shelly told her. "While you're gone, I'll make lunch for both of us. Since it's Sunday, I was planning a proper Sunday lunch. Tim was going to join me, but he's caught a terrible cold and I've told him to stay home and take care of himself instead of sharing his germs with me. How does roast chicken with mashed potatoes and roasted vegetables sound?"

"Fabulous. Are you sure you don't mind? It also sounds like a lot of bother."

"I don't mind. I try to do a full Sunday lunch most weeks, even when I'm home alone. I have to cook the chicken before it goes off, anyway, and adding a few trimmings won't take much more time or effort."

"If you're sure, that sounds great."

Shelly headed back home, taking Katie with her for a play session with Smokey while Fenella raced through her shower and got dressed. She added the least amount of makeup she felt she could get away with, aware that as she crept closer to fifty she was using more and more all the time.

The grocery store was crowded, full of people who seemed to be buying enough to keep them going for a month or more. Fenella could easily get back to the store any day, so she stuck to getting just the essentials. When she got into what she hoped would be a reasonably short checkout line, she glanced down into her shopping cart.

"You're definitely single," she muttered under her breath as she surveyed the cans of soda, packets of potato chips, and ready meals. She was still discovering new ready meals every time she shopped. The idea of individual servings of prepared foods, chilled but not frozen, that she simply had to cook at home, still felt sort of odd to her, but she'd quickly discovered that she loved many of the options. She had a box of cereal and a loaf of bread, but most of the rest of the space in the cart was filled with cat food.

"How many cats do you have?" the girl behind the register asked as she began to scan Fenella's items.

"Just one, but she's spoiled rotten," Fenella laughed. "I like to have lots of variety on hand for her."

"Oh, aye, I do the same," the girl told her. "Mum and I have two cats, but they don't like the same brand of cat food, so I feel as if I'm buying food for one or the other of them nearly every day. Still, they're our family, so I don't complain."

"They're less hard work than husbands," the woman behind Fenella said. "My kitty, Oscar, and I just threw my husband out. We're much happier on our own, I can tell you."

The girl laughed. "Mum keeps telling me to stay single and keep cats. She reckons I'll be a lot happier in the long run."

Fenella felt as if she ought to defend men in some way, but she wasn't exactly sure how. Before she'd worked out what to say, the girl was done and she was paying for her groceries.

"I hope your kitty likes everything you've bought," the girl told her as Fenella pocketed her receipt.

"Thank you," Fenella replied. She smiled at the woman behind her and then made her way back out to her car.

"What would you have said?" she asked Shelly a short while later as they both dug into the delicious meal that Shelly had prepared.

"I don't know," Shelly shrugged. "I mean, John was a good man and

I miss him, but Smokey and I are doing just fine on our own. I enjoy Tim's company, but there was a little bit of me that was relieved when he rang up to tell me he wasn't coming today, too. It's complicated."

"I might have been faster to defend men if I knew what was going on with Daniel," Fenella told her. "Or maybe not."

Shelly smiled and patted her hand. "It will all come right in the end," she said. "Maybe he just needs some time to work out how he feels."

"And maybe while he's working that out, I'll simply move on."

After Fenella helped with the dishes, she went back to her own apartment to freshen up and get her car keys.

"I feel as if we're getting close to a solution on this case," Mona said as Fenella was combing her hair. "Helen may well be the key to the whole thing. Ask her lots of questions."

"We aren't going to talk about Ronald," Fenella told her. "If we do talk about Ronald, I'm not asking her any questions. I'll listen while she talks, of course, but today isn't about the case."

"Of course it is," Mona replied. "Until we find Ronald or his body, every day is about the case."

Fenella didn't argue, she just finished getting ready and then waved to her aunt. "See you later."

"We're going to be early," Shelly laughed as the pair sped toward the south of the island. "Mona's car is fast."

"I can slow down," Fenella offered.

"I don't mind being early, actually. I'd love a chance to catch up with my friend, Martha, before Helen arrives."

"Tell me about her," Fenella suggested.

"As I said, we went to school together, er, a few years ago," Shelly replied. "She moved across and worked for several different restaurants, finally ending up as an assistant pastry chef at some really fancy place in London. When she got tired of the crazy long hours and being shouted at by irate chefs all the time, she moved back to the island and opened the café in Port St. Mary."

"Is she married?"

"No. She's had a few boyfriends over the years and was involved with the head pastry chef at her last job. Apparently he was the one who shouted at her the most, and one of the main reasons she decided to come back to the island. As far as I know, she's been happily single ever since."

"Does she have cats, too?"

Shelly laughed. "I don't think so, but she might. As much as I love her cakes, I don't get down to see her very often. She didn't have any pets the last time I saw her, but that was probably a year ago."

"It isn't even a long drive," Fenella commented as she turned onto the road that would eventually take them into Port St. Mary.

"It's not a very long drive for someone who grew up in America," Shelly countered. "In island terms, it's quite far away."

Fenella nodded. It often seemed that people who lived in Douglas rarely ventured elsewhere on the island. On an island that was only around fourteen miles wide and approximately thirty-two miles long, nowhere seemed particularly distant to Fenella, even if the roads across the island were often winding and indirect.

"I never would have found this without you," Fenella said as Shelly guided her through the back roads in Port St. Mary. "I'll never find my way home again without you, either."

"It isn't that bad," Shelly told her. "Martha's café is just a little off the beaten path."

"Which is odd for a café," Fenella suggested.

"It was all that she could afford when she moved back to the island," Shelly told her. "All she really wanted was the huge kitchen, anyway. Once she'd opened the café, she started offering her cakes to local restaurants, and they were happy to have them. I'm sure I told you that they're how she makes most of her money."

"I didn't know there was much money in cakes."

"She doesn't just do a few cakes here and there. She supplies hundreds of cakes each month to several different restaurants. She also does wedding and other special occasion cakes for restaurants and events. I truly think she only keeps the café open because she's there anyway, baking."

Fenella pulled Mona's car into the tiny parking lot for the café and looked at the small building. "It doesn't look as if it will hold many customers."

"It holds fewer than it should because the kitchen is enormous," Shelly told her. "I've never seen it busy, so we should be okay."

"Shelly Quirk? What are you doing here?" the tall, slender blonde woman who was sitting at one of the tables in the otherwise empty café demanded as the pair walked into the small café.

"I needed a place to meet a friend," Shelly told her. "I thought it would be lovely and quiet down here."

The woman laughed as she got to her feet. "That's my café. Sadly, always quiet."

"Fenella Woods, this is Martha Smith. I know she looks a decade younger than me, but we actually went to primary school together."

"I started school when I was a mere baby, though," Martha told Fenella. "I'm really much younger than Shelly."

Fenella thought that she could almost believe it. It wasn't until they were close enough to shake hands that Fenella was able to detect faint lines and wrinkles on the woman's face. "It's nice to meet you," Fenella said.

"Likewise. I hope things aren't too bad and that you just wanted a quiet place to talk about happy things," Martha said.

"Oh, this isn't the friend who needed to talk," Shelly told her. "She should be here soon, though."

"Shelly was always the best person to talk to about problems," Martha told Fenella. "Everyone confided in her all the time. Why, I've told her things about the various men in my life that I haven't even told my therapist."

"You're seeing a therapist? You never told me that," Shelly said.

Martha laughed. "It's trendy, darling. I see a wonderful man in London once a fortnight. I think the trip to London, shopping and eating at different lovely restaurants, is better for me than the actual therapy, but I'm sure my therapist wouldn't agree."

"Whatever you're doing, it seems to be working," Shelly told her. "You look amazing."

"I have another specialist for that," Martha replied. "I see him once a fortnight, too. I haven't had to do anything too dramatic yet, but I'm sure those days are coming."

"Someone else in London?" Shelly asked.

"Yes, indeed. All the best people are in London," Martha said.

"And expensive," Shelly suggested with just a hint of a question in her words.

Martha grinned at her. "They are, but I'm worth it," she replied. She glanced around the empty room and then leaned in close to Shelly. "About a year ago, a rather famous celebrity-type chef visited the island. He had a piece of one of my cakes at one of the restaurants in Peel. To cut a long story short, he bought my recipe, and he's been back to buy a few more since. I could shut the café and retire to the south of France with what he's paying me, but I'm afraid I'd get bored."

"Congratulations," Shelly said, sounding surprised.

Martha shrugged. "He has a deal with one of the supermarket chains. He supplies cake mixes to them and he's using my recipes for the mixes. Oh, they need a lot of modifications, but as they're based on my recipes, I get a cut of every mix that gets sold. When he first asked about buying recipes, I had no idea how far it was going to go."

"How exciting for you," Fenella said.

Martha glanced around again. "We're sort of romantically involved, too," she said in a low voice, "but no one knows about that part."

Shelly nodded. "Well, they won't hear about it from me or Fenella."

"Good. He'd rather people didn't know. He likes everyone to think that he's single and available. Many of his biggest fans are women."

The door behind Fenella opened suddenly. The trio of women spun around, startling Helen.

"Goodness, hello," she said uncertainly.

"Hello," Shelly replied quickly. "Come in and meet my friend, Martha."

After introductions, Martha pulled out a small notebook from her pocket. "What can I get everyone?" she asked.

"What cakes do you have today?" Shelly asked.

Martha ran down a list of cakes, including descriptions, that all sounded delicious.

"I didn't think I'd want anything after my huge lunch," Fenella said. "But I have to try the flourless chocolate cake."

"Victoria sponge for me," Shelly said.

"Oh, I don't really think, I mean, I wasn't going to indulge," Helen began. "Oh, heck, I'll have the chocolate and vanilla one, whatever it was."

"Thin slices of chocolate sponge cake with layers of vanilla buttercream between them," Martha told her.

"And tea for everyone," Shelly added, giving both Fenella and Helen a questioning look. They both nodded.

"Sit anywhere," Martha told them. "This won't take long."

The trio sat at a table near the back wall of the building.

Helen sat down and sighed deeply. "I don't know if this was a good idea or not," she said.

"You said you needed someone to talk to," Shelly replied. "We can talk about anything you'd like, from what's bothering you to the weather or the state of the Welsh cricket team."

"Does Wales have a cricket team?" Helen asked.

"I think so," Shelly said, "but their players play for England in internationals. Cricket was something of a passion for my husband, so I picked up a few things in spite of my complete lack of interest."

Helen and Fenella both laughed.

"Here we are," Martha said. She was carrying a large tray that she put down on the table next to theirs. Fenella gasped when she saw the huge slices of cake on each plate.

"I bake fresh every day, and it seems very much as if you're going to be my only customers today," Martha explained as she passed around the plates.

"What do you do with all of the leftovers?" Helen asked.

"Whatever doesn't get eaten by closing time goes to the shelter down the road. I've been told more than one person living in the shelter has refused to move out because of my cakes," Martha replied.

Fenella took a bite of her cake and smiled. "I don't think I'd want to leave either," she said.

Martha grinned. "I always get a few last-minute customers near closing time because they know I cut larger and larger slices as the minutes tick past. I used to only do two or three cakes each day to minimize waste, but now that I'm doing better, I can be more indulgent. The vanilla and chocolate one is an experiment, so please give me your thoughts once you've finished it," she told Helen.

"It's amazing so far," Helen sighed. "I'm sure it's like a million calories."

"Probably only half a million," Martha told her. "I'll be in the kitchen if you need anything else." She disappeared before the women could do much more than nod at her.

"I'm going to need a forklift to get me back on my feet after all of this cake," Fenella muttered after another huge bite. "And it will be totally worth it."

Shelly laughed. "I told you she did good cakes."

"If I'd known about this place, I'd have been here before," Helen said. "It was a long drive, but totally worth it."

The threesome chatted about their cakes and the weather for a few minutes before Helen sighed. "I can't stop thinking about Ronald," she said. "I was starting to think that I was getting over him, finally, but now I can't stop thinking about him."

"I'm sorry we mentioned him," Shelly said.

Helen shook her head. "It isn't your fault. The case is all over the local paper at the moment and someone from the paper has been ringing my flat every hour for days. He wants a new statement from me, and I don't know what to tell him."

"You don't have to tell him anything," Fenella told her.

"I know, but I feel as if I should say something," Helen countered. "I was so angry seven years ago that I said a great many things I shouldn't have about how badly treated I'd been. I feel as if I should set the record straight, really."

"You weren't badly treated?" Shelly asked.

"Oh, I was, but at the time I put most of the blame on Ronald. Really, all of the blame should have gone on Cassie, but I was too angry to see it that way back then."

"Surely they should share the blame," Fenella suggested.

Helen shrugged. "Ronald was, well, he was sweet, but not too bright. Cassie was gorgeous and sexy, and I'm sure Ronald was shocked and flattered by her attention."

"I wonder what she saw in him," Shelly said thoughtfully.

"He was smart at computers," Helen told her. "That's how they met, actually. His company came in to repair a computer where she was working. No doubt she thought he'd be useful to her in some way."

"Didn't you say something about him complaining to you about Cassie?" Fenella asked.

Helen blushed and looked down at the table. "I shouldn't have let him come over to my flat, not after we'd split up, but he needed somewhere to get away, and sometimes Gary was busy. It didn't happen very often, but once in a while I'd let him come and tell me about his troubles."

Fenella frowned. "Otherwise he went to Gary's?" she asked, feeling as if she hadn't heard that before.

"Not usually to Gary's flat, but every so often they would meet for a drink or something. They never did it when he and I were involved, but once Ronald took up with Cassie, well, he needed a break, I suppose. Sometimes they'd meet at whatever house Gary was working on at the time. He installs kitchens and things like that, and the process always fascinated Ronald. Gary often worked after hours when homeowners had left their property vacant for the remodel. Ronald used to take computers from the shop with him and work on those while Gary was laying flooring or installing cabinets or whatever. It was just an escape."

Fenella and Shelly asked the woman a few more questions about Ronald's evenings with Gary, but didn't get any more information.

"You said something about Ronald looking for other family members," Fenella changed the subject a short while later.

"Did I? I suppose I did. It wasn't a big deal, but it was something else that interested Ronald. He'd met someone who researched people's family history for them. That was what she did for a living. She complained to him, actually, because previously she'd been paid a lot of money for digging through the historical records at the Manx Museum for people, but now everything was being put on computer and people were able to find what they wanted for free. She'd come into the computer shop to buy a computer of her own that would let her do her research more easily, though, in spite of her complaints."

"Did she do any work for Ronald?" Shelly asked.

"Oh, I don't think so," Helen replied. "He never mentioned hiring her, just said that he thought maybe it was time that he started looking into his own family tree. He said something about having to have more relatives than just Gary, even if they were only distant relatives."

"Do you think he discussed the plan with Gary?" was Shelly's next question.

"I'm sure he did. He and Gary talked about everything," Helen said, blushing. "I'm sure Gary knows far more about me and my relationship with Ronald than I'd like, for example."

Fenella and Shelly exchanged glances. Gary had insisted that he knew nothing about Ronald's efforts to trace their family tree. Was he lying or was Helen mistaken about how much Ronald confided in his cousin?

"How are we doing?" Martha asked as she walked back into the room. "What did you think of the cakes?"

All three women were very vocal in their praise of the different cakes.

"I loved the contrast between the chocolate of the cake and the vanilla of the buttercream," Helen told her. "It was delicious."

"I was wondering about adding some chocolate chips or chocolate shavings to the outside of the cake," Martha replied.

"I don't think it needs it," Helen replied. "And it might mess up the balance between the flavors. I think you should leave it exactly as it is."

"Did anyone want anything else?" Martha asked.

While Fenella was tempted to ask for another slice of cake, she was incredibly full. She shook her head quickly before she could ask for cake in spite of herself.

"You're more than welcome to stay as long as you'd like," Martha told them as she cleared the cake plates from the table. "Does anyone want more tea?"

"No, thank you," Helen said. "I really must be going, anyway. I hadn't planned on staying this long." She got to her feet and then opened her handbag. "How much for my cake and tea?" she asked Martha.

"It's on me," Shelly told her firmly. "I just hope you're feeling better."

"It was good to get out of my flat for a few hours," Helen replied. "When I'm home I spend too much time thinking. Now I need to get some shopping done before work tomorrow, though. Thank you both so much for your time, and thank you, Shelly, for the cake. It was a real treat."

The woman dashed out the door before anyone could reply.

"She has a lot on her mind," Martha said as the door swung shut behind Helen.

"Yes, she does," Fenella agreed.

"Are you sure you don't need anything else?" Martha asked.

"We truly don't," Shelly said. She glanced over at Fenella. "Are you in a hurry to get home?" she asked.

"Not at all," Fenella replied.

"Martha, sit down and tell me all about your fabulous life," Shelly invited.

An hour later Shelly and Fenella had heard all about Martha's life in London, where she spent her time with the rich and famous, on the arm of her celebrity chef boyfriend.

"The island makes a nice contrast, really," Martha concluded. "Here, I'm just Martha Smith who makes nice cakes and runs that little café that no one seems to visit very often. My celebrity chef friend likes to come and stay with me and help out here once in a while. No one recognizes him, and he loves how peaceful it is."

"It wouldn't be nearly as nice if you had to rely on the café for all of your income," Fenella suggested.

Martha laughed. "No, you're right about that. As it is, I run the café at a huge loss, but it's still my favorite place in the whole world."

"Now that I've had your cakes, I'll be back," Fenella promised.

"Let me get you a calendar," Martha said. She walked over to a small table near the door and grabbed a sheet of paper. "I'm only here three weeks out of every month. This shows when the café will be open for the next few months."

"We were lucky today," Shelly remarked as she glanced over the sheet. It looks as if Martha had only just returned from London the previous day.

"We should probably get home," Fenella said reluctantly. "It's getting late and Katie will be getting hungry."

"I suppose you're right," Shelly agreed. They both stood up and Martha gave Shelly a hug.

"Wait here a minute," she told them both before she disappeared back into the kitchen.

"We haven't paid yet, anyway," Fenella said to the woman's departing back.

"She's probably not going to want me to pay," Shelly frowned. "I'd better hide a generous tip while her back is turned."

Shelly slipped two folded twenty-pound notes under her teacup and then quickly tucked her wallet away. The pair were studying a painting on one wall when Martha returned with two large boxes in her hands.

"Here you are. Small samples of some of today's cakes," she said, handing them each a box. "Stick them in the refrigerator when you get home and they should be good for tomorrow, too."

"I can't take this," Shelly told her. "The people at the shelter need it more than I do."

Martha shook her head. "I rang the shelter first to see how many, er, guests they have at the moment. It's very quiet, and I have nearly a dozen cakes for them. That's going to be more than enough for today. Tomorrow I'll bake a dozen more."

"Are you sure?" Shelly asked.

"You can ring them yourself to check if you don't believe me," Martha laughed.

"You should add these to our bill, then," Shelly told her.

Martha nodded. "I'll do that," she said. "Here you are." She handed Shelly a slip of paper.

Shelly read it and then sighed. "Fifty-plus years of friendship does not cancel out our debt," she said.

"It does, though," Martha replied. "If I needed the money, I'd make you pay anyway, but I truly don't. I'm just happy I got to see you."

The pair hugged again before Shelly and Fenella walked out to the car. After carefully putting their cake boxes in the trunk, they headed for home.

"We need to talk to Gary again," Shelly said as they went.

"I definitely don't want to talk to him again before Daniel does," Fenella said firmly. "I didn't like him."

"I didn't like him, either. That's why I think he's lying about Ronald and his search for more family."

"Even if he is, I'm not sure how that relates to Ronald's disappearance."

"Maybe Gary was so irate that Ronald was looking for other relatives that he killed him," Shelly suggested. "Or maybe Ronald uncovered a distant relative that was a criminal and Gary didn't want anyone to know about it."

"The cakes were good," Fenella changed the subject.

"We could visit Eugene tomorrow," Shelly suggested. "Maybe he knows more about Ronald's evening visits with Gary to get away from Cassie. That didn't seem to agree with what Gary said either."

"I don't want to visit Eugene again," Fenella said. "Maybe we should leave everything to Daniel."

"Maybe," Shelly sighed. "But what fun is that?"

Fenella sighed. "I'm not sure any of this has been fun."

"But you did get cake," Shelly pointed out.

Fenella couldn't argue with that.

❧ 13 ❧

Fenella had a quiet evening at home with Katie and Mona, as Shelly needed to do laundry and clean her apartment.

"Tell me everything that Helen said," Mona demanded as Fenella ate a sandwich for dinner.

While Fenella thought about arguing, she decided it was easier to go along with her aunt. As she went through the conversation, she nibbled on one of the cake slices from her box.

"What is that?" Mona interrupted to ask.

"This one is chocolate cake with vanilla buttercream icing," Fenella replied. "I have about ten others, if you'd like to see them."

"Ten other cakes?"

"Slices of cake," Fenella told her. "Just small slices of cake, really."

"That isn't what I would consider a small slice of cake," Mona countered. "That's a fairly generous serving."

Fenella frowned. "It's not that big, and some of the others are smaller. Anyway, I probably won't eat them all."

"Should I ask why you came home with eleven slices of cake?"

"You'd already know the answer to that if you'd let me tell you about our meeting with Helen," Fenella replied. She took another bite of the truly delicious cake and then went back to the story. When she was done, she helped herself to a slice of Victoria sponge and a cup of coffee.

"Gary knows what happened to Ronald," Mona said after a moment. "It's the only thing that makes sense. Why didn't the police arrest him seven years ago?"

"No evidence? No motive? Maybe he even has an alibi," Fenella suggested.

"You need to talk to Daniel," Mona told her. "Ring him and invite him over. He can eat some of that cake for you."

Fenella frowned. She wasn't ready to see Daniel, and she didn't want to share her cake, either. When someone knocked on her door a few minutes later, Fenella shot Mona a questioning look. While there didn't seem to be any way that Mona could have managed it, Fenella couldn't help but wonder if the woman had somehow arranged to bring Daniel to her door.

"Daniel, what a surprise," she said with artificial cheer.

"I can't stay long," he told her, "but I never found the time to ring you back to talk about Gary. I thought it might be easier to do that in person, since I was in the neighborhood."

"Come in," she invited.

"Offer him cake," Mona said loudly. "Tell him you made it yourself."

Fenella glared at the woman and then forced herself to smile at Daniel. "I just made coffee," she said. "Decaffeinated, as it's so late. Would you like some?"

"That sounds great, although I could probably use the caffeine," he replied.

Fenella poured them each a cup of coffee and then hesitated. "I have some cake," she said after a moment. "Shelly and I had coffee at this little place in Port St. Mary today. The owner went to school with Shelly and she insisted on sending us both home with boxes full of cake samples. I'll never eat them all before they get stale. Would you like to try one or two?"

Daniel's eyes lit up. "Cake? That sounds wonderful. What sort do you have?"

Fenella pulled the box out of her refrigerator and put it on the counter. "You can have anything except the flourless chocolate cake," she told the man as she opened the box. "That one is mine."

He laughed and then looked inside the box. "My goodness, did Shelly's friend know you live alone? There's a lot of cake in there."

"Take two or three, if you want," Fenella said grudgingly.

Daniel looked at her for a minute and then looked back into the box. "Every single slice looks delicious," he told her. "Are there any that you know you don't want?"

"The chocolate with coconut icing," Fenella said quickly. She didn't really like coconut. "And the dark chocolate and orange." That one she would have eaten rather than see it go to waste, but it would have been the last to go, probably.

"Those sound perfect," Daniel told her.

Fenella got him a plate and slid the two slices of cake onto it. They barely fit. While she was at it, she put the flourless chocolate cake onto a plate for herself. When the cake box was back in the refrigerator, she sat down across from Daniel and took a bite.

They ate silently for a few minutes before Daniel looked up at her. "Thank you for this. I didn't get any dinner."

"You should have said something. I could have made you a sandwich," Fenella frowned.

Daniel shook his head. "I'm happy with cake," he told her. "Especially this cake."

"It is wonderful, isn't it?"

Once his plate was empty, Daniel took a sip of coffee and then pulled a notebook out of his pocket. "I just have a few questions about your conversation with Gary," he said.

"After I've answered them, I should probably tell you about the coffee today," she replied.

"Where you got the cakes?"

"Yes. It wasn't just Shelly and me. We met Helen for coffee in Port St. Mary."

"Helen Campbell? Whose idea was that?"

"She rang Shelly and asked to see her. She just needed someone to talk to about, well, things."

"Things like makeup and shoes or things like Ronald Sherman?"

"Mostly Ronald Sherman," Fenella told him.

Daniel nodded. "Before we talk about Gary, then, tell me about your meeting with Helen Campbell."

Fenella did her best to repeat the conversation that had taken place at the coffee shop in Port St. Mary. Mona seemed to be listening intently, and Fenella wondered if her aunt was checking to see if Fenella had left anything out of the version she'd told her earlier. When she was done talking, Fenella felt as if she deserved another slice of cake.

"Interesting," Daniel said. He flipped back through the pages of notes he'd taken and then smiled at her. "Question time," he announced.

Half an hour later, Fenella was certain she deserved more cake. Daniel's questions had strained her memories of both the meeting with Gary and the meeting with Helen.

"I think that's all I need for tonight," he said. "Do you know what Shelly was planning to do tonight?"

"Shelly? She was going to clean her apartment and do some laundry," Fenella told him. "Why?"

"I'd like to hear her version of both conversations," he said. "I'm not doubting anything you told me, but it's always helpful to hear more than one account of a conversation."

"As far as I know, she's at home."

"I'll go and talk to her now, then," he said. "Thank you for your time tonight, and also for the cake and coffee."

"Are you going to start interviewing people yourself soon?"

"Tomorrow. I've finally submitted my last report on the incident on the promenade the other night. Now I can focus on Ronald Sherman for at least a short while, barring the unforeseen, of course."

"Great. I hope everything Shelly and I have contributed proves helpful and that you can solve the case quickly."

"Me, too. I'd love to have it all wrapped up by Thursday so that I can enjoy my first American Thanksgiving."

Fenella grinned at him. "It's going to be an interesting evening." Which reminded her that she still needed to get a final count to the caterers. She walked Daniel to the door and then shut it behind him as he began to knock on Shelly's door. After Fenella heard Shelly's door open and close a moment later, she walked back to the table by the phone and looked at the list she'd made.

"Only a few people haven't replied," she said. "I wonder if I should count them in or not."

"I'd count them," Mona said. "You can afford to pay for a bit of extra food, and that's preferable to being embarrassed if there isn't enough."

Fenella nodded. "You're right, of course. I'll count them all. I'm really looking forward to Thursday."

"I've always felt that it would be nice to have a holiday to celebrate being thankful for all of our blessings."

"It's one of my favorite holidays," Fenella said. "It truly is just about being thankful and feasting with family and friends. What could be better than that?"

The pair sat together and watched an old movie on television before Fenella headed to bed. Katie woke her right on schedule on Monday morning.

"It's seven already?" she groaned as the kitten tapped on her nose. "I'm really not ready for morning, yet."

Katie was vocal with her displeasure at Fenella's attitude.

"Okay, I'll get you some breakfast," she conceded. "Then I'm going to go back to sleep."

Once Fenella finished getting breakfast for Katie, though, she wasn't all that tired any longer. Rather than going to back to bed, she headed for the shower. After breakfast she rang the caterers to finalize the plans for Thursday.

"We'll have drinks and starters in the front room and then move everyone into the dining room for dinner," the woman at the restaurant told her. "We'll have three separate buffet stations set up with the same food at each station. A separate table will be set up for pudding. Our chef has been working on perfecting a pumpkin pie recipe since we first spoke and he's confident that he'll be able to make something acceptable for Thursday."

"My goodness, I didn't expect him to worry about it," Fenella exclaimed. "I'm probably the only person who'll eat pumpkin pie."

"All the more reason for him to work to get it just right. You'll know what it's meant to taste like, after all."

"Yes, I suppose so. Is there anything else you need from me before Thursday, then?"

"We've had your deposit. The final bill will be due on Thursday and will be based on the number you gave me today, even if fewer people come than you are expecting. We will charge extra, however, if there are more than two extras over the number you've given me."

"That's fine. I've added in several people who haven't actually told me if they're coming or not, so my number should be high rather than low."

"As I said, you'll be charged for the number of guests you gave me today, even if the actual number in attendance is significantly lower than that number."

"I understand. You'll have food prepared for the number I gave you, even if they don't all turn up. I can take home the leftover food, right?"

"Absolutely. We'll box everything for you however you'd like."

"Perfect. I'm looking forward to it."

"I believe Chef is as well. He loves trying different things, and some of the items you requested are unusual, at least in this country."

With that chore out of the way, Fenella did some cleaning and tidying around her apartment and then had a small sandwich and two slices of cake for lunch.

"I really should have given Daniel three or four pieces last night," she sighed as she put the box back in the refrigerator.

"Yes, you should have," Mona agreed.

Fenella jumped. "Hello to you, too," she snapped.

Mona sighed. "Wouldn't it be easier for your nerves if you simply always assumed that I was here somewhere?"

"Are you here, even when I can't see you?"

"No, but I could always be about to appear, so you may as well just assume I'm always here. Anyway, you were talking aloud, so I assumed you were talking to me."

"I was just talking to myself," Fenella told her.

"That's a bad habit. One day you may have a man stay over. What would he think if he walks in on you talking to yourself?"

"Probably that I'm crazy, much the same as if he walked in when I was talking to you. I don't suppose you'll stay away if I ever have an overnight guest?"

"I suppose I could, but I'd miss you," Mona said in a hurt tone.

Fenella sighed. "It seems highly unlikely that I'm going to have anyone over in the foreseeable future anyway. Let's not worry about it for now."

Mona nodded. "For today we should talk about Ronald Sherman. It's time to work out what happened to him."

"I'm hoping he found a distant cousin in New Zealand and went to visit him or her. Maybe he loved it so much he simply stayed."

"I thought you said he didn't take his passport."

"Maybe he got a second one for some reason or something," Fenella waved a hand. "Or maybe the distant cousin was only in Blackpool or somewhere like that."

"If Ronald was only in the UK, surely he would have stayed in touch with Gary," Mona argued.

"Maybe, or maybe he and Gary had a disagreement about something and that's why he left."

"Or he didn't stay in touch with Gary because he wanted to hide from Cassie," Mona suggested.

"That's a thought."

"Or he wanted to hide from someone else, maybe someone he stole a lot of money from or something like that."

"I can't see him stealing money. Helen didn't think he'd do something like that."

"From what you've said about Helen, she was crazy about the man, even though he'd treated her badly. I'm not sure I'd put a lot of stock in her opinion."

"Eugene did say that Ronald had said something about finding a fortune," Fenella mused.

"You need to go and talk to him again. See if you can't work out exactly what Ronald said, and maybe see if Eugene has any record of what Ronald was working on when he disappeared."

"According to Helen, Ronald sometimes took computers he was working on to job sites where Gary was working. What if they discovered something together? Gary might have helped Ronald get away. Maybe they stole the money together."

"I like that scenario," Mona said excitedly. "Gary helped Ronald get away with the money and they're sharing the proceeds between them."

"Gary doesn't seem rich."

"No, but he has gone into business for himself since Ronald left," Mona pointed out. "Maybe Ronald gave him a lump sum with which to start the business and now he's helping him with the new shop."

"The old shop didn't seem to be doing very well. It's hard to imagine where he's getting the money for another one," Fenella replied thoughtfully. "Especially a new shop that's going to specialize in higher-end finishes in a much more central location."

"We should have had this conversation with Daniel."

"We didn't have any conversation with Daniel," Fenella sighed. "I told him about my meeting with Helen and then he asked me a bunch of questions. That was it."

The pair chatted for a while longer about the case and the various suspects, but didn't reach any further conclusions. When they ran out of things to discuss, Fenella went out for a long walk on the promenade. She was disappointed not to see Harvey and the dogs, but at least she got to stretch her legs and get some exercise.

When she got home, there was a message on her answering machine.

"You'll never believe it, but I actually crashed my computer this afternoon," Shelly said. "I was thinking maybe we should take it to Manx Computer Innovations tomorrow and see if they can repair it."

Fenella called her back. "What did you do?" she demanded.

"I was just trying to surf the Internet and something went wrong," Shelly told her. "I think I picked up a virus."

"Really? On purpose?"

"Really, and it wasn't on purpose, either. I was actually looking at some new software as an excuse to visit the computer shop, and then suddenly the screen went black and the machine switched itself off."

"And?"

"And what? I unplugged it and rang you."

"You didn't try to turn it back on?"

"No. Should I?"

Fenella hesitated. "Maybe not. Maybe we should take it to an expert. I hope you don't have anything too important on that computer."

"It wasn't actually the old desktop that I've been using for my writing. This was an old laptop of John's that I didn't even remember having. I found it when I was looking for something else and thought I would see if I could get it working. I've no idea what's on it, really, but it can't be anything too important, as John hadn't touched it in years and I didn't even remember having it."

☛ "Okay, then, we can take it in tomorrow and see what they say," Fenella agreed. "If they can fix it, it might be easier for you to write on that than on the desktop, right? The laptop will go wherever you go."

"That's what I was thinking when I found it. It seemed to be going so well, too. I managed to connect to the Internet and everything. It was old and slow, but it was working, and it had word-processing software on it, too."

"They open at ten tomorrow. Let's be there when they open," Fenella suggested.

"That sounds good," Shelly agreed. "I'll come by your flat at half nine. It's probably my turn to drive."

"I won't object. Onchan isn't far enough away to make taking Mona's car fun."

Shelly laughed. "See you tomorrow, then," she said.

Fenella made herself another small sandwich and then ate far too much cake for dessert. Wanting to enjoy the cakes at their best, she took a bite of each one of the cakes that remained and then finished off her two favorites. The rest she put back into the refrigerator. Surely they'd still taste good for at least one more day, she thought as she settled in front of the television.

"I'm not sure about this," Fenella said to Shelly the next morning.

"I had a terrible dream about Eugene and Lucas. They were chasing me around and around a giant chocolate cake, shouting at me to buy a new computer."

"You ate too much cake yesterday," Shelly told her. "We're going to talk to them about computers, nothing more."

Fenella nodded, but she wasn't sure she trusted Shelly to stick to her words. Shelly seemed to be enjoying being a part of Daniel's investigation.

It only took them a few minutes to get into Onchan and park at the small strip plaza.

"Since we're early, why don't we take a peek at Gary's new shop?" Shelly suggested.

"Which one is his?" Fenella asked in a resigned tone. She'd known Shelly wasn't going to give up a chance to snoop.

"I think it's the last one in the row."

The pair walked the length of the strip, glancing in windows as they went. The computer shop was dark as they crossed in front of it. Two doors down, at the very end of the row, an empty storefront had paper covering its windows. There was a small sign on the door that read "Future home of Great Kitchens and Better Baths."

Shelly tried to peer in between the sheets of paper that covered the windows from the inside. "There's a gap here," she said excitedly. "I can't see anything," she added sadly after a moment. "It's really dark inside the building."

"Never mind. We can come back after he opens," Fenella said.

They walked back to Shelly's car, got the laptop out of the back, and then headed toward the computer store. Lights were just flickering on as they approached. Eugene unlocked the door a moment later.

"Ladies? What a pleasant surprise," he said as he held the door open for them. "I hope you've come back for that laptop we discussed," he said to Fenella.

"I haven't, actually," Fenella told him. "My friend is having problems with her computer."

"Really? We're meant to only look at computers by appointment," Eugene said. "Did you book an appointment?"

"No, I'm awfully sorry. I didn't realize I needed one," Shelly sighed.

Eugene glanced around the empty store and then shrugged. "I suppose I could take a quick look. It might be something simple that I can repair quickly."

"That would be good news," Shelly said, giving the man a big smile.

Shelly put the computer on the nearest table. Eugene pushed the power button and Fenella found that she was holding her breath as she waited to see what would happen next. Nothing happened.

"Do you have the power cable?" Eugene asked Shelly.

Shelly nodded and handed the man the cord. He plugged the machine in and tried again. Nothing happened.

"It's a pretty old machine," Eugene told her. "Even if I can get it working, it won't be good for much beyond some light word processing or web surfing."

"That's all I need it for," Shelly told him.

Eugene raised an eyebrow and then shrugged. "First things first, then. Let's see if the power cable is good."

He unplugged the computer and took the cable across the room. He plugged it into a small machine and then frowned at it. "I may have found your problem," he said. "Or maybe your first problem. I think the cable is bad."

"It worked for a short while when I first plugged it in," Shelly told him.

"It seems to be an intermittent fault," the man told her. "Let me see if I have the right replacement cable."

He disappeared into the back of the shop, leaving Fenella and Shelly alone for a moment.

"How can we bring the conversation around to Ronald?" Shelly whispered to Fenella.

"Let's not," Fenella whispered back.

The door behind them swung open. Fenella gasped when she recognized Gary Mack in the doorway.

"Where's Eugene?" he demanded.

"He just went into the back to find a part," Shelly replied.

He narrowed his eyes at her and then frowned. "Do I know you from somewhere?" he asked.

"I don't think so," Shelly said quickly, turning herself slightly so that Gary could see less of her face.

Gary walked further into the shop, but was interrupted by Eugene's return.

"Gary, what a lovely surprise," Eugene said brightly.

"What have you been saying to the police?" Gary asked.

"What do you mean?" Eugene replied.

"I mean the police seem to think that I know where Ronald is and I think you've been telling them that."

"All I said was that you and Ronald were close, that's all. I said something like if anyone knew where Ronald was, it would be you," Eugene told him.

"If I knew where he was, I wouldn't have filed a police report, though, would I?" Gary asked.

"No, of course not," Eugene agreed.

"So maybe you should tell the police that," Gary suggested, "and maybe you should think very carefully before you tell them anything else."

Eugene nodded. "I won't talk to them again."

"That's probably wise," Gary said. "Wherever Ronald is, I don't think he wants to be found. We should leave him in peace, shouldn't we?"

"Yes, absolutely," Eugene agreed. "I'm sure the police will drop the case again in another week or so."

"No doubt. Maybe even sooner if everyone stops talking to them," Gary said.

"I won't talk to them again," Eugene told him. "Unless you want me to tell them something specific?"

Gary glanced at Fenella and Shelly and then shook his head. "You know all I've ever wanted was what's best for Ronald. At first I thought that meant finding him, but now, after all these years, I don't think that any longer. Now I think we should just leave him alone. I'm thinking about having him declared dead, actually."

"Dead? That's sad," Eugene said. "I've never thought of Ronald as dead before."

"Yes, but if he's declared dead, the police will stop looking for him," Gary replied. "That seems as if it might be for the best."

"But if he's still alive, won't that cause problems for him?" Eugene asked.

"I don't know. Maybe. But maybe I have to do what's best for me," Gary snapped.

"Will you inherit Ronald's things, then?" Eugene asked, raising an eyebrow.

Gary frowned. "I don't know that Ronald left any things, but I suppose I might. I just hope I don't inherit any of his old bills. He left quite a few of those."

"Well, good luck, whatever you do," Eugene said. "I won't talk to the police or the reporter again."

"What reporter?" Gary asked.

"The one who came in yesterday to ask about Ronald," Eugene said. "He said he was looking for you, too, but I told him I didn't know how to find you."

"That was smart, anyway," Gary sighed. "What else did you tell him?"

"Nothing much," Eugene said, clearly nervous. "We talked about Ronald, that's all. I probably told him the same thing I told the police, that if anyone knew where Ronald was, it was you. The reporter seemed to think that Ronald had to be dead, since you don't know where he is."

Gary frowned. "It's all turning into a mess," he muttered. "Just keep your mouth shut, won't you?" he asked. "I thought we were mates."

"We are mates," Eugene replied quickly. "I didn't say anything different to what I said seven years ago."

Gary stared at him for a long minute and then nodded. "Just keep quiet," he said before he turned and walked back out of the shop.

"He was scary," Shelly said as the door swung shut.

"He isn't, really. It was his cousin that disappeared seven years ago. He's never quite recovered, I don't think. He and Ronald were friends as well as family. I don't think Gary has anyone else."

"We met Helen Campbell the other day. She said that Ronald used to take computers to the houses where Gary was working and they would work late into the night together, Gary installing cabinets or whatever while Ronald worked on repairing the computer," Fenella said.

Eugene frowned. "We were a bit more lax about things in those days. Computers that come in for repairs now never leave the shop. We're very strict about that now."

"Were there problems when Ronald was here?" Shelly wondered.

"No, of course not," Eugene told her, "but we've wandered way off topic. Let's see what a new cable can do for your laptop." He pushed the cable into the computer and then plugged the cable into the wall. When he pushed the power button, the computer began to hum and whir.

"That's a good sign," Shelly said.

A moment later the machine flickered to life. "I'll just run a few little tests," Eugene said.

The two women watched as the man performed a series of tests on the machine. When another customer came in, he shouted for Lucas to come out and help.

"Sorry, I was, um, working on repairs," Lucas said to Eugene as he walked out of the back.

"Yeah, sure," Eugene replied. A few minutes later he looked over at Shelly and shrugged. "I can't find anything wrong with the machine itself. I think the cable was the only problem."

"Really?" Shelly said happily. "That's good news."

"It's a nice machine," Eugene told her. "It's old, but it was well built back in the day. If you only need it for word processing and web surf-ing, you may get a few years out of it." He shut the machine down and put it back into Shelly's case.

"I was really worried that it was going to need a lot of money spending on it," Shelly said as she followed Eugene across the shop.

He grinned at her. "You haven't heard how much that power cable costs."

Shelly frowned. "How much?"

When Eugene told her, Shelly sighed with relief. "You had me worried for a minute there," she said.

The man punched a few numbers into his register and Shelly

counted out the necessary cash. "What about your time and effort testing the machine?" she asked as he handed her a receipt.

Eugene shrugged. "No charge today. I hope you'll come back the next time you need computer services."

"I will, for sure," Shelly told him. "Thank you so much."

She and Fenella walked back to Shelly's car. As Fenella climbed inside, she glanced over at the last shop. "Something looks different," she said.

Shelly followed her line of sight and then nodded. "Something is different," she said. "Let's go and see what it is."

"I'm not sure I'm ready to run into Gary again," Fenella told her.

"We'll just walk past quickly," Shelly said. "We won't even slow down."

They walked along the row, past the shop, and then turned around and walked back to the car.

"He's taken down the sign," Fenella said as Shelly started her car engine. "Why would he take down the 'coming soon' sign?"

"Maybe he's changed his mind about the location," Shelly suggested. "Or maybe he's decided to change the shop's name."

"Maybe. I think we need to call Daniel."

"We were going to do that anyway, weren't we?" Shelly asked.

"Yes, I suppose we were."

When the pair got back to Fenalla's apartment, she rang the station. Daniel was at his desk, and she put him on speakerphone so that Shelly could join in the conversation, too. He didn't say much as Fenella told him about their morning. When she was done, he asked both her and Shelly a few questions.

"Everything you've told me is worrying," he said when he was done. "I'm going to tell you both to stay away from everyone involved in the case from now on. If you have more computer trouble or need a new kitchen, you'll have to wait for a short while, until I've had a chance to finish my investigation."

"That's fine with me," Fenella told him.

"Me, too," Shelly added.

"Not me," Mona said. "I'm not stopping now. Things are just getting interesting."

Fenella frowned at her aunt, but couldn't reply.

"Thank you for that," Daniel said. "I'll be talking to everyone again this afternoon, and I may pull Eugene in for some extra questions, too. If I don't talk to you before, I'll see you on Thursday evening."

Daniel put the phone down before Fenella could reply.

"What should we do now?" Shelly asked.

"Forget all about Ronald Sherman," Fenella told her. "Let's worry about Thanksgiving instead."

❦ 14 ❧

In spite of the assurance that she'd been given on Monday, the restaurant called Fenella three times on Wednesday with last-minute questions.

"I don't know why we put marshmallows on top of the candied yams," Fenella told the woman who called. "I just gave you my mother's recipe. That's how she always made them."

"Chef isn't happy about it. He doesn't like marshmallows," the woman replied.

"I don't even eat the yams, so tell Chef to do whatever he likes," Fenella conceded.

The other two calls were similar, and after the third, Fenella took herself out for a walk. She covered the entire promenade twice, anticipating extra helpings of both apple and pumpkin pie the next day.

"Assuming the pies are even edible," she muttered to herself as she got back on the elevator in her building. "I'm not feeling a lot of confidence in anything at the moment."

She was grateful to find that the messages on her machine when she got home weren't from the restaurant. Her gratitude faded as she listened to two different people cancel for the next night.

"Sorry, but I've a late meeting that I didn't know about," one of them said.

"I need to make an emergency trip to London," the other told her. "I'm sorry it's all so last minute."

"So am I," Fenella muttered as she drew a big red line through both of the names on her list.

When Shelly knocked an hour later, Fenella was grateful for the interruption.

"What are you doing?" Shelly asked as she followed Fenella into the kitchen.

"I've been working on a seating chart for tomorrow," Fenella replied. "The restaurant suggested that it might be easier to assign seats, rather than just leaving people to sit anywhere. They told me to try to match up people who don't know one another to make for more interesting conversations."

"Well, I don't want to sit with strangers," Shelly said quickly.

"I think you know everyone that I know," Fenella laughed. "I was going to have you sit with me, anyway. The problem is where to put Daniel."

Shelly laughed. "Maybe it would be better to just let people choose their own seats," she suggested.

Fenella frowned and then nodded. "You may be right. I don't want to upset anyone, and I've no idea who should sit where, anyway."

"It will be fine," Shelly assured her. "I know the day means a lot to you, but for the rest of us it's just a nice dinner. We'll all be happy as long as we're fed."

"What if the food isn't edible? I'm a little bit worried about the chef now. The restaurant keeps calling to ask questions about the different recipes that I supplied."

"You should be glad they're ringing and not just making things up as they go along."

"I suppose you're right. Maybe I shouldn't have insisted on all of my American favorites. Maybe I should have just gone with their standard menu."

"It's your special day. You should have what you want. Maybe next year you should fly a chef in from the US."

Fenella stared at her friend for a minute and then laughed. "I suppose I could afford to do that, couldn't I? I was thinking that next year I'd just have a small dinner for a few friends here in my apartment, but I could do a lot of different things, really."

"You'll get used to the money eventually," Shelly predicted.

"I hope I don't ever take it for granted."

"I'll make sure you don't," Shelly promised.

"Let's go somewhere," Fenella suggested. "I need to get out of the house and do something so I can stop worrying about tomorrow."

"Shopping? Sightseeing? Walking? Driving?"

Fenella shrugged. "Any of those would be good. I just need distracting."

In the end, they headed to Ramsey in Mona's car and did some shopping in the stores there. They had dinner together before they headed back to Douglas.

"I think you need a trip to the pub," Shelly said as Fenella parked the car.

"I think you're right," Fenella agreed.

It was quiet at the Tale and Tail. It wasn't long before the women were settled in the nearly empty upper level with drinks. A large black cat with white feet jumped into Shelly's lap a moment later.

"Well, hello," she said happily.

The cat looked at her for a moment and then curled up and went to sleep.

"This is strange," Fenella said, looking around the room.

"What is?"

"That it's so quiet in here. The day before Thanksgiving is usually a busy day for bars and clubs in the US, at least for young people. It's when most of the college kids come home for a few days. Clearly, they aren't interested in staying home and spending time with their parents. They're eager to get out and see their old friends and have a few drinks."

"That probably happens here closer to Christmas."

"I suppose so. As most college-aged kids from the island are studying in the UK, the homecomings must feel extra special. It isn't like it was for me. I was only an hour's drive from home."

"Tell me more about Thanksgiving," Shelly said after a sip of her wine. "I understand the idea behind the holiday, but how is it really celebrated in American homes?"

"With food and football," Fenella laughed. "There are a couple of major-league football games on Thanksgiving, and as I understand it, lots of families eat their dinner in front of the television while they watch the games."

"Really? I can't imagine."

"I don't really follow football, but my dad was a fan. Mom used to make him turn the television off during dinner, though. He used to get really cross when everyone went back for seconds and thirds."

Shelly chuckled. "The poor man."

"My earliest memories of Thanksgiving are from when I was in grade school. My parents didn't really celebrate the holiday when they lived on the island, so my brothers didn't care much about it, but I was raised with the tradition. I remember spending time on both the night before Thanksgiving and Christmas Eve helping my mother in the kitchen. My first job was tearing up the stale bread for the stuffing, but as I got older I learned to do more and more."

"Maybe you should cook next year," Shelly said. "I could help. Tearing up stale bread doesn't sound too difficult."

"It was always fun when I started, but then after a while I'd get bored and start making bigger and bigger pieces. I think it made the finished product interesting. The first pieces were practically bread crumbs and the last were huge chunks."

The women finished their drinks and then headed for home. Shelly gave Fenella a hug at her door.

"What time are you going over to the restaurant tomorrow?"

"Probably just after lunch. People are supposed to start arriving around six, with dinner at seven, though, so I'm sure I'll be far too early and just in the way."

"Want to spend the day with Tim and me, instead?"

Fenella hesitated and then shook her head. "I'd be terrible company. I'm better off going and annoying the restaurant staff than annoying you and Tim. You're more than welcome to come early, though, maybe at five if you're free?"

"If I can bring Tim, we'll be there."

"Of course, bring Tim. The more distractions I have the better, I think."

"I'm never going to be able to sleep," Fenella told Katie a short while later. "My mind is racing."

"Merroow," Katie replied.

Fenella crawled into bed and then sighed. "I don't know why I'm so worried about everything. It's only a dinner party. The restaurant is doing all of the hard work. I just have to show up and chat with my friends."

Katie made her way up from the center of the bed to Fenella's side. She snuggled against Fenella's chest and then went to sleep. Not wanting to wake the animal, Fenella lay very still, carefully breathing in and out.

When the phone woke her, she felt disoriented. She was shocked when she looked at the clock. "Are you okay?" she demanded of Katie, who was still in bed with her. "It's nearly nine."

Katie smiled and then raced off to the kitchen as Fenella fumbled for the telephone.

"Maggie? Happy Thanksgiving," Jack said loudly.

"Um, yeah, Happy Thanksgiving," she replied. "What time is it?"

"Time? Oh, it's around four in the morning, why?"

"Why are you up?"

"A few of us went out for drinks last night. I'm just getting home, actually."

Fenella sat up in bed. "You're just getting home?" she echoed in surprise.

"I know, you didn't think I could still have wild nights, but since you've been gone, I've changed."

Katie began to complain loudly in the kitchen. Fenella slid out of bed and headed for the door while she tried to think of how best to reply to Jack's words. "I'm glad you're having fun," she said eventually after she'd switched him to speakerphone.

"I met someone."

"Really? Good for you," Fenella replied as she poured cat food into Katie's bowl.

Jack laughed. "A man, not a woman."

"Oh? Are you trying to tell me that you're gay?"

Behind her, Mona laughed. "That would be interesting news."

"No, not at all," Jack said indignantly. "That isn't what I meant. I met a man last night whom you might know."

"Oh? Would you like to tell me more or are you having fun being cryptic?"

"His name is Peter Grady. He's a physics professor at a university in Liverpool."

"The name doesn't sound familiar."

"Well, I met him last night. He's on a tour of the US, lecturing at various colleges and universities, but he's heading back to the UK in mid-December."

"How nice."

"He has a house in Liverpool, but he also has a house on the Isle of Man."

"Lovely." Fenella was only half-listening as she wandered around the kitchen assembling the ingredients for pancakes. It was Thanksgiving, which definitely called for pancakes with maple syrup.

"I told him all about you."

"Lucky him."

"He mentioned that he knew your aunt."

Fenella raised an eyebrow at Mona, who shrugged.

"Anyway, I told him how much I want to visit you and he offered to let me stay in his house on the island."

Fenella froze, the bag of flour in her hands nearly crashing to the floor. "Really?" she said eventually.

"He even gave me the keys and told me how to get past the security system. He's going to be in the UK for December and January, you see."

"You just met the man last night and he's given you the keys to his house?"

"We bonded over our problems with women," Jack told her.

Fenella opened her mouth and then snapped it shut. There was no reply that she could think of that wasn't nasty.

"Anyway, I've booked my flight for the nineteenth of December.

We'll be able to spend Christmas together, and I don't have to be back for work until the twenty-fifth of January. We can have a lovely long visit before I need to get back."

"What about a passport?"

"Oh, I applied for that ages ago," Jack said. "Well, a week ago, anyway. It should be here in plenty of time."

Fenella looked at Mona and sighed. "I truly don't want to get back together," she said firmly.

"I know you think that now, but I'm sure you'll change your mind once I arrive. I can't wait to see the island. If it's half as wonderful as you make it sound, you may struggle to get rid of me."

Jack put the phone down before Fenella could reply. She pushed the disconnect button on her end and then stared at Mona.

"He's coming to visit," she said in an appalled voice.

"Maybe you should marry Daniel before Jack arrives," Mona replied.

"This isn't the time for jokes."

"What makes you think I'm joking?"

Fenella shook her head. "I have too many other things to worry about today. I'll have to worry about Jack tomorrow."

"And you thought your Thanksgiving banquet was a problem," Mona laughed.

Fenella sighed. "The day can only get better, right?"

After a very late breakfast of pancakes and bacon, Fenella got dressed for the party and headed over to the restaurant.

"Ms. Woods, you really don't need to be here this early," the manager told her when she arrived. "Everything is under control."

"I'm sure it is, but I was too nervous to sit at home any longer."

The man laughed. "Come up to my office. We can chat for a while."

"Are you sure everything is okay with the dinner?"

"I'm positive," he assured her. He led her through the building to a small office at the very back. There was a much larger office next to it. Both spaces had huge windows that let Fenella see the nicer furniture and more attractive design of the larger space.

"That's the chef's office," the manager told Fenella, nodding towards the larger office. "He's much more important for the success of the business than I am." He offered Fenella a chair and then sat down opposite her.

"Someone told me that you're a historian," he said after an awkward moment.

"Yes, I have a doctorate in history," she replied.

"I've been studying my family tree," he told her. "I keep hoping I'll find some long-lost cousin with millions of pounds and no heirs, but I've not had any luck yet."

Fenella laughed. "I knew about my Aunt Mona, but I never expected to be her heir. I didn't realize she had any money, either."

"Maybe one of my aunts is secretly hiding a fortune, then," the man said cheerfully. "That would be a nice surprise for one day."

The pair chatted about the weather and Fenella told him a bit about Thanksgiving, but something kept nagging at her. After a short while, she smiled at him.

"I just remembered that I have to call someone," she said. "It will probably be easier if I do it from home. I'll be back soon, though."

"We'll be here," he replied. "As long as you're back before five, I won't be worried."

Fenella glanced at the clock. It was only two-thirty. "I'll be back," she promised.

It only took her a few minutes to get back to her apartment. She called the police station and asked for Daniel.

"I'm sorry, but he's out of the office right now. May I take a message?" the woman who'd answered the phone told her.

"Please ask him to call Fenella Woods," she replied before she put the phone down.

"What's going on?" Mona demanded.

"I was talking with the manager of the restaurant and he said something about hoping he might find a relative with a small fortune and no heirs," Fenella told her. "I keep thinking about Ronald and his sudden interest in his family tree. What if, when he told Eugene he'd found a fortune, he meant that he'd found a distant relative who was wealthy?"

"I suppose that's one possibility," Mona said. "So what?"

"I don't know. The idea just bothers me, that's all. It feels like another piece of the puzzle."

"Did you ever ask Eugene if Ronald had ever mentioned that he was looking for other relatives?"

"I don't remember," Fenella sighed. "It's stupid, really. It was just a random comment from a stranger, but I really want to tell Daniel about it."

"So ring him."

"I just did. He's not in the office. I left a message."

"Ring his mobile."

"I can't. He gave me that number back when we were, well, I don't know what we were, but we aren't that anymore."

"Text him and ask him to ring you," Mona suggested. "That's better than pacing a hole into the carpet."

As Fenella opened her mouth to argue, the phone rang.

"You rang?" Daniel asked.

Fenella sat down and tried to think. "This is going to sound weird, but I was talking to someone today and he said something that I think might be a piece of the puzzle."

"Go on."

Fenella repeated the conversation that she'd had with the restaurant's manager. "What if Ronald did find a distant relative with money?" she asked when she was done. "What if that was the fortune he was talking about when he was talking to Eugene?"

"I think I may need to talk to Eugene again," Daniel said. "If only to find out whether Ronald really was looking for more family or not."

"It's only Helen who mentioned it, right?"

"I can't talk about people's statements."

"It was only Helen who mentioned it to me," Fenella countered. "I don't think I thought to ask Eugene about it, though. Gary insisted that Ronald wasn't doing any such thing."

"I need to go and try to get some interviews done," Daniel told her. "I'm meant to be at a banquet at six."

"I'll see you later, then," Fenella said.

"I'm looking forward to it," Daniel replied.

Fenella smiled as she disconnected the call. Maybe he was only looking forward to the food, but Fenella chose to believe otherwise.

Feeling as if it was too early to head back to the restaurant, Fenella walked around her apartment for a while, annoying both Mona and Katie. Then she rang Shelly.

"Am I interrupting your day with Tim?" she asked.

"He had to go into work for a few hours," Shelly told her. "He'll be meeting me at five."

"Want to come over and hear my weird theory about Ronald Sherman's disappearance, then?"

"I'm on my way."

Fenella told her friend about the conversation she'd had with the restaurant's manager. "I can't stop thinking that maybe Ronald found a rich relative," she concluded. "And maybe Gary got rid of him so that he'd be the one that inherited the fortune."

"It doesn't seem as if Gary is doing all that well, though," Shelly pointed out.

"Maybe the rich relative hasn't died yet," Fenella guessed.

"I suppose that's possible," Shelly said.

"Daniel is going to talk to Eugene to see if he knew anything about Ronald researching his family history. He's also going to talk to Gary again."

"I hope he isn't late for dinner."

Fenella nodded. "Oh, but I nearly forgot to tell you the worst thing," she exclaimed.

"What's wrong?"

"Jack is coming to visit."

Shelly frowned. "Oh, dear. Are you sure? I mean, he has lied to you in the past, hasn't he?"

"Well, yes, I suppose so, although it was often more stretching the truth than lying," Fenella said, feeling stupid for defending the man. "I suppose he might have been doing the same again this time, but he sounded very sure. He met a man who offered to let him stay at his house, apparently."

"Pardon? A total stranger offered to let Jack stay in his house?"

"It was something like that, anyway," Fenella replied. "Apparently the man is a university professor in Liverpool with a second home on the island. He and Jack met last night and he gave Jack the keys to his house and told Jack he could use it for December and January."

"That's really odd. No one does that. If I were Jack, I think I'd be worried about being arrested for breaking and entering or something. Maybe the man is angry with his live-in girlfriend and is sending Jack to stay as revenge."

Fenella stared at her friend and then laughed. "What a wonderful idea," she said. "I should warn Jack."

"Why don't you wait and see what he says the next time he rings. You don't want to ring him and make him think that you're really worried, do you?"

"No, I suppose I don't, at that."

"And now we should get going, I think," Shelly said, glancing at the clock.

Fenella nodded. "I'll just freshen up," she said, fleeing into her bedroom.

"What's wrong with you?" Mona demanded as Fenella tried to reapply her lipstick with a shaking hand.

"I'm nervous. I've never thrown a big party like this. What if it all goes wrong? What if people are bored or the food isn't good or we run out of wine?"

Mona shook her head. "You're paying other people to worry about those things. You're just meant to go and have a wonderful time."

"I'll feel better once it's over."

"Then you can start to worry about Jack."

Fenella made a face. "Maybe I don't want it to be over too quickly."

"That's the spirit," Mona told her.

When she rejoined Shelly, Fenella was feeling more in control of her emotions. "I've never hosted an event like this before," she told Shelly as they began the short walk to the restaurant.

"Mona loved this sort of thing. Just channel her spirit and you'll be fine," Shelly replied.

Fenella swallowed a laugh and then led her friend into the restaurant. Tim joined them a minute later. They had drinks in hand before the manager found them.

"Come back to the kitchen with me," he suggested. "Chef has a few samples for you to try. If anything isn't quite right, we might have enough time to change it before the guests start to arrive."

Fenella and her friends tried three or four different dishes, and by the time they were done, Fenella felt much better about the evening ahead.

"The stuffing isn't exactly like I was expecting, but it's delicious and I don't want you to change it," she told the chef. "Everything else is wonderful, and the turkeys smell good, too."

The chef nodded and then glanced at the clock. "We'll be getting the starters into the oven soon," he said. "Would you like the first tray out a little early?"

Fenella glanced at her friends and then nodded. "Not too early, as I don't want to fill up on them before the food is served, but as we're already drinking, we probably should be eating, too."

A short while later, as Tim entertained the women with stories about his younger days in the band, a waiter entered with a large tray of appetizers. "Your starters," he said with a bow. He left the tray on the table next to Fenella and she and her friends helped themselves.

"Everything is delicious," Shelly said after a few minutes. "Everything."

"I don't like the green ones," Tim frowned. "They taste almost healthy."

Fenella laughed. "The manager told me we should have something healthy on the tray. I don't think they're too bad."

The first guests began to trickle in a few minutes before six, and by half past the party seemed to be in full swing.

"It's lovely," Shelly whispered to Fenella as they crossed paths a short while later. "Everyone from the band is having a wonderful time."

Fenella nodded. Nearly everyone who'd agreed to come was there, except for Daniel. She found herself watching the door far more than she knew she should. When he walked in, she had to remind herself not to rush over to him. It didn't take her long to make sure their paths crossed, though.

"You made it," she said softly.

"I did. Mostly because I couldn't track Gary down. I'll have to talk to him tomorrow."

"Did Eugene have anything interesting to say?" she asked. Before Daniel could reply, she held up a hand. "I know, you can't answer that."

A passing waiter offered them drinks. Fenella took a glass of wine, but Daniel shook his head. "I'm driving," he explained.

"The glasses with the white stems are non-alcoholic," the waiter told him. "Or you can get a fizzy drink at the bar."

Daniel picked up a glass with a white stem and took a sip. "Fizzy apple juice. Nice."

The man nodded and then walked away.

"For what it's worth, Eugene didn't really tell me anything. I think Gary's warning that you witnessed was effective. He wouldn't answer any questions or even confirm answers he'd given me before. It was very frustrating."

"Can you trace Ronald's family tree?"

"Maybe. I mean, I can't, but if we need to, we can have someone do it for us. I'm not sure if it's worth the time and expense, though. I'll give it some thought after I talk to Gary tomorrow."

"If you can find him," Fenella suggested.

"I'll find him."

The food in the buffet lines looked delicious, and Fenella circulated among her guests as they helped themselves to the many different offerings. She had to explain a few of the dishes to her guests, and she enjoyed their reactions to the candied yams and green bean casserole.

"They're traditional," she explained for the tenth time. "At American Thanksgiving meals, anyway. And yes, people truly do eat them. I've never liked either of them, but lots of people do."

Eventually she filled her own plate and then found a seat between Shelly and Daniel.

"Everything is delicious," Shelly told her.

"It really is," Tim agreed from his seat on the other side of Shelly. "I even like the candied yams, but I've had them before. I celebrated a few Thanksgivings in America with a former girlfriend."

"You never mentioned that before," Shelly said. "Tell me more."

Tim grinned. "I'm going to get myself in trouble now, I think."

Fenella looked over at Daniel. "What do you think?" she asked.

"I think we need to talk," he replied. "Maybe after everyone else has gone, I could walk you home?"

"Sure, that sounds good," Fenella replied, feeling slightly sick to her stomach at the thought.

The dessert table was a thing of beauty, to Fenella's mind, anyway. Pumpkin and apple pies alternated between plates of chocolate chip cookies and rich chocolate brownies. Iced sugar cookies in the shape of autumn leaves were dotted everywhere.

"I ate too much food," Shelly sighed. "I don't have room for pudding."

"Take something home with you," Fenella suggested. "I'm sure they can put some pie into a box for you."

Shelly wasn't the only one who felt too full to indulge in dessert. Three waiters were kept busy for several minutes boxing up slices of pie and piles of cookies for the guests. Fenella nibbled her way through a chocolate chip cookie as she wandered around talking to everyone. It didn't seem long before the room began to empty as people headed for home.

"What usually happens after dinner at an American Thanksgiving?" Shelly asked as she joined Fenella near the dessert table.

"People usually have dinner earlier, like around two or three," Fenella replied. "That leaves the late afternoon and early evening free for family games. That was what happened in my family, anyway. It was the one day of the year when we'd actually play board games for hours."

"Do people still play board games?"

Fenella shrugged. "I haven't played one in years. I suspect most kids these days have electronic games they'd rather play. I remember loving board games when I was younger, though. It really brought the whole family together, too. Everyone would play, from the smallest child to the oldest adult. My father always cheated, but deliberately badly, so that he'd get caught. When I think about it now, he used to get banned from playing and then go and watch more football. No wonder he cheated."

Shelly and Fenella both laughed at the memory. "I think Thanksgiving sounds like a perfect holiday."

"In my memories, it always was," Fenella told her. "I think I said it before, but it really marked the beginning of the whole Christmas season. Everything seemed more exciting and wonderful from Thanksgiving right through the new year. I can remember one of my father's cousins arriving on Thanksgiving for dinner. She always brought Christmas presents for my brothers and me when she came because she didn't come for Christmas. There was something about knowing that those first presents were in the house that made it all the more magical."

"Did she give you wonderful things?" Shelly asked.

Fenella laughed. "I suppose that depends on how you define wonderful. She loved to knit, so she usually knitted something for each of us. It was always the same item, just done five times over. I remember hats, scarves, mittens, and slippers. Mine were always pink, as I was the only girl."

"I hope you liked pink."

"I didn't, really, but it would have been rude to tell Aunty Blanche that. She meant well, and when I think back now, I'm grateful to her for the time and effort that she put into everything she made for me. At the time, of course, I would have preferred a toy or a book."

"I had an aunt that always knitted things for me, too," Shelly told her. "She did beautiful work, and I didn't properly appreciate it until I was much older. I still have a few blankets that she made me. I can't bring myself to use them, as I'd be upset if anything happened to them."

"My mother knitted me a gorgeous blanket when I was a child. It had tassels all along the ends, and I used to tie them around my neck and pretend that the blanket was my cape," Fenella laughed. "I'm sure I ruined all of my mother's very hard work, but I did love that little blanket, right into bits."

A loud ringing noise startled Fenella. She looked over at Daniel, who was standing nearby. He pulled his phone out of his pocket and frowned at it. As he walked away, Fenella and Shelly exchanged glances.

"I'm sorry, but I have to go," he told Fenella a few minutes later. "There's been an accident."

"Oh, dear. Anyone I know?" she replied.

"Eugene Matthews. He's at Noble's. I don't know any more than that at this point."

Fenella frowned as she watched Daniel leave the room.

❧ 15 ❧

"How was the banquet, then?" Mona asked when Fenella let herself into her apartment an hour later.

"It was good," Fenella replied, carrying several large boxes of leftovers into the kitchen. "I think I have enough left over for a week or more, although a lot of it is pie."

"Pie? What sort of pie?"

"Apple. I had a piece of pumpkin there and that was enough pumpkin pie to last me until next year."

"Tell me everything," Mona suggested.

With nothing better to do, and feeling something like post-party letdown, Fenella did just that. When she got to the part where Daniel had to leave, Mona got excited.

"Gary tried to kill Eugene to keep him quiet," she said.

"Daniel said it was an accident. Anyway, what makes you think Gary had anything to do with it?"

"It's the only answer that makes sense," Mona replied. "Ronald found out that he and Gary were heirs to a fortune and he told Gary. Gary decided that he'd rather have all of the money to himself, so he killed Ronald."

"Where's the money?"

"The relative probably simply hasn't died yet," Mona waved away the question.

"I'm not going to bother arguing with you. It's one possible solution, anyway."

"It's the right one, you'll see," Mona told her.

Fenella took off her party dress. Jeans and an oversized sweatshirt were just what she needed as she curled up with a book and a few leftover brownies. The box with cake slices was still in her refrigerator, but now it was nearly inaccessible behind all of the other boxes.

She was thinking about heading to bed when she received a text message.

Are you still up? Daniel asked.

Yes, she replied.

Instead of a response, she heard a knock on her door.

"Hi," Daniel said softly when she opened the door.

"Hi," she replied. "Come in."

"Thanks. I should have just gone home and gone to bed, but I didn't want you to have to read everything in tomorrow's paper."

Fenella led him into the living room and offered him a drink. He shook his head as he took a chair.

"So, what's happened?" Fenella asked, trying to ignore Mona, who'd taken the chair next to Daniel. "You said Eugene had an accident?"

"He was hit by a car in the car park outside the computer shop," Daniel told her. "It was a desperate act by a desperate man."

"Gary?"

"Yes."

Mona grinned. "I knew it!" she exclaimed.

"You're sure it was Gary?"

"Eugene is sure it was Gary, and we have witnesses, as well. They were all able to describe Gary's car fairly accurately."

"Please tell me you have Gary in custody."

"We do. And he's talking."

"That's good, right?"

"Yes, although I would prefer if Gary would limit his confessions to me, rather than sharing them with Dan Ross."

"Oh, dear."

"Dan was trying to talk to Eugene when Gary tried to run Eugene over," Daniel explained. "Gary drove away after the accident while Dan rang 999. I arrived at the same time as the ambulance. Eugene was shouting all sorts of accusations about Gary and Dan was taking careful notes."

"Dan must have thought it was Christmas."

"If he didn't think so at that point, he must have when Gary returned to the scene of the crime a few minutes later."

"He did what?"

Daniel shrugged. "As I said, he was desperate. The new investigation into Ronald's disappearance has been worrying him. I think the stress made him a little bit crazy."

"He killed Ronald?"

"At this point, he claims it was all an accident. Ronald was visiting a home Gary was remodeling, and allegedly Ronald slipped and fell and hit his head on a countertop."

"So why not ring 999 and try to get him help?"

"Gary claims Ronald died instantly and he panicked."

"And did what?"

"He hid the body behind a fake wall that he built into the house he was remodeling," Daniel told her.

"That's insane."

"It certainly suggests that Ronald's death wasn't an accident, anyway. Tomorrow I get to tell a homeowner that I need to tear apart his kitchen, which won't be fun."

"Any idea why Gary would have wanted to kill Ronald?"

"That's where Eugene comes in, although I don't think Eugene ever realized what he knew. According to Eugene, Ronald told him about researching his family tree but asked him not to tell anyone. Apparently, he wanted to surprise Gary with what he'd found."

"Any idea what Ronald actually found?"

"Exactly the sort of thing you suggested. Ronald found a distant cousin worth millions. Gary admits that Ronald had just told him about their unexpected potential good fortune before his unfortunate accident, but claims that had nothing to do with what happened to Ronald."

"You think Gary killed him so that he could be this cousin's sole heir?"

"That seems like the most likely explanation at this point," Daniel replied. "Gary filed papers to have Ronald declared legally dead. That was one of the reasons why I reopened the case, actually. He also had a ferry crossing booked to go across to the UK in early January. He was planning to stay at a hotel in the village where his wealthy cousin lives. I believe he was going over to make contact with the man in hopes of getting added to his will."

"That makes it all seem like some very long-term planning went into Ronald's murder."

"I don't know anything for certain yet, but I suspect a lot of the planning started after Gary found himself standing over his cousin's body," Daniel said. "He seems the type to do something completely impulsive and then scramble to deal with the consequences afterwards."

"Poor Ronald," Fenella sighed.

"I solved his murder, anyway," Mona said happily,

"It may be a while before we fully work everything out, but I'm satisfied that I know what happened to Ronald. Tomorrow we'll work on finding the body. Gary will be behind bars for the attack on Eugene while we decide what to charge him with for Ronald's death."

"Not exactly a happy ending, but the case is solved, anyway," Fenella said. "Whatever he says, I believe Gary killed Ronald. I'm very glad he's behind bars now."

"That just leaves us with one thing to discuss," Daniel said.

Fenella frowned. She wasn't ready to talk about their relationship, but she knew it needed to be done. "Oh?" she said, glancing at Mona, who was clearly paying close attention.

"I met a woman in Milton Keynes," Daniel told her, looking down at the floor.

"Tiffany?" Fenella wondered.

"Tiffany? No, not Tiffany. I mean, I met her in Milton Keynes, too, but she's far too young for me. I was just trying to help her find another job, that's all."

"Really? Because she seemed quite attracted to you."

Daniel flushed. "There were five or six of us who became good friends during the course. Tiffany was sort of on the fringe of the group. The rest of us were older and had been on the job for a while, and she seemed to enjoy spending time with us and hearing our stories. At the end of the course, Nancy invited everyone from the group to come and stay with her for a few days."

"Nancy?"

"She's the woman I was talking about earlier," Daniel said, not meeting Fenella's eyes. "We became very good friends while doing the course."

"How good?" Mona demanded.

Fenella shook her head. She didn't want to know the answer to that question.

"Anyway, Nancy lives on one of the Scottish islands. It's a tiny island, and she's pretty much the island's entire police force. We were all intrigued by the idea of life on a very small island, so six of us went and stayed with her for a weekend. Tiffany invited herself along. When it was time to leave, she asked if she could come here and stay with me for a few days. I felt sorry for her. She'd lost her job and was trying to work out what she wanted to do next. What could I say?"

"No," Mona said firmly. "The correct response would have been no. You don't understand women, do you?"

Fenella shrugged. "She stayed for a lot longer than a few days."

Daniel nodded. "Once she was here, I couldn't seem to get rid of her," he said. He glanced at her and then sighed. "I know, I should have just told her to go, but I was upset about Nancy and you, and having Tiffany here gave me some space to think. I'm sorry."

"You and Tiffany were just friends?" Fenella checked.

"Not even that by the end," Daniel chuckled. "I barely knew her when she first arrived. I was just trying to help her out. By the time she left, I was quite happy to see her go. She slept in her own bedroom the entire time she was here, if that's what you're really asking."

Fenella blushed. "What about Nancy?"

"She slept in her own bedroom, too, and I didn't sleep with her. It would have complicated an already difficult situation. Nancy is really special, and I think I could have fallen for her if things could have been different."

"What things?"

"She has a part-time constable and a part-time civilian assistant. The island where she lives can't afford two inspectors. They can barely afford her, but she loves it there and would never move."

"So you split up because you can't work together?"

"We weren't together enough to actually split up," Daniel told her. "We were attracted to one another and we talked about the possibilities, but in the end we both realized it would never work."

"But you still miss her," Fenella said, picking up something in the man's tone.

"I don't know. She was special, but so are you. I'm confused."

"So what do you want to do?"

Fenella stared at Daniel until he lifted his head and let his eyes meet hers. "I want to kiss you," he said softly, "but I think that might be a bad idea."

Fenella swallowed hard. "Maybe you should think about what you want for a while before we try that."

"I have been thinking. That's the problem. I reopened Ronald Sherman's disappearance mostly so I'd have an excuse to see you and talk to you. I knew you'd be able to help me work out what had happened to the man. I didn't mean to involve in you in another murder investigation, though."

"I suppose I'm flattered."

"Maybe we could start over," Daniel said after a long pause. "I mean, almost like we've just met for the first time. We could get to know each other again and see what happens from there."

"Maybe."

Daniel stared at her for a minute and then sighed. "You're angry."

"I'm sad," she corrected him. "I wasn't expecting you to fall in love with someone else."

"You were here, going out with Donald nearly every night."

"Yeah, but I was never going to fall in love with Donald."

"I wish I'd known that."

"It was pretty obvious," Mona muttered.

"I think you need more time to think," Fenella told him. "And I have enough problems right now, anyway. Jack is coming to visit."

"Jack? The man you were with for ten years?"

"Yeah, that Jack," Fenella sighed.

"I didn't realize you'd invited him to visit you."

"I didn't invite him. He invited himself. Or rather, he made himself a friend and got given a place to stay. It's all very odd."

"How so?" Daniel asked.

Fenella grinned as the man suddenly switched into police inspector mode. She told him the entire story that Jack had told her.

"That is odd. I'm going to see what I can find out about Peter Grady," Daniel said when she was finished. The words were hardly out of his mouth when his mobile buzzed. He glanced at his text messages and sighed. "And now I have to go. Apparently Dan Ross tracked down the couple who own the house where Gary claims he hid Ronald's body. They're understandably upset."

Fenella walked him to the door. "Thanks for filling me in on what happened," she said.

"Thank you for your help with the case. Thank Shelly for me, too, please."

"I will," she promised.

The man looked at her for a minute and then leaned over and kissed her forehead. "Maybe we both need some time," he muttered as he turned and walked down the corridor.

"Maybe you need to find a new man," Mona suggested as Fenella shut the door behind Daniel. "I still think you should get married before Jack gets here."

ACKNOWLEDGMENTS

My beta readers are a huge help and I'm grateful to all of them.

My editor works hard to correct my (many) mistakes and I truly appreciate all of her effort.

Linda at Tell-Tale Book Covers does amazing work and I'm thankful that she continues to create the wonderful covers for this series.

And I'm always grateful to my readers for sharing Fenella's world with me.

JOY AND JEALOUSY

An Isle of Man Cozy Mystery
Release date: February 15, 2019

Fenella Woods is excited to be celebrating her first Christmas on the Isle of Man. She's less enthusiastic that her former boyfriend, Jack, is coming for a long visit. While they split up months ago, before Fenella moved to the island, Jack seems to be having trouble accepting that the relationship is over.

Jack managed to get himself an invitation to stay with Dr. Peter Grady, a university professor who has a second home on the island. Dr. Grady isn't home when Jack and Fenella arrive, but a string of beautiful women looking for the man turn up almost immediately. When one of the women discovers Dr. Grady's body in the master bedroom, Fenella finds herself in the middle of another murder investigation.

Letting Jack stay at the house Fenella owns on Poppy Drive is necessary. She doesn't want him staying with her in her apartment on the promenade. The house, though, is right across the road from CID Inspector Daniel Robinson's home. Daniel and Fenella are still trying to work out where their personal relationship is going. Now he's investigating a murder where Jack could be considered a suspect, but also might be the killer's next target.

Can Fenella help Daniel solve the case and keep Jack safe? Can she incorporate American traditions into her first Manx Christmas? And what do you get a ghost for Christmas?

ALSO BY DIANA XARISSA

The Isle of Man Romance Series

Island Escape

Island Inheritance

Island Heritage

Island Christmas

ABOUT THE AUTHOR

Diana grew up in Northwestern Pennsylvania and moved to Washington, DC after college. There she met a wonderful Englishman who was visiting the city. After a whirlwind romance, they got married and Diana moved to the Chesterfield area of Derbyshire to begin a new life with her husband. A short time later, they relocated to the Isle of Man.

After over ten years on the island, it was time for a change. With their two children in tow, Diana and her husband moved to suburbs of Buffalo, New York. Diana now spends her days writing about the island she loves.

She also writes mystery/thrillers set in the not-too-distant future as Diana X. Dunn and middle grade and Young Adult books as D.X. Dunn.

Diana is always happy to hear from readers. You can write to her at:

Diana Xarissa Dunn
PO Box 72
Clarence, NY 14031.

Find Diana at: DianaXarissa.com
E-mail: Diana@dianaxarissa.com

215
178
___
37

Made in United States
Troutdale, OR
05/19/2025